LIGHT
OF THE
DAMNED

LIGHT

OF THE

DAMNED

F. JOHN HURR

To order additional copies of this book, contact:
Xlibris
800-056-3182
www.Xlibrispublishing.co.uk
Orders@Xlibrispublishing.co.uk
701084

My grateful Thanks
To Linda, my lovely wife who never gave up on me, but constantly told me I was a good writer, even when I didn't believe it myself.

FOREWORD

In this, the twenty-first century, when science and technology have advanced at an exponential rate to such a degree of wonder and discovery, still there are profound gaps in our understanding of the way the universe works. Scientists can map the smallest of molecules, trace the passage of invisible neutrinos through matter, and send unmanned rockets to the outer reaches of the solar system with pinpoint accuracy. In a short time, we are told, when the mystery of the Higgs boson particle is finally solved, we shall know the answer to the ultimate question of how and when matter was formed in the very first instant of time.

Yet we remain so limited and bound to the confines of our own planet's time and space. The English author H. G. Wells, in his famous science fiction stories, shone a light on the hopes of mankind in the hope that we would one day transcend our human limitations and journey beyond the most restrictive aspects of humanity. He also gave us a warning, that there are many hazards to be faced in the pursuit of the limitless. The real danger is that in becoming superhuman we may paradoxically become enfeebled, not empowered, as idealistic dreams would have us believe.

We have built the magnificent Large Hadron Collider yet cannot measure the soul or the spirit of man. We have the means to look into the far reaches of space and to delve into the microscopic world of molecular cells, yet we do not have the sight to see as cats do and as owls see, we do not possess an ear to rival canines and bats. In a very real way these creatures live and inhabit a very different world to us, that we are both deaf and blind towards.

I believe that there may indeed be other spheres of existence in addition to the one our five senses perceive. Strange alien and foreign worlds that despite all our exquisite knowledge and sophisticated ways of recording phenomena, we cannot see hear or fathom. Yet, in some rare moments, certain individuals do at times catch fleeting glimpses of these other worlds and even of a sixth sense awareness of nonhuman inhabitants who walk like spectres on the human plane.

A wise man once declared, "Demons exist whether we believe in them or not." Indeed, God and His angels exist whether we believe in them or not. In a morbid way, we all want the supernatural to exist. We crave stories of ghosts, hobgoblins, werewolves, vampires, and forest fairies. We delight in being frightened. We love the chills and thrills of a good ghost tale. But what we absolutely do not want is to encounter the paranormal in its raw evil form which may cause us harm. We desire supernatural experiences, but only on our own terms. Despite circumstantial evidence and extensive folklore, the creatures I've mentioned above probably do not exist, mainly because there are no universal origins from which their creation might ensue. But angels and demons? Well, that is a different matter altogether.

If we had eyes to see and an articulate suite of new senses, we might observe supernatural comings and goings all around us. Perhaps in every city and town, on Main Street and at the heart of your own community, you might with these senses be fully cognizant of angels helping and guarding the people and places that God in His wisdom holds dear. You would have a glimpse of another world intimately co-existing with ours. A world that is more wondrous than you could ever imagine.

Of course, where there are angels, there are their fallen brothers. Demons, we call them now, not wishing to bestow on them any residual fragment of their previous angelic nature. They stick as close to us as we allow. We are their 'reason' for existence—they are intent on doing us harm and, by doing so, strike at God's own heavenly kingdom. The psalmist asks God, "What is man, that thou art mindful of him?" (Psalm 8:4). Man has been made "a little lower than the angels," but we carry within our spirits the very nature of God. As the Bible says, we are made in His own image. Being like Him is to know love, to know truth and to be set free. True unconditional love is the greatest gift ever given to man. But the gift carried a high price, such a terrible price, paid by His Son on the cross at Calvary. In bestowing His love, He also gave us a free will. We all possess the awesome ability to choose to love or not to love. Sadly, the absence of love can manifest itself as evil in its most brutal forms. The Bible tells us that we should treat strangers with respect, with love even, for we may be entertaining angels unawares (Hebrews 13:2). However, the Good Book also says to be watchful and wary, to be discerning, because we just might be inviting a dark angel into our lives.

All that is necessary for the triumph of evil is that good men do nothing.
Edmund Burke
1729–1797

ONE

Maynard Jones was the curate at St. David's, though he had not been seen at the church for several days. He had missed morning prayers, evening prayers, and all of his other daily duties that fell in between.

He rolled over in bed and half opened his eyes. It was still dark outside. A gust of wind rattled the window frame of the old cottage. The bedchamber was littered with unwashed clothes left on the floor where Jones had carelessly discarded them, and dirty cups sat on the bedside cabinet and on the chest of drawers. On the floor beside the bed was an empty bottle of cheap scotch. Everything in the room spoke of disorder and neglect.

Jones was a shadow of his former self. Not long ago, he was one of those people everyone liked to be around. Tall, blond, and genial, he was now a pitiable and pathetic creature. Wearily, he pulled himself up and struggled out of bed. He didn't bother to switch on the light. Staggering blindly across the landing to the bathroom, he stood in front of the washstand and urinated into the basin. In the medicine cabinet he found some tablets his doctor had prescribed for headaches. Tipping the toothbrush and paste out of the mug into the stained porcelain bowl, he filled the mug with water from the tap and then swallowed four of the pills.

He made his way downstairs, stumbling and slipping precariously on the stairs. He managed to catch the rail to stop from falling headlong into the front hall. In the kitchen he put the kettle on to boil, sat wearily on a stool, and waited. He made himself a mug of tea and then worked his way back up the stairs. Sitting on the bed, he pushed aside the empty cups and set down the fresh made tea. His body was failing fast, and he knew it.

Spying the bottle of scotch at his feet, Jones picked it up and dangled it over his open mouth. A lone bead of golden liquid slowly dripped onto his tongue, but nothing else. He cursed and threw the bottle across the chamber. Switching on the bedside lamp, he winced as the light penetrated his eyes. He pulled open the drawer of the bedside cabinet and searched among the discarded pills and empty boxes. He found a plastic strip of antiretroviral pills. His CD4 cell count had been under two hundred for a long time.

Pressing out two of the tablets, he put them on his tongue and took a large swig of tea and then coughed violently. Jones switched off the lamp and fell back onto the bed, exhausted. He closed his eyes, but there was no peace in this world for him. Just a terrible, unending pain, that pulsed interminably through his body. And always the throbbing, tortuous ache in his head that never left him.

Curling up like a foetus in the womb, he tried hard to pray, but in the gloomy darkness it felt as though he was fumbling in the dark for a lost jewel and never finding it. His faith could not overcome the anguish he felt. The sickness was the enemy of his soul, and it was winning the war of attrition. If only he could just glimpse the light! To his dismay the heart of darkness enveloped him every time he tried to reach out to God. The persistent pain wore him down leaving him feeling debilitated and defenseless.

Longing desperately for sleep, he remembered the sleeping pills. Turning the light back on, he scooped up a handful of *Temazepam* that he had dropped on the floor from the bottle the night before. For a moment, with several capsules held tightly in his hand, he thought of swallowing them all. Peaceful oblivion could be his. He smiled at the idea ruefully. Dragging the mug of tea to his lips, he shoved a few of the pills into his mouth. He dropped the remaining pills carelessly onto the bedspread. He closed his eyes, hoping that sleep would come quickly and release him from torment, yet knowing all the while it would take hours for the drugs to work. He knew their effectiveness diminished each time he took them, but still he carried on, and sometimes, like tonight, taking them twice in the evening, only a few hours apart.

Later, in that twilight place between dull consciousness and the deep slumber he so longed for, he began to see visions. Suddenly, the bedroom became ice cold. He dragged the covers up around his ears. Strange, haunting sounds invaded the room. Muffled sobs and cries reached his ears. Drawing the covers over his head, he hid beneath their scant protection like a frightened child. The nightmarish manifestations came every night now to terrorize his soul.

As he fell in and out of consciousness, Jones had no way of knowing what was real or a dream. The sounds that had disturbed him faded, and then he found himself standing on a hill. An eerie half-light covered the land. In the desolate landscape ahead of him three rough-hewn timber crosses stood with bruised and broken men hanging upon each. Roman soldiers gazed up with some interest. Jones stood behind the crucifixes and could not see who was dying there, though the awful tortured cries of these poor suffering souls rang out plaintively. They pleaded in vain for sudden death to release them from their agony.

Jones's own body doubled up in pain. The shock of it was too terrible to bear—he could feel what they felt. He screamed aloud and collapsed on the earth.

Below, crowds of people laughed and jeered. They threw stones at the wretched men hanging there. They shouted curses and blasphemies and taunted the central figure, saying, "If you are the Son of God, come down from the cross and save yourself." From his knees, Jones looked up and saw the crown of thorns and wept bitterly.

Then he heard the voice, utterly devoid of power, piteously cry out to heaven, *"Eloi, Eloi, lama sabachthani?"*

"No, no! Take him down," Jones wailed. "Save him, somebody, please help him . . . help me. Help me, for God's sake."

In his state of delirium, he saw a grinning demon standing near to him and ripping the pages out of a holy book. The torn pages were carried away on the wind. The demon, laughing, threw the profaned book at Jones, striking him on the head and knocking him down. Jones picked up the book and tried to read the words, but the pages were covered in fresh blood. He tried to wipe it away with his hands. His fingers dripped with blood—not his own, but Christ's. The words in the book detached themselves from the pages and floated before his eyes. He mouthed the words: "Eternal death . . . everlasting life . . . sin . . . atonement . . . forgive them for they know not . . . they know not . . ."

He feared for his soul. Suddenly, he was on his knees and naked, with his hands bound tightly behind his back. He struggled to free himself but found he could not. He was now in the doorway to St. David's. Past the nave, deep in the dark recess of the building, he could see several men dressed in white robes standing beside a burning altar. The smoke from the fire billowed upwards to the roof timbers. His head was suddenly pulled violently back by his hair, forcefully gripped by someone who straddled his body. Jones was terrified to see Reverend Stannard over him. The vicar held a gleaming knife at his exposed throat. Stannard was dressed in the full regalia of a high priest of Israel after the order of Aaron. Upon his head sat the golden crown inscribed with the words *Holy unto YHWH*. Over the priestly robe he wore the ephod, and on his chest the *hoshen*, the breastplate which held the *Urim* and the *Thummim*.

"I have the sacrificial man, holy and blameless without spot! Perfect atonement for the sins of the world," intoned the vicar.

The men in the church all shouted, "Then let atonement be done. Slaughter the sin offering and sprinkle his blood upon the mercy seat."

Jones felt the blade touch his neck.

Then he heard the Son of God cry out, "Father, into your hands I deliver my Spirit."

The blade cut deep into him, and he felt his own hot blood flow. Then a suffocating dark oblivion surrounded him. He fell through emptiness into an endless void, all the time desperately reaching out for salvation that did not come to him. Now he had only one thought in his deranged mind: *Is this death?* He was utterly alone. Alone for all eternity.

Then horrifying scenes of war and destruction bombarded him. He stood naked amidst the carnage. The noise of war was deafening to his ears. Acrid smoke filled his nostrils and mouth. He could hardly breathe. Brutalized bodies of women and children lay abandoned by the wayside. Columns of distraught and despondent people, thousands of them, trudged slowly along the road amid the stench of burning and rotting flesh. On either side of the road were the ruins of once grand buildings, ravaged and torn apart by bombs and exploding artillery. Overhead there screeched flying beasts, demons with eyes of red searching for fresh prey. They swooped low to harry the pilgrims with whips and rods of iron, beating all the more those who stumbled and fell. Jones saw in the distance a burning city. The sacred city from whence these unfortunates had fled.

Some of the people cried out and wailed in distress, "O woe is Jerusalem! Jerusalem is no more!" Jones felt a stabbing pain in his chest as a passing devil pushed the tip of a spear into his ribs. Holding up his hands, he saw blood flowing from his palms, from which protruded iron nails. He tried to walk, to flee from this nightmare, but he fell down—his feet were crippled, bloodied and crushed by a pair of iron spikes.

All will be well.

The scene slowly dissolved into black nothingness, and an overwhelming silence filled his brain, crushing his spirit.

All pain passes.

All will be well.

Then came a brilliant recrudescence of light, and his pain was gone.

Before him now lay an exquisite landscape. The endless sky was a pure azure, and the sun shone golden on the horizon. A becalmed lake of silver water with numerous fountains and swans gliding upon its surface made him long for a taste of life-giving water that would banish his thirst forevermore. Broad willow trees lined the banks, their long, sinewy branches dancing in the light breeze. Swifts and swallows darted across the cool waters of the lake. He wondered if he was in Eden.

He saw a young man in a white robe standing by the water's edge, his back to Jones. He recognized him, and his heart flooded with joy. It was Roger, his school mate, his best friend. Jones ran forward wildly and tried to cry out, but no sound issued from his mouth. He stumbled and fell in the grass. Rising, he ran on, worried that the apparition might disappear. At last, he reached the lone figure and excitedly clasped the shoulders of his friend.

"Roger! Roger, it's me, Maynard!"

The figure turned around slowly and smiled.

Jones cried out, "No, no!"

The figure was not Roger . . . but was the risen Christ.

Jones covered his face with his hands, fearing to gaze upon those terrible, infinite eyes.

Absurdly, among the trees, a telephone started to ring.

Jones began to rouse himself from the deep troubled sleep. The ringing persisted. His eyes tried to focus on something, anything. The lampshade in the ceiling appeared hazy and blurred, swinging to and fro.

Ringgg . . . ringgg!

Leaning over the bed his hands fumbled on the floor until his fingers found what he was searching for. He pressed the mobile phone to his ear.

"Yes, who . . . who is it?" His voice sounded empty, weak.

"Who is it?!" the voice blasted. "It's me, for heaven's sake. Where are you?" Without waiting for a reply, the voice clamored on. "You're supposed to be here. Helping me, remember? It's Sunday. Where are you?"

Not waiting for Jones to reply Stannard added viciously.

"You are utterly worthless to me!"

"Reverend, I'm sick. . . so very ill. I can't. . . I can't—"

"What's wrong with you, Jones? Where have you been? You are a malingerer, Jones, a complete wastrel. I should never have agreed to take you on."

"Stannard, listen to me. I beg you, for mercy's sake. I am ill. I need a doctor, urgently. Please, please help me. . . pray for me!"

His plea was cut short as the phone went dead.

Jones dropped the phone onto the floor. Cradling his head between his knees, he groaned and writhed in agony. Suddenly, his body went into violent spasm. He coughed and vomited, throwing up the remains of his last meal all over the carpet and onto his bare feet. Then he fell back heavily onto the bed. Wiping his mouth with the soiled sheet, Jones passed out into his own personal oblivion.

TWO

The sunlight shone brightly through the stained-glass windows, casting multicolored replicas of the saints on the grey flagstone floor. Motes of dust hung in the air, accentuating the silence of the nave. The great bell in the stone tower had just struck three in the afternoon. It was Tuesday—market day in the village of Penrhos Bay—and St. David's was empty. The voices that had filled the chancel on Sunday in worship of God were no more than faint residual echoes of the past.

High above the nave, at the zenith of the church's gothic arches, medieval sculptures depicting gruesome images of demons and devils looked directly down on the pews where the small congregation sat every Sunday. Evil eyes, set deep in stone sockets were untouched by the light. The distorted faces and mocking grins of the crude effigies served to remind parishioners that Hell cordially reserved a special place for all the unrighteous.

The perfect silence that pervaded the sacred building was disturbed now by the creak of rusty iron hinges as the great west door swung slowly open. Jonas Silth grasped the cumbersome latch in his rough hands and closed the door firmly but quietly behind him. The hooded man padded stealthily forward on grubby cross-trainers, moving quickly across the wide narthex and slipping behind a huge stone column. He remained there awhile, holding his breath and listening intently for any sound that might betray the presence of another in the hallowed space. Finally, Jonas decided that he was alone in the church and it was safe to go about his business.

He slipped off the hood, revealing a wan, wasted face, one that had gone unshaven for days. He retraced his steps to the west end of the nave where books and pamphlets had been neatly set out on tables for maximum visibility. Prominently displayed in the centre of one table was a large black book. Beside it was a pen with which well-meaning visitors to the church could leave their mark. Jonas opened the book and read the most recent entries. Boring and banal statements littered the pages. The word *lovely* was used a lot. *Lovely* this and *lovely* that. All, no doubt, written by tourists who had come inside simply to get out of the rain or to sit in a pew and eat their homemade sandwiches in peace and quiet. He flipped the page and, for a moment, had the urge to add his own contribution. He tried hard to think of something clever and witty to write, but nothing came to him.

At the end of this small side chapel of books, cards and leaflets, Jonas spied something much more interesting: Attached securely to one of the stone columns was a wooden box, with a notice above it that read, *Donations—Give generously.*

Excitedly, Jonas Silth grabbed the box with both hands and tried to wrench it from the wall. It didn't budge. From a soiled canvas knapsack, he withdrew a handful of tools and chose a well-used metal jimmy, a small crowbar designed to lever things open, like this box. The donation box had a small clasp and lock at the front that kept the contents safe under normal ecclesiastical circumstances.

Jonas looked furtively over his shoulder before swiftly inserting the jimmy under the lid and levering it upwards with all his might. The top of the wooden lid splintered noisily. The metal lock was still attached, but one half of the box could now be forced open to reveal the contents. He covered his hand with the sleeve of his jacket to ward off splinters and then lifted the shattered lid. He let out a low excited whistle. "Hello, hello! What have we here?"

The box was by no means full, but a quick glance told him that the collection of notes and coins probably amounted to at least twenty pounds. Reaching into the box, he quickly grasped the wad of money, leaving only a few copper pennies behind for charity's sake. He returned the jimmy to the knapsack and stuffed the money into his pocket. Patting his pocket, he whispered to himself, "Tonight we'll drink to God's wonderful bounty. Amen!"

Looking upwards, Jonas raised his right thumb to his forehead in a sign of thanks to the Almighty and made a comic bow. *Time to leave,* he thought. *Don't want to get nabbed now, do we?*

Back at the entrance vestibule he inched the large oak door open a crack. Not a soul in sight.

He swung the door open wide, but as he sprang forward to cross the threshold of the great doorway, he was thrown violently back. Stumbling, he tripped over his own feet and fell awkwardly onto his back.

"What the—?" He pulled himself up onto his elbows and looked at the open door in confusion. Clambering to his feet, he ran at the arched doorway, determined to make a fast exit. This time, his head encountered an invisible barrier as strong as a wall of solid bricks. Again, he careered backwards, this time holding his head in his hands and uttering a string of curses.

Jonas felt as though he had been hit over the head with a policeman's stick, a feeling he knew only too well. He could not comprehend what had happened to him. He massaged his sore head and thought; *maybe it's one of those electric gadgets, some kind of force field like in* Doctor Who. *There's got to be another way outta here.*

He ran down the nave, looking to the right and left. Arriving at the chancel he tripped over the first step of the altar, stumbling and knocking over a lectern with a Bible on it. The crash of the heavy brass lectern hitting the stone floor reverberated through the building like a large clanging bell.

Hurriedly picking himself up from the floor, he kicked the Bible out of his path. He had noticed a small door to the left of the sanctuary. Not wasting a second, he ran to it, grabbed the handle of the door, and pulled hard. It held fast. Using his body as a ram, he threw himself against the door with all his might. All he got for his efforts was a sore arm.

Turning around, he ran back to the crossing of the nave and transepts. He placed both hands upon his bald head in a gesture of dismay.

"Mary, mother of Jesus, for Christ's sake, help me!"

Confused and shaken, he was beginning to lose his nerve. He dragged a heavy oak table up to the side wall, clambered up, and tried to release one of the stained glass windows. But they had not been opened for centuries.

He spent the next ten minutes frantically searching for another way out, but his attempts were all in vain. As he stood in the centre of the church, it began to dawn on him that he was trapped. Frustration welled up inside of him until he let loose a scream. "Yaghhhhh!" The sound was like the desperate cry of a broken and wounded animal. Gulping in deep breaths, he tried to calm himself. Narrowing his eyes, he again studied the main door, which was still standing wide open, just as he had left it.

He then began walking slowly and meaningfully with measured steps toward the open door. Instead of rushing headlong at the problem, Jonas moved forward cautiously, stopping a few inches from the threshold. He scanned the edges of the door jamb and the masonry of the arch overhead but could find no evidence of security equipment. No wires, no cables, no beams of light, nothing.

He could see out into the churchyard, where rows of old headstones stood to the right and left of the gravel path that led away from the church. He could even hear the hum of traffic beyond the church property. But these things may as well have been on the other side of the world. Jonas was beginning to crack.

"This is madness! Just walk out, you stupid bugger!" he yelled.

But he felt his head again and his courage deserted him. A large lump had risen on his forehead where he had hit the invisible force.

Hit what, though?

Jonas resolutely curled his right hand into a clenched fist. "Right then! I've had enough of this. Here goes!" he muttered.

Just as if he was aiming at someone's chin, he threw his best punch. He put all his strength into the swing—a knockout blow, if ever there was one. His knuckles rebounded immediately and painfully, and he staggered back in horror.

The pocket at his side suddenly felt heavier. Then an idea slowly began to take shape in his mind. At first he dismissed it as sheer nonsense. *No. No, never! It couldn't be. It just couldn't be. . .*

But the thought would not go away. Indeed, it became the only thought inside his throbbing head. Without further protest, he went to the shattered donations box and lifted the broken lid. Scooping the wad of cash out of his pocket, he threw the money back into the box. He was just about to leave when another thought pricked his conscience. He thrust his hand deep into his jacket pocket to make sure that he had indeed returned *all* of the money to the box. Finding a hole in the lining of his pocket, he ripped the hole wider and found a single penny within the recess.

He held the small coin aloft between his finger and thumb, showed it to each of the four corners of the church, and then ceremoniously waved the coin at the statue of Jesus hanging on the cross. "Look, I'm taking it out and putting it back where it belongs, okay?" Dropping the coin into the box, he closed the lid and backed away slowly toward the west door.

At the exit, he made the sign of the cross on his chest and then cautiously extended his fingers across the threshold, as if to gently caress the unseen. To his utter amazement and delight his outstretched fingertips felt?. . . nothing. His arm followed his hand as he stepped out the door. This time he encountered no resistance.

Freedom at last! Once outside, he hesitated for the briefest of moments to glance back at the doorway. His countenance registered a look of utter consternation, but his fear had turned to wonder. Then he ran as swiftly off as fast as his legs could carry him.

THREE

"What was that all about, may I ask?" There was a note of playful sarcasm in the captain's question.

"Well, I, er. . . that is, I was just, um. . ." The youthful watcher shifted his feet nervously before. "I was protecting the Lord's property. I mean, people give generously. Should we just stand by and see it stolen by some lowlife thief?" His confidence returning, he stood up on the crest of the roof.

"Sit down, Samuel." It was an order, not a request.

The two angels were perched atop the church, unseen by human eyes. Seated side by side, they surveyed the streets. It was late afternoon, and the sun making its descent toward the cliffs that walled in the seaside town. The taller and broader of the two was Bezalel, the captain of the Lord's Guard, who had been bloodied by many skirmishes with the hosts of hell.

"Let me ask you a question. You see all those people down there going to and fro. Can you tell which of them belongs to our Lord just by looking at them?"

The youthful angel looked at his companion quizzically. "Is this a trick question, sir? I mean, is it part of my probation test?"

"No, Samuel. It's just a question, okay?" The captain revealed a note of exasperation in his voice.

"Well, from here, sir, I suppose not. From this vantage point I can't see into their souls, can I?"

Sighing deeply, the captain said, "Well then, how could you tell that the thief in the church was a 'lowlife,' as you so colorfully put it?" He waited a moment for the truth to sink in. "He could have been a desperately hungry man. Or perhaps he needed that cash for his children who are ill, or to buy some flowers for his dying mother. If you haven't been given the means to comprehend the nature of their souls, are you telling me that you, a mere watcher, have somehow acquired some deep spiritual discernment in the first month of your field training?"

The captain waited patiently.

"No, sir I guess not, Sir."

"Now we are agreed on something. So did you think that you could read the thief's heart and soul?"

"No, Captain." Replied Samuel, quietly.

"No, Captain." Bezalel repeated Samuel's words more loudly and with more emphasis. "Have you already forgotten that one of the most important rules of engagement is not to intervene in human affairs unless absolutely necessary?"

Samuel hung his head.

The captain put an arm around the shoulders of the young angel. "Even in the direst of circumstances"—the captain's manner was gentle, but the voice stern—"even if it's life or death for some poor individual, we do not act. Understood?"

"Yes, sir perfectly understood."

"And certainly not for our own private amusement." The captain stood up to his full height and towered over the new recruit. "Although in the case of this thief, I have a feeling the Lord will use it to his benefit. For the record, Samuel, this particular lowlife is actually close to the kingdom of God."

"Praise God!" Samuel rose up and stood beside his mentor.

"Yes indeed, praise God. Come with me into the church. There are some other circumstances I need to acquaint you with."

Inside the building, the two angels stood together at the centre of the nave.

"Your little escapade was witnessed by the enemy," Bezalel said. "The strange behavior of our little friend trying desperately to exit the church aroused the curiosity of a passing demon."

"But, sir, I had been there all afternoon, watching as instructed, and I can assure you that no other—certainly not one of them!— entered the church. I would have seen . . . I mean, surely I would have noticed . . ."

The captain was shaking his head. "Listen, I had the same problem when I was a raw recruit. Loads to learn, full of enthusiasm. You know you're on the winning side, so what could go wrong? You did exactly what I did all those eons ago: You underestimated the stealth and cunning of the enemy."

Samuel was now paying full attention.

"There *was* someone here. He could see you. Watching the watcher, you could say. But he made certain that you couldn't see him."

"But where was he?"

The captain pointed to the carving at the highest point of the main arch. "Inside that gargoyle. A fitting place for an enemy spy, don't you think?"

Samuel shivered involuntarily.

"It was a good thing for you that whilst he was so intent on spying on you, he did not register my presence. He was so sure of himself that he made the same error as you. Your good fortune was that if he had decided to strike, I was nearby to save you." The captain paused before adding, "This time."

Samuel's inner light glowed a little less. "Yes, sir. Please forgive me. I will be more careful next time."

"I know you will, Samuel. We learn from our mistakes even when they are well meant. Remember this always: We are like spies in the land of the enemy. Our Lord does not reign here. His adversary does! So be vigilant at all times."

The captain pointed to the gargoyle again. "Go smell that ugly face up there and tell me what your senses detect."

Samuel rose swiftly and took a deep draught through his nostrils. At once, he recoiled away from the arch. "What is that foul stench?"

Smiling, Bezalel said, "It's the residual odor left by the demon who was observing your antics."

"That's quite disagreeable, sir! Like a whiff from Hades."

The captain laughed. "What did you expect, frankincense?"

Samuel hovered, his fingers pinching his nostrils tightly shut. "Sir, may I come down now?"

The captain nodded. Now sitting in a pew seat, he looked at Samuel and said, "What troubles me is that I think I know who that unpleasant odor belongs to. As soon as I caught a whiff of him, I knew it was Gathan, a very powerful and artful creature, a high servant of Rim—" He was about to utter the name but then checked himself. "Well, we won't mention his name in this sacred place. But what bothers me is why he is in this neighborhood."

Rising straight up and through the timbers of the roof, the captain shouted, "Come on, we have some urgent work!"

The two angels, now soaring above the rooftops of the town, turned heavenward and simultaneously vanished in a flash of light.

In the ancient storehouse of Heaven, the captain spoke to one of the curators. The angelic ward led them to a chamber that was bathed in a soft, golden light. Delicate sounds of a great angelic choir humming exquisite musical chords and notes hung upon the air, giving Samuel infinite pleasure. The feeling of utter joy was so strong that Samuel quite forgot why he was there.

"Samuel! Get yourself over here!"

"Apologies, sir, I was enraptured."

The curator smiled at the captain.

"Well, bring yourself back here and take a handful of these."

The curator carefully placed several small golden implements that were fashioned like hanging flutes into Samuel's outstretched arms.

"What are these, sir?" Samuel asked.

"They now serve as warning chimes. Once, a long time ago, the pieces you see here were the finest of instruments that played the music of praise to our Lord. Their sounds rose directly to the ears of the Ancient of Days. These chimes were crafted by the Lord's own smiths from the precious metals wrought from the wonderful instruments of the Fallen One, once our own dear brother Lucifer, now called Satan, the prince of darkness."

Samuel dropped the chimes in terror. The curator stooped low to pick them up and handed them back to Samuel. "They cannot harm or corrupt you. They serve only holy purposes now."

The captain also held several of the chimes in his grasp. Addressing Samuel, he said, "We must return to the church. We haven't a second to lose. And Samuel . . ."

"Sir?"

"No more of your tomfoolery."

Back at the church, the captain explained the significance of the chimes to Samuel. "Whenever a demon approaches, the chimes begin to resonate, emitting a sound that can only be heard by angels of the Lord. Utterly outside the hearing of the fallen ones. The greater the evil of the form detected, the higher the pitch—something you will learn in good time."

Samuel nodded, wisely preferring not to say anything about his own special talents.

"We place the chimes strategically around the structure, both inside and out, so as to completely cover the surrounding atmosphere."

"But won't the demons be able to see them?"

"No. Just as they cannot hear them, so they cannot see them."

After they had positioned the chimes, the angels resumed their surveillance of the neighborhood around St. David's. There was nothing going on, and soon they began to relax and converse.

The captain asked, "So how did you come to be transferred to my unit, anyway? Forgive my bluntness, Samuel, but you are definitely not the sort of material I usually get in my platoon."

Samuel's face dropped. "Well, sir, until recently I was in the third rank of the Heavenly Choir in the celestial outer courts."

"That's an unusual honor for someone of your maturity isn't it?"

"It certainly is," said Samuel. As he spoke, he began to visibly change before the captain's eyes. He seemed to glow with an inner light. Suddenly, it dimmed. "But I failed my probation there."

"Why?"

"Well, my voice has an unusually beautiful timbre, and my range is so great that I can sing as no others have sung before."

The captain waited patiently. Samuel sighed and continued. "But with such a gift I simply could not contain myself. I wanted to praise Him at every opportunity and to the best of my ability . . . and that's where the problems began."

The captain listened intently.

"Whenever the choir was singing *sotto voce*, I was unable to resist the urge to soar above them. Like a climbing eagle, I would allow my chords to ascend to the highest notes—all, I might add, in harmony to the melody being sung. But I was strident and loud, and my voice would grow louder every second until the choir had to stop their ears."

The captain nodded. "I begin to understand the problem. All talent and no discipline, eh?"

"Yes. So the Choir Master, although appreciative of my God-given talent, pointed out to me in an extremely kind way that perhaps I could do with some training of another kind, namely, as you have so keenly observed, in discipline. He did say, however, that my place in the choir would remain open until I return . . . in a few centuries or so."

The captain laughed. "Well, if discipline is what's needed, you're in the best place." The captain looked at Samuel thoughtfully. "And perhaps you will be able to interpret the chimes more quickly than I thought."

FOUR

In a dank and dark cavern at the bottom of a deep mine shaft, under the Great Ulm and not far from the church, an unholy gathering was taking place. Conditions were fetid and claustrophobic in the cramped chamber, but to those congregating there, the atmosphere was anodyne, the fouler the air, the better. A couple dozen gruesome beings stood silent, shuffling to and fro with impatience. No human who unwittingly stumbled into this lair could have hoped to survive an encounter with such undiluted iniquity. The faces and shapes of these beings were hideous caricatures of angels and humanity. Their eyes burned with malevolence, and from their mouths dripped venomous saliva that seeped slowly through their blackened and sharp-set teeth.

None dared speak as they waited for something wicked to come. Their commander was an unnatural and powerful beast, an entity far more unpleasant than these lowly demons could ever aspire to be. He was a loathsome being who, in an age long past, had been pure, without sin in thought and deed, and gloriously counted among God's host. Now he was totally degenerate, ungodly in every way and an enemy of Jehovah for all eternity.

This company of demons, subordinates of Hell, had inhabited their present form for thousands of years and, like their master, were once angelic. But evil had long ago crippled their hearts, twisting their minds and bodies. Yet, for all their deformities, they possessed a strength far greater than that of any mortal.

At the front of the chamber, there was a dais upon which stood an ornate chair. This was no ordinary piece but a throne fashioned from ebony and ivory. Dark jewels studded the arms and legs—misshapen rubies, sapphires, and emeralds that shone with a dark light which glowed from within the crystals. The intricately sculptured details of the throne depicted evil forms performing all kinds of cruelty and bestiality. The devils confined in this place knew that to even touch this throne was to suffer extinction at the hands of the master, such was his reputation.

The attention of the fiendish gathering was now drawn to the centre of the throne where a greenish light appeared and began to grow in power and energy. At the heart of this manifestation a form slowly began to take shape. The servants of Satan murmured to each other and trembled in fearful expectation. This was no ordinary visitation. The demons shuddered as they began to comprehend the form appearing before them.

The figure, changed from phantom to solid aspect, was now seated on the throne. His body, arms, legs, hands, and head had metamorphosed into a palpable entity of diabolical stature. He was neither angel nor man, not animal nor beast, but a foul fiend of unremitting iniquity. Pungent, sulfurous smoke issued from the base of the throne and swirled about the figure. Eyes of evil incarnate searched the gathering, seeming to focus on each demon in turn. None could hold his head high when confronted with those terrible, barbarous eyes. As their gaze met his, their very essence shook with fear, and they wished in their dark hearts that this inquisition would not last long.

With heads bowed low in obeisance, they knelt and waited to be addressed by their master, Prince Rimmon, lord of lightning and storm.

When Rimmon spoke, the words were not like those any human could utter. His voice was like that of a ponderous bell tolling a funeral dirge, and it held the listener with an occult power that could not easily be denied. The sounds that issued from the mouth of this creature were like dark waters tumbling over a hellish waterfall. Every syllable commanded attention, and each phrase resonated deep within the black hearts of his servants.

"Rise up, my lieutenants. I see you hang upon my words for news, but I bring tidings that will not please your ears."

The demons became restless, disturbed.

Prince Rimmon raised his hand to quell the muttering voices. "Be still! Let us get to the point. I have received alarming reports of rampant goodness in this area of late, and this has drawn the attention of our great lord in Hades."

The very mention of Satan made them even more fearful.

Rimmon changed his tone to one of mock sympathy.

"I know that some of you have been too long in the company of the saints. And yes, I know that I have promised you leave from this odious place. But my master, the lord of darkness, knows what sacrifices you make. He is cognizant of the privations and pains you suffer in His service."

He paused.

"But He is also aware that each of you has more to give. You are not weaklings, not mere wimps like those doltish harp-players of Heaven. You are warriors of Lucifer, the invincible god of the earth! No soldier of the enemy can match you in battle, and every mortal trembles in abject fear at your presence. I have informed our great lord that you will gladly endure the agonies of Hell to carry out any deed necessary to add to the myriad names inscribed in his black book for all eternity!"

The demons raised their fists and cursed the name of God in honor of their lord Rimmon and his majesty Satan.

Rimmon stood and stepped off the throne. He raised a fist and said, "Great deeds will achieve great rewards. These will be given to those who succeed in the glorious name of Satan!"

The demons congratulated each other with a grisly glee.

"But," Rimmon roared, "for all those who fail, unspeakable torment awaits you at the hands of the master himself."

The mood in the chamber turned black.

"I need not elaborate, do I?"

The devils shrank back, frozen into a shocked silence at the mere thought.

Rimmon allowed them to imagine such a fate for a moment longer and then said, "I know you shall not let me down."

"No, master, no! We will not fail you!" the demons shouted.

At this moment, the prince's form and countenance began to change. The loathsome figure began to undergo a strange metamorphosis. He now resembled a human youth in his prime—a thing of great beauty and strength, like a naked David confronting Goliath. His muscles were lean and strong, the lithe body perfect in form, the head noble and true. Yet the transition did not ultimately and completely materialize but wavered back and forth from dark to light, from beauty to corruption. The centuries of degradation could not be held in stasis. Rimmon's powers of sorcery could not overcome the curse of corruption that he carried in his heart. The illusion of beauty was flawed. It was skin deep only, for the pale translucent flesh exposed Rimmon's true essence.

The demons cheered wildly at this display of occult transformation.

The beautiful figure towered over them, no longer benign in appearance, but taking on a new form of malevolence. The gaping mouth of the fiend took a deep intake of breath, sucking through its parted lips strange sinuous strands of sulfurous smoke. As the green-black smoke swirled around him, Rimmon's form changed into a scaly creature whose arms and legs ended in sharp gnarled talons. His head

was disfigured with suppurating boils, and his mouth boasted sharp
fangs that could easily rend the flesh from man or beast. The demons
in the front rank instinctively shrank back. The stench of death
pervaded the cavern.

The beast now sat upon the throne. A long, spiked tail curled
around the base of the dais. The whole body was a malformation of
natural animal life, an abomination, a creature that had never lived
or ever existed among the fauna of the earth. Its countenance was
malevolent. In its lustful eyes there flashed a dark brilliance—an
evil intelligence determined to entice, deceive, and subjugate every
foe. The subdued demons were held in awe of their master's powers.
They all knew that what they had witnessed had been not only a
demonstration of Rimmon's power but also a spectacle meant to
invigorate, a parable whose meaning was understood by all present:
*Use every fiendish device at your disposal to deceive and destroy and lay claim
to these souls for the Dark One.*

The demons began to chant, the sycophants among them
genuflecting in the dirt.

The beast reveled in their subservience.

Now Rimmon began to change, resuming his own form.

"My subjects, let us return to the business at hand. I am fully
aware that there is a phenomenal proliferation of sin in this place, and
I congratulate you all. I discern with great enjoyment and satisfaction
that murder, greed, idolatry, debauchery, adultery, ignorance, and
cruelty abounds in this cesspool of a town. There are some, I am told,
who worship our master with corruption and lies, spreading iniquity
with little help from us.

"You have heard it said that where there is evil, goodness shall
abound. So seek it well and stamp it out. I suggest that you add
kidnapping to the list of your menaces. That will stir things up! And
target the enemy's leaders. Discover their weaknesses and exploit
them, especially those of the flesh. Give them whatever their stupid
hearts desire! There is not one so-called follower of Christ who does

not have his price. If it is wealth, then set gold in their path. If it is lust, then tempt them with the most sensuous of Jezebels. If it is pride and self-righteousness, then arrange titles and accolades beyond their wildest imaginations."

The gathering was growing excited, feeding on their lord's dark wisdom.

"If you cannot tempt or corrupt, then simply kill them."

The demons' distorted lips drooled at the thought of the many kinds of murder they could employ to destroy and dismember their victims.

"And as for our erstwhile companions of creation, I don't need to tell you what to do if you come across them."

The whole contingent went into a frenzy of imagined actions. In their minds they rent and tore and thrust their swords into holy flesh. The brutal cacophony of cries and shouts was deafening.

Rimmon grinned at their antics. Then after a few moments he raised his hand to bring attention back to him. "But as I said, something is amiss. What of this rumor of an increase of holiness in and around St. David's church? I find this most surprising and deeply disappointing. I thought that this putrid edifice, this lackluster jewel of Christianity, was firmly in our grasp. Is it not?" The question went out among the assembly like an arrow searching for a target.

No one volunteered an answer.

"Where is Jusach? Is he among you?"

"I am here, my lord." An elderly, bloodied entity stepped forward from among the front lines and knelt with his head bowed low.

"I wish I could say it is good to see you, old friend. Rise and tell me—what of the churchman? Is he not still in our service?"

"Yes, my lord, without a doubt he is. And no, he does not guess that he is under our power. But his behavior of late causes me a modicum of concern."

"Why so?"

"I think he has discovered a new religion, and I am not sure . . ." Jusach paused at this point. He may have been enlightened from—forgive me, master, for even daring to speak of the enemy—from on high. We may be losing him, I fear."

Rimmon did not like this news, and his displeasure showed.

The crowd of devils behind Jusach shifted nervously like a pack of frightened animals as they subtly inched away from their colleague.

"I can only describe what I saw," Jusach continued, "for I did not comprehend the actions of the man. He was seated at his desk in his private study and had several books open before him. In his hand was a large magnifying glass, through which he studied strange hieroglyphs on the pages of a great book open at the centre of his desk. I inched closer and peered over his shoulder, and I could see that he was studying small bits of colored paper on the surface of the pages of the book. He was arranging and rearranging them into a kind of pattern. Every now and then, he would open a wooden box and retrieve more of these tiny parcels of paper and place them into the great book. I could only think he was creating a sort of—forgive me again, sire—a new gospel, in some strange new language entirely unknown to me. And there was another great book at his right hand. It was called *The Philatelist's Bible*."

Suddenly, the seated figure rose to his full height and, throwing his arms wide, burst into uproarious laughter. The other demons, not comprehending Rimmon's intentions, dove away from the vicinity of Jusach.

"You idiot! You dolt of dithering demon, you are an imbecile!"

At this, the elderly Jusach prostrated himself on the slimy floor and pressed his face hard against the earth, expecting any moment to be struck a fatal blow.

"Philately!" Rimmon shook with guffaws of laughter. "Get up, you fool! This is no new religion, though it might just as well be. Some of the crass humans worship these bits of paper—'stamps,' they are called—as if they were depictions of gods. Ha! This is *good* news.

Whilst this man of God should be about his Father's business, he has locked himself away to pore over silly scraps of meaningless paper! This is great news, indeed. It will be easy to control this man, and you shall give him some rare delights to divert him from ecclesiastical matters."

Rimmon turned excitedly to a nearby lieutenant. "Ganymede, dispatch a note immediately to all our legions to acquaint them with this hobby of stamp collecting. We must include it in our arsenal of spiritual distractions, especially for clergymen! They do seem uniquely susceptible to this childish behavior."

Ganymede mumbled something under his breath.

"What did you say?" Rimmon said imperiously.

"Train sets, my lord. Stamps and little train sets seem to take up a lot of their personal time."

"Whatever train sets are, add them to the list," barked Rimmon.

"Consider it done, my lord."

"Now, tell me about the unfortunate curate Jones. Is there anything in his life that is attracting goodness? No? Excellent! I hear that he is suffering, the poor soul, and is not long for this world. My first thought was that we should continue his soul's angst in Hell. But then I had a second, more delicious thought. Why not let the 'old and decrepit man' upstairs have this miserable wretch? Let's face it, from the reports I've received of late, Heaven is rapidly becoming a nursing care facility for the virtually insane. All the best people—or should I say *worst* people?—come to us, many of them by their own choice. As one of their own once said, 'The great masses of people will more easily fall victims to a big lie than to a small one,' and the greatest falsehood ever is that we don't exist!"

The demons chuckled nervously. The master had made a joke.

"So tell me, Jusach, can I assume that you torment this man daily?"

"Most certainly, master. I work on him daily and, indeed, nightly. I am by his side twenty-four/seven, as the humans like to say. The man is in such turmoil and anguish that he has become his own worst enemy. At times, all I have to do is sit and watch. He has taken the reins of his own downfall."

Rimmon smiled at this. "And our esteemed ally and friend, the Most Reverend Stannard the Philatelist," Rimmon sneered as he mouthed the words, "is he at all inclined to help the younger man?"

"On the contrary, my lord. He has washed his hands of the curate and is content to mind his own business. I think he actually loathes Jones and will not lift a finger to give him aid of any sort."

The prince rose from his throne, took a step forward, and placed a claw-like hand upon Jusach's shoulder. "You have done well. I am not unpleased with you. This Stannard sounds like a credit to our cause."

Jusach bowed and stepped back into the ranks.

"Now where is Aggra? Step forward."

From the rear, another demon barged his way through the assembly. He was very different from Jusach, noticeably younger, leaner, and clearly capable of great agility.

Aggra knelt before his master.

"Sire, I am at your command."

"I have a special mission for you. Go immediately to Lord Salus in the east and make enquiries regarding rumors of a replacement for our ailing curate. Find out all you can and report back to me swiftly. Give Salus my greetings of affection and *try* to sound sincere."

Aggra bowed low again and vanished.

The great devil sat back upon his throne and addressed his minions once more. "It is vital that you do your utmost to ferret out anything holy brewing in this backwater. Meanwhile, I want you to redouble your regular efforts. Generate slander and cruelty wherever you can. Keep a watchful eye for any individual whom you even suspect is about to choose benevolence over balefulness. Wherever you see kindness, sow envy, increase gossip, foster ferocity, and make it easier for them to choose violence over virtue, especially amongst the drunken youth under the cover of night. Be merciless when it comes to persecution and intolerance and hatred, in particular where there are different races. You know the drill. Now get out and see it is done! And remember, Halloween approaches—use it to your advantage."

The demonic horde clamored and cheered at the mention of All Hallows' Eve. Slowly, the figures began to fade away like apparitions through the rock walls and the vaulted roof of the cavern.

Rimmon shouted, "Gathan! Stay behind. I would have words with you." A solitary figure turned back toward the throne, knelt with his head bowed low, and waited. Soon the chamber was empty, and only the master and his single servant remained. Gathan was a demon of brutish intelligence, a rare breed in the ranks of the damned. He was utterly committed to mayhem and destruction.

"About this holiness business," Rimmon began, "it is his majesty's view that something is happening in this insignificant town. He tells me that strange emanations of light are moving to and fro, as if taking up position. Yet I sense nothing at all. What about you?"

"Lord, I sense nothing untoward. There appear to be only the most ordinary activities, small sparks of spiritual awareness in the humans that are easily extinguished by well-timed disruptions to their despicable lives."

"So there is nothing unusual happening? No new clergymen or visitors to the town?"

"I believe the reigning bishop has not long to live, so there will be a new bishop arriving. But bishops generally come and go without bothering us. If there were others of significance, I would know immediately. My spies are everywhere."

"What about the enemy?"

"Again, I see nothing out of the ordinary. Just a few angels passing through on their way to more important territories like Birmingham and London. There have been riots recently in the capital, as you know, but all we get here in this accursed town are minor angels, apprentices mostly. They send them here to this innocuous place to learn their trade. I myself witnessed the inept antics of one of them today at the church where the Reverend Stannard is posted. It was actually rather comical to see this fool trying to protect the church offerings—"

"Did he see you?" The master's tone turned ugly.

"Nay, lord, he did not. I hid myself inside a gargoyle and was completely unseen by him."

"We know that the enemy spies on us, as we spy on them, but I do not want them becoming aware of your presence or knowing that any high-ranking demons are in the area. That would alert them to our plans. I cannot be bothered to have to fight a battle for this tawdry, degenerate place."

Gathan said nothing.

"And what of global reports that are filtering in, of spiritual revivals in some of the major cities across the planet?"

"I could not say, my lord, but our network would know in advance of any meaningful disturbances, surely?"

An expression of thoughtfulness passed over Rimmon's face. "Be vigilant, Gathan. Do not become complacent. I want no mistakes. I am sent here on a special mission because the Dark One believes something heavenly is soon to occur hereabouts."

"Here, lord? In this God-forsaken place?" Gathan looked incredulous.

Rimmon looked straight at his understudy. "Bethlehem was an inconsequential, 'God-forsaken' place until . . ." Rimmon trailed off, pondering.

"Sire, surely not? But an event of that significance would indeed be a catastrophe! The Second Coming? Here, of all places?"

"No, certainly not, you idiot! Satan forbids it!"

The senior devil looked at Gathan thoughtfully. "Yes, well, Bethlehem was a long time ago. It has been quiet for more than two millennia, apart from a few sporadic outbreaks of accursed revival. Who had ever heard of Loughor in the south of this country before the intervention of the Holy Spirit. . ." Rimmon shuddered at the mention of that name. "We lost thousands of souls, more than a hundred thousand, in fact, and the effects reverberated around the globe. The only satisfaction from that troublesome episode is that we were able to spiritually emasculate Evan Roberts so that he couldn't do further harm to our cause." Rimmon leaned forward. "I hope you were not part of our defeated forces at Moriah Chapel in Loughor. Did you have a hand in that debacle, Gathan?"

"No, sire. In 1904, I was in Austria, fermenting discontent among the Baltic states."

"I am glad to hear it. I would not like to think that one of my top lieutenants had taken part in that disaster."

Rimmon stood and paced about the gloomy cavern. Gathan stood to attention and kept a close eye on his master.

"As you know, Gathan, ordinarily I adore catastrophes, but not the kind that originates from the kingdom above. So if a flame *is* kindling in this town, we must find out where it is and strike quickly to smother it—and early enough so that it cannot spark and grow beyond our control. Search hard, Gathan. Search every road, every street and alleyway. Look into every dwelling and every church in this ridiculous town and report back promptly."

FIVE

The lone figure lay on the altar steps, fully prostrated beneath the life-sized figure of Christ on the high wooden cross. Maynard Jones's body convulsed with sobs and desperate cries of anguish. Muffled utterances came from his mouth, which was pressed hard against the rough crimson carpet. Disparate thoughts, confused words, and jumbled verses issued forth like so much flotsam on a turbulent sea.

The church lay in semi-darkness. A soft ethereal light filtered through the windows from the street lamps outside, yet there was a sense of desolation in the air. Bezalel's chimes set inside and around the perimeter of the church rang out their warning that a demon had entered the hallowed sanctuary, but there was no sentinel to hear the call. A few feet away from Jones, unseen by him, sat the loathsome demon Gathan watching in an bemused way the miserable demise of this once godly man. The foul being grinned as he came closer and hissed and whispered into Jones's ear. Gathan longed to murder this unfortunate soul, but God's own were protected against such direct violence so he would to have to be especially devious to end this petty clergyman's life.

The curate struggled to get up, rising slowly to his knees. With trembling hands he wiped the tears from his face. He lifted his head and fixed his attention on the crucifix. Raising his outstretched hands, Jones sought absolution and mercy from the cold and lifeless statue figure hanging there. In a pathetic voice he called out, "Forgive me, Lord! I am the worst of sinners!" A whimper escaped his throat. "I cannot go on anymore. My soul is in turmoil. My sin is too great to bear. I have condemned myself to suffer Hell and all its torments. I am not worthy."

Standing, he backed away from the altar and made his way slowly to the front of the church. Gathan gamboled ahead of Jones, beckoning him by dark means. Jones obediently followed, as if pulled by an invisible leash. He brushed aside the heavy curtain that hid the door to the bell tower. He opened the door and began to climb the steep winding stone stairway.

Out of breath, Jones stumbled up the last few steps and stepped out onto the roof of the high tower. Gathan was there to welcome him. "Yes, yes! This way, my friend!"

Jones staggered to the edge and looked over the stone parapet to the ground far below him. The lights of the village shone bright and clear, as the stars shimmered brilliantly in a cloudless sky. Jones began to feel nauseated and dizzy from vertigo. His eyes tried to focus on the street lamps, but all was just a pulsating blur of illumination. His head pounded and ached, and he shivered in the cold night air.

Gathan, seeing his prey falter, urged him on.

Gripping the rough stone of one of the pinnacles, Jones heaved himself up with his last ounce of strength until he stood precariously on the edge of the parapet. His legs went weak, and for a moment Jones's head began to clear a little. He became suddenly frightened. What was he doing here? Fear gripped his insides, and at that moment demon stepped up beside Jones and whispered into his ear, "Nearer to God are ye, my friend. Heaven is just at hand."

Jones steadied himself and stood upright, now balanced between life and death. Gathan maneuvered himself away from the curate until he was suspended in midair a few feet away. The demon allowed himself to materialize in part, and Jones misguidedly thought the presence to be angelic. He called out, "O Lord, take me into your arms! Save me!"

His foot slipped, and he almost fell. Beyond his reach, Gathan had transformed himself into an apparition of someone whom Jones desperately longed to be with in his hour of direst need. Before him now was the figure of a handsome young man, smiling and holding out his hands to Jones in a gesture of warm embrace. Surely Jones's prayers had been answered: Roger had come to escort him to paradise.

He heard his friend's voice, clear and sweet, speak to his heart. "Come, Maynard. Come into my loving arms. I am here for you."

The figure drifted slowly toward Jones. Without hesitation or fear, Jones stepped forward, eager to grasp the hands held out to him. But at the very moment his hands met the apparition's, the appearance of the figure changed, and Jones now beheld a malevolent creature so terrible in appearance that his heart went cold with fear and loathing. The figure still resembled Roger, but the eyes of the creature smoldered red, and a thick, black liquid oozed from its mouth and nostrils. The very flesh of the thing seemed to decompose before his very eyes, and parts were detached and carried away on the wind, gradually revealing the white of the bones beneath. A foul stench began to choke Jones's throat until he convulsed and wretched up the contents of his stomach.

Gathan laughed as he reached out a calloused hand to tenderly caress the curate's head. Then the awful bleeding mouth spoke. "Come near to me, Maynard. Am I not your lover? Find eternal peace in me." Jones struggled to free himself, to recoil from the demon's embrace. He tried desperately to maintain his foothold.

Mocking him, Gathan said, "No, my friend, come. There is peace in my arms. I am Roger." The demon's tongue caressed Jones's ear, all the while whispering evil endearments. "Come, come to me."

Gathan's arms encircled the doomed curate's body, and Jones's spirit finally gave in, his will to live drained away like water from a sieve. There was no resistance left in his pitiable soul. Gathan felt the victory and screamed aloud, "Satan is lord!"

At that instant, Gathan was struck with terrific force. He lurched violently sideways, but like a hawk a precious kill in its claws he kept hold of his prey. Twisting around, he saw the angel Samuel frantically clutching at Jones, trying to free him from the demon's grasp.

Gathan spat venom at Samuel and laughed derisively. "Do you think you can subdue me! I am Gathan the Great, destroyer of men and angels!" Without letting go of the curate's limp body, Gathan released his right hand and took hold of Samuel's neck. With terrible power he hurled the angel away, far off into the night.

Samuel tumbled over and over, unable to control his flight. Finally gathering his bearings and his wits, he charged back toward Gathan faster than light. He managed to catch the demon from behind, and wrenching his face backwards, he dug his fingers into Gathan's eye sockets. The demon faltered and released his captive. Jones fell through the cold air like a stone.

Alerted to the danger, Samuel swooped down and caught the curate before he hit the ground. As the angel attempted to carry Jones to safety, Gathan grabbed the feet of his heavenly foe in an icy grip. Samuel kicked with all his might, but the demon held him fast. The demon then slowly pulled Samuel up until they were face to face with each other. The stench of Hell exuding from Gathan almost overpowered Samuel, but his resolve, though surely tested and shaken, remained true. Jones lay lifeless in the angel's arms, unaware of the battle raging for his life, his soul.

"I can crush you, Samuel, like a sparrow in an eagle's talons! I can rip you apart." Gathan had grabbed Samuel's left arm and was turning him over and over as the angel clung desperately to the curate.

Samuel realized he could not win. Gathan was just too powerful. His only hope was to summon help. He gathered all the power of his voice and called, "Brothers! Angels of the Lord, come to my aid. I am attacked by Hell's own!"

At the sound, Gathan shuddered and placed his free hand over one ear.

Samuel looked out into the darkness, but there came no answer to his call.

"It seems you are alone with me, pathetic one!" Gathan now seemed to grow in stature and power, and seeing this, Samuel's heart sank. Gathan grasped the angel's head and twisted him around with terrible force until Samuel cried out in agony and let go of his charge. The demon took back his prize, stared into Samuel's eyes, and then simply let Jones slip from his fingers.

Samuel could do nothing but watch helplessly as Maynard Jones fell to his death.

Jones's body hit the stone flags of the pathway with a resounding *thump*. His skull hit the ground with such force that it splintered into myriad pieces. His inert body lay spread-eagled, crumpled and broken. The cracks in the stones began filling with his lifeless blood.

The evil deed was done.

Gathan released Samuel and began to rise into the night sky. "And you believe your God is greater than my lord!"

Samuel, bruised and battered, knelt beside the now lifeless body of the curate. He cradled the man in his arms and looked up at Gathan. "Curse you, Gathan!"

Gathan stopped in midflight, grinning back at Samuel.

"It is too late, my friend. I am already cursed and damned by one much greater than you."

All was quiet now. No vehicles moved along High Street. Dark clouds moved slowly across the night sky as a light drizzle of rain fell upon the prone figure.

Samuel and the captain stood beside the dead man. Samuel, shoulders dropped and head hung low, looked forlorn, sorrowful, and altogether crestfallen.

"Come, soldier, you couldn't have done any more than you did."

"I should have been here. I was too far away and didn't hear the alarms in time."

"You should have been here. But I don't think the outcome would have been any different." Bezalel put an arm around his companion's shoulders. "You could not have defeated Gathan. He is too clever and too strong. The Lord knows, even I might have been defeated by him."

Samuel looked up disbelievingly.

"He has no scruples, no compassion, and that can give him an advantage in battle."

In his despair, Samuel wasn't really hearing the captain's words of comfort.

"I could have gone for help. I should have called to you sooner!" Samuel pulled away from the taller angel.

"Samuel, listen to me. Even if I had received your message, I was too far away to help. Even if I had arrived in time . . . I might have chosen to restrain you rather than assist."

Samuel looked up in dismay. The rain fell heavier now, and puddles began to form around the body of Maynard Jones.

"Why didn't He send help? He sees all and knows all!"

The captain sighed. "Yes, He does. But this world belongs to Satan, and his demons have dominion here. Humans have been given the will to decide. Jones chose his own fate."

"Did he, sir? I saw him being deceived by that pestilence!" He broke off, unable to hold back his sobs. "If we cannot protect the innocent . . . then what are we here for? What use are we?"

"It is not for us to make those decisions, Samuel." Bezalel spoke tenderly, trying to console his charge. The captain drew him away from the body.

"Samuel, let me tell you something that is truly awesome, for it reveals the amazing heart of the God we serve. Mark this well: When our Lord Jesus was praying to His Father, the night before his crucifixion, He begged to have the burden taken from Him. His agony was so great that His sweat fell to the ground like great drops of blood. He asked if there was another way to atone for the sins of the human race, that He might be able to go that way rather than face the horror of death upon the cross. The Father's heart must have been breaking. But for salvation to work, it had to be done. There was no other way. Without our Lord's dreadful sacrifice upon the cross, all humanity would be doomed to a holocaust of corruption and final annihilation. Even the armies of the angelic host cannot begin to comprehend the courage of our Lord in that moment. He feared and dreaded the execution that awaited Him, yet he acquiesced, saying 'Father, your will be done, not mine.'

"We all know of the trials of the cross, but do we ever stop to think what the Father was going through? What anguish He must have felt in commanding His only Son to endure crucifixion? To be beaten, humiliated, and broken on the journey to Golgotha for mankind's sake? Do you think because He is Almighty God that He was somehow immune from the pain?

"In that moment before physical death, Jesus knew the heart of darkness. He was truly separated from the Father in Heaven. Jesus had taken upon Himself all the sins of the world, and the Father spurned the Son utterly, irrevocably. I am certain that Satan and his hordes rejoiced when they saw that the Father was abandoning His Son to apparent oblivion. All the demons of Hell gathered there on that hill outside Jerusalem to mock the Christ. They spat on Him, they abused Him, and they sang profane songs in celebration."

Samuel, his face still pale, looked into Bezalel's eyes and understood.

"Samuel, I know all this because, along with thousands of angels chosen by God to be witnesses, I was there. We did not know about the resurrection at that point. For all we knew, the blessed Trinity was being rent asunder, yet we could do nothing. We had been commanded to watch and wait. Many of your brothers that night wept bitterly as they saw Satan rejoice in debauched merriment."

Then Bezalel's face changed, and he exclaimed with unbridled joy, "Jesus had sacrificed Himself that all might live. Salvation came at a terrible cost, but the greater truth of love triumphed over evil. The Father's plan was truly finished, and nothing would ever be the same! I would have given my right arm to have seen Satan's face that Sunday morning when some unfortunate demon brought the news that Jesus lives!"

Samuel's heart began to beat fast.

The captain smiled at his charge. "Like the Father, we too must sometimes witness evil, feel hurt and pain, but we must never forget nor lose sight of the truth that our Lord reigns in Heaven and that we will, one day, see the ultimate destruction of Satan and all his demons, including Gathan.

"So there's no need for you to curse our enemy, Samuel. Heed my words and never utter a curse again—even to demons—for its evil intent will come back upon you. Curses will not add to Lucifer's misfortune or to that of his demons, for they are most certainly eternally damned."

SIX

Cutting across the churchyard toward High Street, a solitary man walked briskly into the wind and pouring rain, smartly holding onto his umbrella with both hands. With the rim of the umbrella obstructing his view, he almost stumbled over the body of the curate. Stepping back in horror, he instinctively averted his eyes from the gruesome scene. Turning back, but not looking directly at the corpse, he struggled out of his raincoat and threw it over the curate's shattered head.

The clock in the village struck six in the morning.

Standing in the lee of the church tower wall, the man's shaking hands fumbled in his pocket for his cell phone. Shortly after, the police arrived, followed by a single ambulance. A uniformed policeman opened the double iron gates at the side of the church so that the ambulance could drive onto the grounds to get near to the body. A few onlookers on their way to work had paused along the boundary wall, trying to figure out what had happened. The pedestrian's coat had been removed, and a police photographer was taking photographs of the splayed corpse. The paramedics waited patiently for the go-ahead from the detective in charge to bag up the body. After about an hour, but not before all the necessary procedures were complete, the body was taken by stretcher to the waiting ambulance. Within minutes, the vehicle was driving away down High Street. No siren was used to make its grim delivery to the town morgue.

Finally, it had stopped raining, and the skies were clearing. One of the policemen said to another, "It looks like it might be a nice day after all, so I'm thinking of going fishing." Nearby, the church's caretaker was busy with a broom and water hose, trying to eradicate the blood that stubbornly stained the pathway.

In the shelter of the main entrance, Inspector Paul Stewart was talking to the man who had found the unfortunate curate. The detective scribbled notes in a small black notebook as the man answered his questions.

"So you're sure you saw no one else in the vicinity of the body when you arrived?"

"No. But I wasn't really looking. I mean, I was really shaken, but I don't think there was anyone else about."

"And for the record, you didn't move the body?"

"What?! Are you mad, Inspector? I was horrified by the whole thing. I've never seen a dead body before, let alone one in that state." He put his hand to mouth, recalling the sight of the dead man. "No, all I did was toss my coat over the man, and then I backed away. Over there." He indicated the wall where he had stood to call the police. "And believe me, I didn't want to stick around, let alone look at it again."

"Well, thank you, sir. You've been most helpful. Can you give your contact information to the sergeant over there, in case we need to reach you again?"

"Is that likely?" There was a note of apprehension in the man's voice.

"We have your statement, and that may be enough. But it all depends on the coroner, you see."

"Oh, yes, of course. I understand."

The plainclothes detective shook the man's hand and watched him walk away.

Inspector Stewart put the notebook back into his pocket and stepped over to where the body had lain. Something didn't add up. He had been a cop for nearly thirty years, and he'd come to trust his instincts. He always seemed to know right off whether or not a case was going to be a straightforward one. At this moment, as he surveyed the scene, all his senses were clamoring loudly that something about this case was strangely wrong.

Stewart relished a challenge, but they were few and far between these days. He had started his career in London, where there was never a day or night when he wasn't tackling a serious crime. He was a good, honest cop, conscientious and always loyal to his bosses, willing to take on the dirty jobs that his colleagues studiously avoided. But as the years went by, he was repeatedly passed over for promotion, so he eventually moved on to other forces. After London, he went to Birmingham, and a few years later drifted to Liverpool, always enduring the same stagnation, facing the same issues. Life, he thought, was against him, and that's all there was to it. He had developed a phlegmatic view on this subject. Then his marriage had broken up when his wife found someone else who was a bit "luckier" than him. Eventually, Stewart had ended up in this little Welsh backwater, working out the dull days of his final years before early retirement. And beyond that? Well, he had no idea really, other than a vague notion of traveling abroad, perhaps to America to see the sights.

He looked again at the stones where now only traces of blood remained. The caretaker had done a thorough job. Then he gazed up at the top of the tower thoughtfully and puffed on a cigarette, his fifth this morning.

"Llewellyn, come over here a minute, will you?"

The detective sergeant dutifully obeyed. "Yes, sir?"

"Does anything strike you as odd about this business?"

"Odd? In what way, sir?"

Stewart indicated the top of the tower with his hand. The sergeant looked up to where he was pointing.

"Do you think the curate, even with a running jump from the top of the church, could have landed here where we're standing?"

The sergeant seemed to be doing some sort of calculation in his head, and then said, "I see what you mean."

"How far are we from the base of the tower?"

The sergeant ran over to the church wall and methodically paced out the distance in long strides. His last step brought him to the point where Stewart stood.

"About twenty feet, sir."

"Sergeant, you any good at the long jump?"

"Well, at school I was pretty good, but running was my best sport."

"Well . . . what do you think?"

"No, I guess not."

"Have you been around to the other side of the church?" Stewart asked.

"No, sir. But the forensics people have, I think."

"Do me a favor, lad. As you are so fond of running, sprint around the building and tell me if you see any sign of building works—ladders, scaffolding, and the like."

The sergeant took off in one direction, and within minutes, he reappeared from the opposite side of the church, puffing and holding his sides.

"Well?"

"Nothing at all, sir. Not a 'mewp' in sight."

"Not a *what* in sight?"

Llewellyn stood upright, pleased that he knew something the inspector did not.

"MEWP. It's an acronym. Stands for 'mobile elevated working platform.'" He had a smile on his face. "My brother-in-law Mick operates one. He's in the building business."

The inspector gazed studiously at Llewellyn but said nothing.

After a few moments of silence, the sergeant asked, "Why did you want me to check?"

"Because if the curate did fall from a great height, but not from the tower, then what did he fall from?" Then he smiled and said, "And I wanted to eliminate . . . MEWPs from the enquiry."

"Oh, I see. Yes, sir. Very clever, sir."

Stewart had started to walk back to his car when he heard the sergeant shout, "Sir, could he have fallen out of an aircraft?"

The inspector kept on walking, not saying anything.

Later, at the forensics lab, Stewart was inquiring as to whether the pathologist had determined the cause of death. The pathologist, taken aback, looked at with some surprise.

"Well," she said, and by the tone of her voice Stewart knew she was laboring the point, "the body struck a hard, immovable object—in this case, the ground—after being propelled by a force—in this case, gravity—which resulted in multiple fractures to the bones of the face, skull, neck, spine and chest area. This in turn caused massive trauma to the body's vital systems, thus resulting in immediate and fatal consequences—that is, the death of said victim." Her technical command of English was very good, but Stewart detected a strong accent.

The inspector thanked the pathologist for her description. "I daresay you are right, but—

"You *daresay* I am right? With all due respect, Inspector—"

Stewart cut her off. "Please, humor me, Miss Padelski. Just for a minute."

She folded her arms over her blood-stained lab coat and leaned back against the long metal table. "Actually, it's *Doctor* Padelski."

Stewart ignored this last remark. "What I need to be absolutely clear about is this." He held up his hand in a gesture indicating *Stay with me for a moment, please.* "Could this man have met his end by any other other means? For example, could his injuries have been inflicted by another individual who, say, beat him to a pulp with a blunt instrument? I mean, is it possible?"

He looked into her eyes, hoping for a yes.

She sighed. "In my professional opinion, the simple answer is emphatically NO. I could show you dozens of photographs of people beaten with all types of weapons, blunt and otherwise, but none of their injuries would resemble those of Curate Jones." Dr. Padelski cocked her head to one side and raised her eyebrows. "I can also show you photographs of people who have fallen, been pushed, or thrown themselves from high places onto concrete, tarmac, or stone, thus sustaining injuries that would resemble those of Mr. Jones."

The inspector shrugged.

"Now, if you will excuse me," she said, smiling, "I have to clean up. I have a date, and I would like to freshen up a bit beforehand."

SEVEN

The doorbell rang at the rectory, the vicar's home on the church grounds. Reverend Stannard's elderly housekeeper, Mary, opened the door and was surprised to find a pair of strangers there.

"Good morning, ma'am. I am Detective Inspector Stewart, and this is Detective Sergeant Llewellyn." He showed her his ID. She squinted at the plastic card and nodded her head but didn't actually read what was written on the card as she wasn't wearing her reading glasses.

"Is it possible that I could have a word with Reverend Stannard?"

Mary hesitated, and the inspector added, "Please tell the vicar that I apologize for the early call, but it is important."

It was just before nine in the morning, and Stewart had already been at work for over two hours. The Reverend Stannard, however, had not even risen from his bed.

Mary said, "Excuse me a moment, and I'll see if the reverend is available." She was about to shut the door when the sergeant placed his foot on the doorstep so that she could not close it. She looked at his foot and then said, "Well, I suppose you had better come inside."

Once in the hall, she said, "He hasn't come down yet for breakfast, but if you care to wait, I'll let him know you're here."

At the top of the wide oak stairs, Mary tapped lightly on the vicar's bedroom door.

"Reverend? Hello sir? Vicar, sir!" she called in a loud whisper, her mouth close to the door panel.

The door opened a few inches wide, and a bleary-eyed Stannard looked out. "What on earth is it, Mary?" There was more than a note of irritation in his voice.

"Pardon me, sir, but there are two police officers downstairs in the hall. One of them's an inspector, wanting to see you right away. He says it's important."

Stannard opened the door wider so that he could see down into the hall where the two policemen stood waiting.

"Very well, tell them I'll be down as soon as I can."

The vicar pulled on his dressing gown and tied it securely at the waist in a double knot. He stepped into his bedroom slippers and smoothed his hair flat with a brush from the bedside table before going downstairs.

Stewart stepped forward to greet the vicar as he appeared at the foot of the stairs. The vicar was a full head taller than the inspector.

"Good morning, sir." Stewart held out his hand, but Stannard placed his own hands into the pockets of his gown.

"Now, what's this all about? I hope it is something important for you to intrude upon me at this hour of the morning."

Mary stepped back into the kitchen but did not close the door behind her. She was out of sight but listening intently to the conversation in the hall.

"Well, sir. I believe a Mr. Maynard Jones is your man at Trinity Church."

"Yes, that's correct."

"Well, I am sorry to inform you that his body was found this morning at the foot of the church tower. The first indication is that he fell or perhaps jumped to his death sometime during the night."

There was a cry from the back of the hall.

Only Llewellyn turned towards the sound. The vicar showed no emotion at all.

Stannard spoke in a cold, dispassionate tone. "And what . . ." He seemed to be searching for the right words. "What exactly do you wish *me* to do, Inspector?"

Stewart raised an eyebrow at the vicar's disinterested response to the sad news. "I must ask you a few questions. Perhaps if we could sit down, I'll go through them as quickly as I can and let you get on with your day."

For a moment, Stannard looked as if he might refuse the request. Then the expression on his face changed from one of annoyance to reluctant compliance. "We can go in here." He motioned them to follow him into his study.

"Perhaps your housekeeper could offer us a cup of tea or coffee, sir. We have been hard at it this morning."

Stannard ignored the suggestion and closed the study door behind them. He then sat down behind his desk and, allowing his guests to continue standing, waited for the inspector to begin.

Inspector Stewart took out his notebook and pen. Llewellyn stood fidgeting by his side.

Stewart saw that Stannard's desk was littered with books and albums full of postage stamps, both rare and old. "Ah, I see you are a stamp collector, vicar. I myself had a collection when I was a boy. I recall many hours of pleasure poring over—"

"Yes, I am sure of it, Inspector. But I am not a stamp collector; I am a philatelist. And a very prominent one at that."

"Yes, well . . ." All Stewart could do was nod. "The church caretaker, Mr. Wilson, identified the deceased as Maynard Jones, your curate. However, we will need to contact Mr. Jones's next of kin to make a formal identification. Can you help us with our enquiry?" Stewart had given up addressing the vicar as "sir."

"I believe both his parents are dead. I am not aware of any brothers or sisters. In fact, I don't believe the man had any close relatives. He had a . . ." Stannard hesitated, "a *friend* in London, but I have no idea where." He said "friend" in such a way that made it clear Stannard held the relationship in contempt.

"I see. Well, in that case—"

"In that case, Inspector, I shall make myself available to verify the body as that of Mr. Jones."

"I ought to say he's in a pretty bad shape, but I suppose the coroner will, um, tidy things up."

"Inspector, I saw action in the army. The dead and dying do not shock me. Can we move on?"

"Yes, of course." By this time, Stewart had begun to have his fill of this man, though couldn't reconcile in his mind the vicar's attitude with his being a man of the cloth. "I will contact you, then, about viewing the corpse."

"Is there anything else?" Stannard was half rising out of his chair.

"Yes, there are a few other details." Even if there hadn't been, Stewart would not be rushed. "Was the curate in his post long?"

Stannard sat down again. "He joined my church about two years ago. He came, or rather, he was *sent* by his former bishop in an agreement made with my own diocese. Calling in a favor, you might say."

"A favor?" Stewart looked puzzled.

"Do I have to spell it out, Inspector? Ecclesiastical privileges! And anyway, *de mortuis nil nisi bonum!*'" Stannard looked at them scornfully. "Your Latin a bit rusty, Inspector? Roughly translated, it means 'Say nothing but good about the dead.'"

"Didn't someone once say the dead deserve the truth?"

"You are quoting Voltaire, Inspector, the despised French polemicist. Not someone I would have thought you'd have much interest in," Stannard replied with undisguised sarcasm.

"Quite right, sir. I overheard it in a pub quiz. Anyway you were explaining about the curate . . . ?"

The vicar continued. "He was sent down from London because of some ecclesiastical misdemeanor. At first, I was not in the slightest bit interested in the man's shortcomings—or in his sins, at that—just as long as they did not interfere with his duties at Saint David's and left me free to pursue mine."

"And did they?" Stewart asked.

"Did they what?"

"His misdemeanors. Did they interfere with his duties?"

The vicar looked pained. "Not exactly, no. But his health over the past six months has failed him. And his duties too, I might add."

"You surely can't blame the man for being ill, can you?"

Stewart did not expect a reply, but he got one.

"In this particular case, Inspector, I can hold the man to account, for it was his lifestyle choices that resulted in his infirmities. These in turn rendered him unfit to serve the church."

Stewart glanced down at his notes. "And his misdemeanors? What are we talking about here, exactly?"

"Nothing for you to be concerned about, Inspector. No felonies of any criminal sort. However, there was a time," he mused, "when such things were considered most properly to be within the compass of the law."

"I see . . . well, no, I don't actually. Can you be more specific as to the nature of these issues?"

Stannard raised his hand to let them know he was done. Standing, he ushered his guests to the door. "Inspector, I have religious duties to attend to. Perhaps you would be so kind as to put down on paper any other questions you have, and I will endeavor to answer them at a more convenient time. Let me know when you wish me to identify the body." As an afterthought, he said, "Oh, and very remiss of me under the circumstances. Let me know when you can release the body. I will arrange a suitable funeral." Then he called down the hall, "Mary, show these two gentlemen out."

With this last remark, Stannard turned and went back into his study. The click of the metal latch had a sort of finality to it. The interview was definitely over.

Mary rapped lightly and then opened the study door. Stannard had a magnifying glass in his hand and was closely examining some stamps in a book on his desk. With fresh tears welling up in her eyes, she dabbed at her face with the hem of her floral-decorated apron.

"Oh, sir, what a terrible thing to happen."

Looking up from the book, Stannard gazed at her with pure disdain. "Yes, yes. Have my breakfast ready by nine-thirty, will you? I have to go out. And for God's sake, woman, don't burn my toast again."

Outside, Stewart asked Llewellyn, "Well, what did you make of him, Sergeant? Quite the model of the caring Christian minister, eh?"

"Well, sir, in my humble opinion, I thought he had more of the undertaker about him than the church."

Stewart could not stop himself from laughing out loud. "You're dead right there."

"Dead right! A good pun, sir."

Early the next morning, Stewart sat in his car, waiting for the vicar to leave the rectory. He knew that with the curate gone, the minister would be taking morning prayers at the church. He lit up a cigarette, then tossed the spent match out the open window and into the gutter. Stannard soon emerged from the house, and Stewart watched the tall figure in black until he disappeared from sight at the top of the road. Giving him a few more minutes, just in case he'd forgotten something and had doubled back, the inspector climbed out of the vehicle. He stubbed the cigarette butt out on the pavement, and then walked across to the rectory and rang the bell. He heard it ringing at the back of the house. The housekeeper came to the door, drying her hands on a checkered tea towel.

"Oh, hullo, Inspector. I'm afraid you just missed the reverend. He's gone over to the church."

"Oh? When will he be back?"

"In about an hour, I should think."

"Perhaps I'll try again later, then." He half turned as if to go. "Actually, it wasn't anything serious. I just wanted to have a look at the curate's lodgings. I assume he lived in town. It would help me finish the paperwork, tick boxes, et cetera. A copper's work isn't done until the paperwork, you know . . ." He let his voice trail off. "Perhaps I don't need to trouble the vicar. He's a busy man, after all. Can you point me in the right direction, Mary?" He smiled his most sincere smile.

"Well, if it's just routine, I guess it won't do any harm. I'll just get you the spare key to the cottage."

As she turned back along the hall, Stewart grinned and congratulated himself.

"Here you are, Inspector. It's just up the hill from the hotel. A little white cottage, last one on the row."

"Thank you, Mary. I'll have it back within the hour," he lied. "You have a good day now."

The cottage was the last one of a terrace of six dwellings, probably built in the mid-nineteenth century for the slate quarry workers. Whitewashed stone walls, grey slate roofs, and small wooden windows. Stewart knew before he went inside that it was a "two up, two down" residence with no garden. There was, however, a small paved yard where the outside privy would once have stood.

Opening the door to the hall, the first thing that hit him was the smell. Stewart instinctively placed his hand over his nose and mouth. The dwelling reeked of rotting meat.

He stepped into the kitchen, drew back the curtains, and threw open the windows as wide as they would go. Retreating to the hall, he left the front door ajar and went in search of more windows he could open to let in some fresh air.

Seated unseen at the bottom of the stairs was the elderly demon Jusach, who was to report back to his master when the new holy man arrived. He watched with amusement as Stewart continued trying to dispel the fetid air. Jusach thought the stench just right for his tastes, but he was glad of the interruption as he was getting quite bored of house-sitting.

The inspector returned to the hall and, looking up the stairs, stepped right through Jusach, who did not bother to move.

On the upper landing, there were three doors leading to bedrooms. The room to the left of the bathroom was being used as a storeroom and was filled with several unopened tea chests and cardboard boxes, probably left over from when Jones had moved in. The inspector slit the tape that sealed one of the boxes and peered inside. Nothing unusual at all, but then what was he expecting to find?

Other large cartons contained clothes, all neatly folded. The remaining boxes housed dozens of books and a few old Bibles. The tea chests contained bric-a-brac, personal items, and breakable ornaments packed in paper and straw. All pretty normal stuff. Stewart sat down on a tea chest that was sturdy enough to hold his two hundred pounds. He withdrew from his jacket pocket a pack of cigarettes and, without thinking, put it between his lips. Striking a match, he hesitated before lighting the cigarette, considering what exactly he was looking for. The match was burning perilously close to his finger when Jusach, now sitting beside him on another box, snuffed out the flame with his fingers. Surprisingly, this obtained no reaction from the man. The inspector placed the burned-out match back into the box and withdrew another. It flamed when struck, but this time, just as he was going to ignite the cigarette, Jusach blew it out.

"I think someone is trying to tell me I need to give up smoking."

Placing the cigarette back into the pack, Stewart stood and found the bathroom. He thought about making use of the facilities but changed his mind when he saw the state of the toilet and wash bowl. The once-white porcelain bowl was encrusted with the remains of Jones's last supper, and the toilet was equally malodorous. Several huge bluebottles buzzed around the lavatory. The mirror on the wall was cracked, and Stewart couldn't even see his face for the coating of heavy dust on its surface. On the floor of the bathroom lay a bar of soap, a pair of flannels, and numerous tablets of differing sizes and colors. Stewart bent down to examine them closely, thinking they might be illegal drugs. He poked at a few with the sharp end of his pen. They all appeared to have inscriptions. These were prescription tablets, legally obtained.

Stewart began to think that there was nothing suspicious about this man. He saw no evidence of crime or serious wrongdoing. As Stannard had confirmed, the man had been sick. Perhaps all that met the eye here was just as it should be. He was just another pathetic individual who had chosen to take his own life. The nagging thought returned, and he spoke it out loud to give it credence. "So how did the body get so far from the tower?"

Jusach sat on the toilet and laughed. "Oh, there is a remarkable answer to that question, but you will never wise up to it you stupid cretin!" Jusach studied Stewart. "This man is not a holy one, I am sure," he said with a deep sigh, "which means that I have to remain here."

Leaning against the door jamb, Stewart was suddenly overwhelmed by a wave of tiredness. He didn't like this place. Not only did the surroundings depress him, but he sensed that there was something not right about it. And that awful stink that seemed to follow him around! He was now dying for a smoke. He remembered there was a good pub at the bottom of the hill, The Tram's Halt. His face brightened as he recalled that opposite the public house there was a fish-and-chips restaurant where he could have his lunch after a pint. He glanced into the main bedroom without stepping in, surveyed the mess, and thought to himself that there was nothing of significance to discover here.

He shut the windows and locked the door on his way out. Not looking back, he put the matter out of his mind. He was already anticipating a pint or two, a cigarette, and then fish and chips to round off the morning.

Stewart didn't see the malevolent, grinning face of the demon Jusach watching him from the upstairs window as the inspector made his way down the hill.

EIGHT

The curate's body was released for burial. However, Reverend Stannard had other plans. There would be no burial, no ceremony. Instead, Stannard instructed the undertakers to take the body to the local crematorium for incineration. A member of the crematorium staff unceremoniously scattered the ashes amongst the leaves and cigarette butts where staff and mourners often stole a quick smoke between services. The vicar had managed to suppress all but the most innocuous reporting of the Jones's death in the local newspaper. The published item that appeared at the bottom of page six simply read, "Tragic Death—Local curate falls from church tower whilst carrying out maintenance."

During the Sunday service following the disposal of the remains of the curate, the vicar delivered a short obituary, telling the small congregation that Maynard Jones would be missed. He then instructed the congregation to turn to hymn 501 in their hymnals.

Monday morning started much the same as any other day. The Reverend Sydney Stannard sat down to breakfast in the dining room of the rectory. Mary brought in a tray with a selection of lightly boiled eggs, buttered slices of white bread, toast in a silver rack, a porcelain jar of the finest marmalade, and a pat of warm salted butter. She returned with a cafetière of freshly brewed coffee. Reverend Stannard placed one egg in a wooden egg cup, sliced off the top, tipped a little salt from an ornate shaker onto the soft, steaming yoke, and then topped it with a smidgen of butter to complete the ritual. He dipped a slice of bread into the egg and mused over the headlines in *The Times*.

The news was always the same, he thought. He was sure that if he scanned the headlines of *The Times* for the past forty years, the essence would be the same. Wars, famine, societal violence, the rich getting richer, and the poor getting . . . well, more unpalatable. He smiled as he took another bite of the egg and bread.

He folded the newspaper and placed it carefully beyond the marmalade. He then picked up the latest copy of *The Stamp Collector* and studied the front page, which included a photograph of a very rare stamp discovered quite by accident within the pages of a nineteenth-century ladies' magazine. The lucky collector had been leafing through the old magazine in a second-hand bookshop and had recognized immediately the worth of the stamp. The person had purchased the magazine without declaring the find. The magazine was priced at a couple of pounds, and the person had purchased the publication and its contents quite legally. Everything was aboveboard.

The Reverend Stannard had moved on to his second egg, a little disappointed that it was not as soft as the first. He must have a word with Mary about it. Surely she could stagger the cooking schedule to get it right. He raised his eyebrows and sighed.

His thoughts returned to the rare stamp displayed on the cover. *Yes, I would have done the same. There is no crime in such a thing. Why, the stamp could have easily been worthless! Would one have to declare the existence of a worthless stamp inside a magazine? I think not. So logically it would follow that the deed and, therefore, the acquisition of the valuable stamp are blameless.*

He smiled at the cleverness of his logic and then began to reminisce about his days as a student at Oxford after the war.

The Reverend Stannard picked up a little silver bell off the white tablecloth and gave it a shake. Mary entered the dining room a few moments after.

"Sir, is everything quite all right? With your breakfast, I mean? I done it just as you always like it."

He winced at her grammar and thought of the second boiled egg.

"Yes, well, it's fine. What I was going to say was this: We do not have a curate at present to cover my day off . . ."

Mary looked down at the carpet, a little embarrassed, recalling the unfortunate death of the late Curate Jones.

"However, I do intend to take this day off as usual. I don't think there is anything pressing on the church calendar, and I have an important meeting in Chester. If anyone telephones, please take a message and I'll return their call tomorrow. Will you do that?" It was a statement rather than a request. "If you will be so kind," he said with exaggerated politeness.

"Yes, of course, sir. And will you be home for dinner, sir?"

"I shall be back around seven. That is, of course, as long as the train is not delayed."

"Will that be all, Reverend Sir?"

Stannard nodded, and Mary did a clumsy curtsy and left the dining room, closing the door behind her as she went. The vicar poured himself a cup of coffee and added two cubes of brown sugar. As he sipped at his coffee, he leafed through the philately magazine, searching for an advertisement at the back of the periodical. Withdrawing his half-hunter watch from his waistcoat pocket, he noted the time. It was almost 8:30 a.m. He still had time to catch the 9:20 to Chester. Before he rose from the desk, he wrote a note to himself on a scrap of paper: *Get a new curate!*

The train pulled into Chester Station on time. It was a short walk to the busy town centre and just a few streets beyond to a quieter street where the Masonic rooms were situated.

Inside, the main hall was filled with dozens of stalls manned by private sellers, the Royal Philatelic Society, local organizations, the major auction houses, and a few renowned purveyors of rare postage stamps. Chrysalis, Larmondy, and Allen were represented by stands that were a cut above the rest, and behind these tables stood solemn men in dark pinstriped suits ready to politely exchange rare stamps for substantial sums in cash or bank drafts.

There was an enthusiastic buzz emanating from all corners of the hall. Here and there, earnest negotiations were being enacted. There was no laughter in the room. This was serious business, after all, and all transactions were carried out with polite servility and with lightly fingered handshakes. Briefcases were clutched tightly, for even here, wolves milled about in sheep's clothing, hoping for an easy take.

Reverend Stannard strolled slowly through the hall, taking his time to survey the offerings. He disregarded those stalls bent on removing hard-earned cash from enthusiastic amateurs and instead honed in on the booths where the truly valuable stamps were displayed under glass covers. Here, small gatherings of serious collectors bowed low over the merchandise, their magnifying glasses and monocles held close to the stamps, the expert eyes of the initiated fully appreciating and studying the wares. Stannard hovered at the rear of these small groupings, eavesdropping on conversations and weighing the possibilities before making up his own mind which stands to focus his attention upon.

Walking slowly away from one such stand, he noticed another clergyman in his collar clutching his briefcase close to his chest and anxiously looking about. Stannard watched as the man climbed quickly up a wide staircase to the balcony area where seats and tables had been set out for coffee and tea. Stannard followed the man upstairs and, seeing him settle at a nearby table, decided to join him.

Standing over the man, Reverend Stannard introduced himself. "I see you are a man of the cloth. I am also, but as you can see, I am in civvies. It's my day off."

He held out a hand to the seated man.

The man in the collar got up from his chair and, still clutching his case to his chest, held out his own hand. "Pleased to make your acquaintance, Reverend. I am Alexander Martin." They shook hands. As Martin took his seat once more, his eyes darted left and right in an agitated fashion.

Stannard sat down across from him. "Please forgive me for asking, but you seem troubled. Can I help?" He chuckled. "We ought to be of help to each other, I suppose, being men of God."

The man shuddered involuntarily. "Yes, I suppose so . . . help, well, I don't know. I *am* in a bit of predicament. I traveled from Norwich last night and planned to spend the day here at the sales, hoping to sell some of my collection. There is a dire need in my parish, and I thought by selling my collection I could help to meet that need. But I am at my wit's end to know what I am going to do now, for I have just received a message from the bishop's office to return straight away on an urgent matter."

Stannard was intrigued. "I am myself a serious collector. I came today intending to purchase some interesting exhibits, though not *too* highly priced." He smiled.

The clergyman returned a very weak smile.

"Do you think this meeting—between us I mean—could be the Lord's doing?"

Reverend Stannard shifted uneasily in his chair and said, "I suppose it could be." The thought of what might be in the priest's briefcase caused his mouth to water. "The Lord does move in mysterious ways."

Suddenly, the seated man stood up and thrust the briefcase into Stannard's hands. "Look, I've got to telephone the church office to let them know I'm returning on the next train. Please take a look at the collection and let me know how much you are willing to for it. I'll be back momentarily. Please take care of the stamps. I've had them since I was a boy."

With that he turned, descended the staircase, and disappeared into the crowd.

Stannard wiped his mouth with a white handkerchief he carried in his jacket pocket. He placed his own case safely between his legs and started to open the straps of Reverend Martin's brown leather case. He laid the case flat on the table and clicked open the catch. Inside he found a battered old stamp album, the sort that was sold on almost every high street toy shop in the 1940s and '50s. Before removing the album from the case, he looked to see if anyone was watching him. Everyone else seemed to be engrossed in their own affairs. He took the album out and laid it on the table before him. He wiped his mouth again, this time with the back of his hand. For no good reason, he began to tremble a little. This perfectly ordinary child's stamp album held his fascination, and the level of anticipation made beads of sweat break out on his forehead. He felt like an archaeologist about to open a newly discovered tomb in the Valley of the Kings.

He carefully opened the album and scanned the first few pages, but all he saw were the most common of stamps usually bought in packets from mail-order advertisements. These packets, cheaply sold for a few pence, contained hundreds of colorful stamps from all over the world, and many a boy and girl had spent numerous hours posting them into their prized albums. His own interest had started in this selfsame way.

Stannard shut the album. He wasn't going to rummage through all the stamps in the book. It was obviously a cheap and nasty little collection. He thought of what he was going to say to the clergyman when he returned. *Perhaps I should just put it back in the case and leave it here*, he thought. *It's worthless, after all.*

But his curiosity niggled at him, and he opened the album once more. He flicked casually through the pages, only half noticing the common collection of stamps on every page. Then he caught sight of something different from the norm: a faded brown envelope. He withdrew the envelope from between the pages. There was no address or name on the front or back. He opened the envelope and drew out the contents slowly. What lay before him now was a collection of intense black and grey Victorian one-penny stamps in mint condition. His heart began to race. He placed the palm of his hand quickly over the packet of rare stamps. He guessed there must be a dozen or so. To purchase such a set from one of the vendors here today, he would need at least 20,000 pounds. His breath raced as his heart beat faster and faster.

"Calm yourself, Sydney," he berated himself. "For God's sake, maintain your sense of decorum."

At that moment Reverend Martin returned, looking flushed and red-faced. He looked down at the album under Stannard's hands. "I see you have looked at the stamps. I know most of them are not valuable, but I thought that some expert here might take a look and find something of interest. Something of value."

Stannard drew a deep breath in. "I quickly looked over your collection." He paused before continuing. "To be honest, there isn't much there, I'm afraid. But having said that," he managed to add cheerfully, "there are a few items that would certainly grace my own collection."

The clergyman sat down with a weary look on his face. "I haven't much time. I was hoping to get about four or even five hundred . . ." His voice trailed off as if he had uttered an absurd sum.

Stannard took his hand off the album to show that he was not desperate to buy. He placed his hands in his lap. He had about £600 with him and had been prepared to spend it all. "I tell you what. I could go as high as 350 pounds. The stamps are not worth more than 200, but let me add a generous amount to help a brother in need. Would that help meet the need in your parish?"

"I wish it were that simple." His eyes begged Stannard to offer more. "The money is needed rather urgently for a poor fellow who has hit hard times."

Stannard did not want to think about the true value of the Victorian stamps he'd found. Then again, he deliberated, they might be forgeries. This clergyman might not be what he seemed to be. He might be a con man, a fraud. But Stannard couldn't very well take the stamps downstairs to be verified, as that would raise Martin's suspicions.

"Would you accept four hundred pounds? In cash of course. You'd be lucky indeed to get two hundred from the dealers down in the pit. I'll take the extra from my own poor fund."

"You have it with you?"

"Yes. I have been saving up funds for quite some time."

The clergyman stepped closer to Stannard. "You are an answer to prayer. Let us shake on it, then. And I thank you for your generosity! I am sure the good Lord will repay you."

Stannard counted out the money, and Reverend Martin carefully folded the notes. He shook Stannard's hand again warmly and hurried out of the building.

The vicar seated himself at the table and gestured to a waitress. "A cappuccino. And bring me some brown sugar. And mind, not in those awful paper things."

Stannard slipped the album into his case, and patting the side, congratulated himself. He then said under his breath, "God forgive me."

NINE

A year earlier on the other side of Great Britain, in Essex, another personal drama had been unfolding. Richard Benton had spent twelve long months as assistant to the bishop of Helmsbridge at the diocesan headquarters. A graduate of Oxford University, Richard's duties included fetching the bishop's morning tea, acting as messenger boy between the various clerical departments at the cathedral, and tidying up the bishop's desk every day before His Grace arrived. The high point of the week was when the bishop entrusted him to proofread some of the weekly missives before they were e-mailed to the outlying parishes.

Even as a teenager, Richard had known he was called to the ministry. He had studied the Word of God from a young age and had listened intently to all the Sunday sermons exhorting young men to enter the mission field. He fostered great ambitions in his heart. He hoped to emulate the Christian heroes and the modern-day saints who had risked life and limb to carry the gospel to the far corners of the world. As a boy, Richard had been enthralled with *Butler's Lives of the Saints*, with reading of a faith in Christ that never wavered despite enduring terrible tribulations. How brave these men and women had been in the face of persecution, torture, and all manner of privations. St. Stephen, for instance, when faced with imminent death, refused to recant his beliefs and chose to praise God even as he was being stoned.

Richard harbored hopes of going to China, like Hudson Taylor or Gladys Aylward, or perhaps going native in the wilds of Africa or South America to bring Christ to the heathen masses. He wanted to follow in the footsteps of those intrepid souls who had crossed hundreds of miles of desert on foot and then fought through dense jungles to reach distant tribes. He was willing to brave the dangers of disease, wild beasts, cannibals, and head-hunting savages in order to shine the light of the gospel in the darkness.

He had nurtured these dreams throughout college, even though he had discovered from historical accounts that a certain amount of exaggeration and hyperbole had crept into many stories of the great heroes of the faith. Yet his vision to serve God in the mission field never wavered. These stories, no matter how fantastic, had stirred him to do the same as they, whatever the personal cost.

Sadly, Richard knew, workers were needed in his own country. The mission field here was ready for harvest, and the laborers numbered lamentably few. Could it be that the mission ground for him was not to be in far-flung places, but in the isles of the United Kingdom? Perhaps for him there would be no jungles or deserts; maybe he would have to be content with the mundane streets and houses of Birmingham, and Manchester, for in this century it was certainly true that peoples from all the wild and wonderful lands of the globe had migrated to the United Kingdom.

At Oxford, Richard had studied and worked diligently, knowing that a degree would be his passport to success as a clergyman or missionary. He possessed no ambitions of becoming a bishop or a charismatic leader to a large flock. He felt his calling was to the poor and the sick, to bring them the truth that could set them free from poverty and ignorance. Doing well academically was simply a means to an end, but he had been sure that top results would command respect from his peers and future employers. He hoped also that graduating at the top of his class would grant him a certain amount of flexibility in choosing his own path.

He had met his future wife, Sarah, at a student party. Although both tended toward shyness, they soon found that they shared ideas about how the Christian faith could make a real difference in today's society. They had similar backgrounds, having been brought up in middle-class churchgoing families, where God was acknowledged during "grace" at evening meals but otherwise went unmentioned from Monday through Saturday. Their parents' faith extended to attending church twice on Sundays and depositing a few pounds in the offertory. Richard and Sarah both instinctively knew there was much more to be experienced in Christ than the mere convention of weekly church services.

They sat in a corner at the party, sipping juice from wine glasses and exchanging views on the state of the world. They shared their dreams and aspirations and talked of what they would do after graduation if presented with the opportunity. After an hour or so, when the music became too loud for them to talk without shouting— when their friends had begun to get visibly drunk—Richard and Sarah stood up and left together. They took a slow walk back to the college. It was a pleasant evening in late autumn when the evening chill has not grown too cold to bear. The pavement was covered in a carpet of yellowing leaves, fallen from the old oak trees of Oxford. The stars above the city shone bright in a black, cloudless sky. As they approached the university lodgings, Richard surprised himself by boldly slipping his hand into Sarah's own. The act seemed so natural, as if it was meant to be. They stopped under the stone arch of the gate that led into Sarah's college, and she turned to say goodnight and smiled expectantly, as though waiting for Richard to kiss her. He did, but so clumsily, she must have sensed immediately that he had never kissed a girl before.

During the next few months, a mutually deep expression of affection had grown between them. Richard had no doubt that God meant for them to be together. In sharing their thoughts, he was often amazed at how compatible they were in so many ways. At times, it all seemed too good to be true. They seemed to have no differences or disagreements, and they never argued about anything. They decided early on they would spend their lives together as man and wife. Both knew deep inside that their future happiness was to be found in surrendering every part of their lives to God, including the much-awaited sacrament of marriage. To Richard's surprise, Sarah's parents gave full consent, and the Bentons were married in Oxford early in the new year.

After the wedding, they moved into a cheap one-bedroom flat in the suburbs of Oxford, where they lived an idyllic life. Days were spent happily attending lectures and tutorials, while their evenings consisted of studying side by side on the sofa, their hands often intertwined whilst flipping pages of textbooks, only letting go when a free hand was needed to jot down notes. On Sundays they attended a local Anglican church, entering into the fullness of worship. After church, they'd often laze around at home, talking about what the future might hold and where the Lord might send them. Richard still dreamt of exotic places far from England, and Sarah listened with a calm, if restrained, enthusiasm as Richard waxed lyrical about his passion to serve God abroad. They would pore over maps of the world, tracing out South America and the Far East with their fingertips, dreaming of the places where the good news of the gospel needed to be preached. Sarah was always quick to voice her support, saying she would follow wherever Richard wanted to go, wherever he was sent. To her mind, meekness was a sign of spiritual strength, not weakness, and she fully intended to obey her husband in all things, as she had promised in her wedding vows.

Richard Benton received a first-class honors degree in theology and divinity, as expected, and Sarah obtained a creditable 2:1 in English literature. They discussed their options and decided he would apply for a position with the Church of England, rather than with a denomination with which, to be honest, they had had little or no contact. Sarah aspired to be a children's teacher, but it was agreed she would put her own career on hold until Richard had obtained a preferred permanent position.

Richard was quickly invited to several interviews. The *Church Times* employment page was full of vacancies. There may have been a recession in the land, but it would seem there was an acute shortage of clerics. Richard knew he could easily get a post as a curate or as an assistant vicar in any one of numerous parishes throughout England, but one morning, while scanning available situations, he had noticed a posting for an assistant to the bishop of Helmsbridge. The advertisement indicated a preference for a first-class honors degree from a leading university. As Richard read the notice again, the idea of being an assistant to a bishop delighted his ego. He felt a high degree of satisfaction from holding a first-class degree with honors from Oxford, which everyone knew was the finest university in the land, possibly the world. He glanced up with pride at the framed certificates on the wall. He didn't need a colorful imagination to see himself strolling through the cathedral and diocesan corridors carrying an armful of important papers and chatting with the bishop and his archdeacon about great ecclesiastical affairs.

Sarah asked, "What are you smiling about?"

Richard returned from his reverie. "Nothing, really . . . There's a job here, that's all, as assistant to the bishop of Helmsbridge. I was just imagining what it might be like. You know, rubbing shoulders with the high and mighty. Did you know that the cathedral in Helmsbridge was constructed in the thirteenth century?"

"Really? That old? As for what it would be like, I think it would be very much like being at Oxford: musty old buildings and stepping aside for crusty old men wearing funny gowns and hats."

Richard looked a trifle peeved. "Well, I imagine it would be like stepping back to the early days of the church. To be at the spiritual heart of England . . ." His mind wandered off again.

"Richard," she exclaimed incredulously, "That was then and now is . . . well, it isn't quite like that now, is it? I thought you wanted to get started right away and minister to the poor and the needy? Isn't that what you wanted?"

He fidgeted beside her on the sofa, and as he spoke, he averted his eyes from her. "Yes, I know," he said a little too forcefully. "But I've been thinking about that—"

"And praying about it? This is the first time you've mentioned it to me."

"I just feel that a spell in the bishop's palace, at the hub of things, I might learn . . ." He paused, searching for the right words. "I might pick up some valuable skills and insights that would benefit us later in the field. Becoming friends with a bishop may prove useful, too. Simply being a subordinate to a vicar wouldn't give me those chances."

Sarah looked at her husband. She wasn't sure that his argument was a valid one, but she considered that perhaps it couldn't do any harm to delay their original goal. And anyway, she mused, this might be part of God's plan. If it wasn't, they would soon find out.

"So when's the interview?" she asked brightly.

The interview with Bishop John Laidlaw went well, and indeed it seemed that Richard was a perfect fit for the job. As it turned out, the bishop had attended the same college at Oxford as Richard. He confided to Richard that he'd been unimpressed with the other candidates, who were mostly from inferior universities, and offered him the post on the spot. Richard told him he would like a few days to think it over and pray about it. The bishop had smiled but said somewhat peevishly, "Well, let's hope the Lord isn't too busy to get back to you with a swift reply. Call me by the end of the week with your answer."

Richard had to be sure that this was the right thing to do, but in truth he made up his mind on the train back to Oxford. He prayed about the matter with Sarah that evening, and they interpreted the

Lord's silence on the matter as an indication that no obstacles stood in their way and the door was open. Richard called the bishop's office the next morning to accept the job and to say that he could start right away. That night the young couple celebrated by dining at their favorite Italian restaurant.

The next few weeks were filled with the ordinary tasks of settling into the job and a new home. Richard and Sarah borrowed money from their parents to tide them over for the first few months. They put down a deposit on a spacious flat in a large Victorian house located on a leafy avenue on the west side, barely a fifteen-minute walk from the bishop's offices. The flat was near to the municipal swimming pool and the bustling centre of Helmsbridge.

Sarah wasn't idle during this period. She spent time shopping in secondhand stores for inexpensive furniture and household appliances that had not been supplied by their new landlord. Now and again, over a cup of coffee, she scanned the "help wanted" section of the local newspaper for job possibilities. In association with a local Christian charity, she spent one day a week at a homeless shelter, preparing food and handing out soup, sandwiches, and smiles to the less fortunate of this otherwise wealthy community. Richard noticed that she was usually in good spirits after spending the day at the shelter. Clearly, Sarah's vocation was to minister to those in need.

As the months passed, the shine wore off the newness of the work for Richard. Yes, he attended several paid courses on church management, both fiscal and parochial, and he did learn much about the day-to-day running of a cathedral and diocese. But he began to feel that something was missing in the daily ordinances. He began to wonder if he had indeed made the right choice in taking this job. Whenever he tried to bring up the subject of his career, of his desire to grow spiritually and find his place in the church, Bishop Laidlaw was always too busy to listen. It also was a disappointment to Richard that he had not managed to make any friends or find a suitable spiritual

mentor and confidante among the many other clergymen with whom
he worked.

The atmosphere of the diocesan office was like that of a place of
commerce or a private company, with endless rounds of meetings,
deadlines, targets to meet, programs to organize, and schedules and
minutes to be typed and distributed. Though all was done in the name
of God, this was not a Christ-centreed operation; it was a corporation,
where profit-and-loss values were prioritized over spiritual pursuits,
where financial spreadsheets were the Scripture, and where stocks and
shares took precedence over charity and alms.

As for the work itself, Richard's duties had become ever more
mundane. He was given no real responsibility. He had begun to find
the daily routine tiring, as if he were drowning in a sea of tediousness.
Worse, he no longer felt in control of his life. As a student at Oxford,
he had been highly respected. Here he was just a little cog in the great
machine that was the Church of England.

He had tried to offset his gloom by snatching moments of personal
prayer in the shadowy corners of the cathedral, but these sessions paled
under the pressures of work. Oddly, he never saw anyone else take
time out to pray. Yes, there were prayers in the morning and evening
as church convention dictated, and sometimes before important
meetings, but the latter were perfunctory and never lasted more than a
few minutes. True, the rituals of high office were observed every day.
The never-ending work of "religion" was carried out to the letter of
the law, but where was the spirit?

After six months of this, Richard had become sorely disheartened
and was rapidly descending into depression. There was no one from
his past or present that he felt he could turn to, not even Sarah. To
unburden himself to her would seem like an admission of failure,
so he kept his feelings to himself and maintained the pretense that
everything was fine at work. It wasn't long before he had to lie to
her to maintain the charade. Guilt quickly followed and grew more

burdensome by the day, as though a heavy weight were pressing down upon him.

Richard Benton was very close to a nervous breakdown. He prayed to God more than ever, but it was a one-sided business. His were the prayers of a desperate man, full of inconsistencies and self-pity. He knew he was no longer intimate with Christ.

The Word of God, the Holy Scriptures, seemed dead in his hands. The words that had in times past leapt off the page to fill his heart and soul with joy were now silent and barren. Dark feelings and thoughts began to fill the void in his aching mind. The book of Job, which had once been for him the very font of wisdom and hope, now seemed to speak only of despair. Richard felt that he, too, was caught in the devil's ash pit without hope of rising. Here he was, at the very heart of one of England's most influential dioceses, serving a much-respected bishop, yet the very core of his belief was eroding. He felt that his faith was slowly crumbling to dust under the sheer monotony of his work.

All this was happening while he was ostensibly serving God in his chosen ministry. The dreams that once fueled him had now faded, and he had almost given up hope of his situation changing for the better. In moments of deep despair, he had thoughts of leaving the church—just giving up and disappearing into the secular world.

Then one day he received a message from the bishop to come without delay. Richard ran to the bishop's office and tapped nervously on the door.

The bishop shouted in his commanding voice, "Enter!"

Richard went in and closed the door behind him.

Without looking up from his papers, the bishop said, "Sit down, Mr. Benton. I have some news for you."

Richard settled uneasily into the straight-backed leather chair that faced the bishop's imposing desk.

Bishop Laidlaw continued for some moments to shuffle papers around his desk before picking up a pen and tapping it against a letter he was holding. "Yes. Yes, I have some news I hope you will consider good tidings. I have received a communiqué from an old college friend who is now the vicar of Saint David's Church in Penrhos Bay. That's in North Wales. A delightful place, I am told. It seems he has an urgent need for a curate—he lost the previous fellow to illness. Passed away rather suddenly." He put the pen down, and with his elbows on the desk, clasped his hands together as if in prayer. He stared at Richard with a studious expression. "It's a stipendiary appointment, and the position comes with a small cottage, I believe, apparently rent-free. A gift to the church from a deceased benefactor."

Richard began to understand the significance of the bishop's words, but all he could stammer out was "I— I see."

"The vicar, Reverend Stannard . . . he's a good man. Perhaps not bishop material, but solid and even-tempered. And I know old Stanners, he'll probably let you do the job without looking over shoulder every five minutes."

Richard was just about to ask a question, when the bishop cut him short.

"I know you've been happy with us at Helmsbridge and would no doubt be content to stay for many years. But sometimes the Lord moves us on. I want you to take this job, Mr. Benton. It would help me repay an old debt, if you catch my drift." He paused for a second or two before carrying on. "Good. That's settled then. Good man. I knew I could count on you. And take my word for it, such opportunities are rare, so my advice is, make the best of it."

He then added thoughtfully, "And if it doesn't work out, you can always return here after a couple of years, and I would be glad to have you back. You have proved to be a valued member of my team."

The bishop rose from his chair and held out his hand. Richard stood and had to lean over the desk to reach the bishop's outstretched hand.

"Speak to the administration department. They have all the details. Your transfer papers have already been drawn up."

The interview ended abruptly, and the bishop returned to his work.

Richard was left standing and looking at the top of the bishop's head.

He turned and left, closing the door behind him. He tried not to slam the door in his growing excitement. Once in the outer office, Richard felt like leaping and shouting for joy. Instead, he simply looked up at the ceiling, put his hands together and silently formed the words on his lips: "Thank you, God!"

TEN

Samuel was standing guard at the curate's cottage, just as the captain had instructed. Bezalel had told him that a new curate would be arriving that day with his wife. They were a young couple, and given the awful events of recent days, the captain felt it was prudent to keep a close eye on them in case of further demonic interest. Samuel had not quite gotten over the death of Maynard Jones and the bitter part he had played in the whole affair. The pain was still raw, but the wise words of comfort that Bezalel had spoken to him were having a healing effect.

The sun shone brightly in the blue sky, and a fresh breeze came off the hills, making for an unusually beautiful day. Samuel loved the sea and was content to sit for hours simply watching the waves ebb and flow over the sand beyond the promenade. There weren't many people out now, as the summer season had not yet begun in earnest. Most visitors to the town came only on weekends, and several of the smaller hotels and guest houses would remain closed until the tourist traffic picked up.

Cleaners had been in and out of the cottage the last few days and had removed the personal belongings of the late curate. Books, clothes, and boxes of ornaments had been disposed of, tossed into a garbage truck without care or ceremony. Samuel was saddened to see the remains of a man's life being so carelessly discarded, but he was reminded that humans come into the world with nothing and leave the same way, so perhaps he was just being sentimental in light of the recent tragedies.

Samuel shifted his position from the garden wall to the roof, where he could better see the ocean. A white steamboat was moving so slowly across the horizon that it seemed frozen in place. A light breeze tickled the back of his neck, and he raised a hand to scratch the spot. This happened a second time, and without thinking, he swatted at the disturbance, thinking it might be a fly. When it happened a third time, Samuel spun around and was surprised to find another angel smiling at him.

"Hello, brother. Forgive my little trick. I'm in a playful mood today."

Samuel stood and, backing away, took a good look at the new arrival. His appearance was that of a handsome youth, tall and lean, yet with obvious vitality in his limbs. His hair was long and hung about his shoulders and shone with a golden sheen. His eyes were a sparkling blue, and his full lips were curved into a welcoming smile. Yet despite his angelic appearance, there was something odd about this manifestation.

"Friend," said the stranger, "why do you retreat from me? I give you no cause."

"Who are you?" Samuel demanded. "Where are you from? For I know you not."

"Thank for your kind enquiry. Perhaps now we can proceed on a sociable level."

Samuel found the stranger's mannerisms and patterns of speech oddly ancient.

"My name is Ganymede, and where am I from? Why, I originated in heaven just as you did, my friend, created by the Ancient of Days."

"You may have been created by my Lord, but whom do you serve now? I perceive a vanity in you which none of my brothers possesses."

Ganymede laughed. "Does not the preacher say in Ecclesiastes, 'Vanity of vanities, all is vanity,' so how we can escape it?' Is it my fault that I was created beautiful?"

Samuel found the stranger's voice alluring, even entrancing, but he remained on his guard for he knew this attractive being was not one of God's anointed. "Beauty is in the soul," he answered, "not on the surface of things. And those things which are mere verisimilitudes will perish in the end."

"Ah, the 'end,' about which much is spoken in the book of Revelation. But who can truly know the future, my friend? Did not the Lord make us creatures of free will, masters of our own destiny? May we not assume that anything can happen, even a future of our own design?"

"That is blasphemy! The end of the world and of your kind has been ordained by Almighty God. Your pleasant form cannot mask your seductive ways, Ganymede. Your words beguile and cajole, but I will not hear any of it, for you are false." Samuel retreated to the ground and took up a position in the entrance to the cottage to bar Ganymede's way should he try to enter.

Ganymede watched this with some amusement, and then followed the earnest angel to the earth until he stood just a few feet away.

This time it was Samuel who spoke. "What are you doing here? What do you want?"

"I want for nothing, my friend. I am complete, and I am content. And as for being here, well, is it not a delightful spot?" He paused, looking about him as though taking in the scenery. "But in truth I came to visit you, Samuel. My odious colleague Gathan boasted that he had pulverized you. He is indeed a brutish fiend." With a deep sigh he added, "He is suited to his tasks, I suppose, but there are some among us who are more civilized, more sensitive. You must not judge us all by the actions of one mindless, obnoxious beast."

Samuel was becoming perturbed and was at a loss how to deal with this silver-tongued demon.

Ganymede stepped closer to Samuel and, placing a hand upon his shoulder, asked, "Are you quite recovered from your injuries? I have commanded Gathan not to come near you again, so you need not fear him in the future. I have seen to that for you."

Samuel twisted his body away from the demon's touch. "I don't need your assistance! I am under the protection of the Almighty!"

"Come now, don't be so churlish. I am only trying to help."

Samuel stared at the demon in anger.

"Samuel, don't look at me like that. It makes me feel unwelcome. Truly, I mean you no harm."

Samuel blurted, "All demons are liars!"

Ganymede chuckled. "You can say that, but what if I say, 'All demons are not liars'? Where does that argument take us? Into doubtful disputations, I should think. I cannot answer for my confederates, but speaking openly and honestly is part of my nature."

"I don't believe a word you say." Samuel's voice revealed how anxious he was becoming.

Ganymede pretended not to notice. "Alas, even when I speak the truth, you do not believe. How sad that is. You must be more discerning if you are to make a success of your assignment on earth."

Samuel wondered if he should simply draw his sword and attack Ganymede, but his recent encounter with Gathan made him hesitant to engage in open hostilities.

At that moment, the captain appeared behind Ganymede, and relief flooded the junior angel.

Without turning and still smiling at Samuel, Ganymede said, "Greetings, Bezalel. We have not crossed paths for such a long while. How good it is to meet again."

The captain stepped menacingly between Samuel and the demon and stared down his longtime foe.

"Oh, come now," Ganymede protested innocently, "I meant your friend no harm. You know me better than that."

The captain moved closer to Ganymede, and Samuel saw, for an instant, the smile on Ganymede's face change into a frown. But even this frown was disingenuous. The demon was still playacting.

"Do you threaten me, Bezalel?" Ganymede exclaimed with amusement. "Have you forgotten we were once the dearest of companions? How we swore to be friends forever?"

The captain was silent but remained resolute.

"Perhaps you have also forgotten that I always bested you in swordplay."

"That was a long time ago, Ganymede, in another age when . . ." Bezalel stopped, sorrow and pity showing in his eyes.

Ganymede finished the sentence, "When we both served our Creator."

"Yes, before you chose to betray Him."

"I betrayed no one, my old friend. I simply saw what you still fail to see, what my master had the courage to challenge: that Yahweh has corrupted this world by raising man to an exalted place in creation. We, who were the elect of God, have been degraded to mere servants of these ridiculous humans."

The captain was about to draw his sword when Ganymede rose in the air.

"Put your sword away. I am unarmed. You disgrace yourself, Bezalel. Do you not see how your own passion has been spoiled by the absurd gesture of your Messiah? Redeeming the human race! Why, most of these pathetic individuals want nothing to do with your Christ. You will see the truth one day, and then perhaps you will join us and we can be friends once again."

"That will never be. I order you to depart, Ganymede. Do not return, for we have no need for conference with your kind. I warn you, next time I will strike without hesitation."

Ganymede ignored the captain's oath and gazed past him, speaking to Samuel. "You and I should be on the same side, Samuel. Let the brutes like Gathan and Bezalel fight it out amongst themselves.

Whichever lord they serve, they remain brutish and boorish. Goodbye, my friend, until we meet again." Ganymede signaled to Jusach, who had observed this exchange from his hiding place on a nearby hill. "Come, grubby fellow, it seems we are not wanted here."

In an instant, the demons vanished and were gone.

"Did you know of the other one?" the captain asked, staring at the space where the demons had last been.

"No, sir. I fear that Ganymede had hypnotized me with his subtle speech."

"That's Ganymede, all right. You describe him well."

The captain turned to Samuel, who was visibly shaken by his encounter with Ganymede. He grabbed the junior angel's shoulders with both hands. "Are you okay? Do not ever underestimate the foul Ganymede. His appearance is meant to deceive. There aren't many like him. He emulates his own master, the Father of Lies. His treachery is far worse than any assault Gathan could throw at you. That is not even his real name, just an affectation. His name was once Andreas, but now he goes by that despicable name given to him by Satan. There is nothing of Andreas left in that twisted heart. Pray to God, Samuel, that he does not return."

Samuel looked at his captain and asked, "Does the appearance of Gathan and now Ganymede mean that more terrible things are going to happen here?"

The captain's face darkened. "I don't know, Samuel. But their presence almost certainly means that Rimmon, one of the high lords of darkness, is also here. We must be vigilant."

Eleven

The quaint cottage had been built into a cleft cut out of the hill overlooking the town of Penrhos Bay. Constructed of stone and slate and partly covered by ivy and flowering climbers, the house blended into the steep face of the Great Ulm, the ancient name for the hill. From here could be seen the entirety of the town and the pier that reached out into and the deep waters of the Irish Sea. Beyond the rows of homes and hotels, the swelling sea rolled and broke, wave upon wave, onto wide sandy beaches that looked as though they would not have been out of place in the south of France.

The pier was the town's main attraction, with its café, shops, and stalls selling all kinds of seaside bric-a-brac. The promenade and pier had been built in the late Victorian era, when day-trippers flocked to Penrhos Bay boat and train from the industrial cities of Liverpool and Manchester. They came by the thousands every Saturday afternoon, in cheap summer suits and dresses, to escape their dirty hovels and put the working week behind them. When the summer weather was kind, many would sit or sleep on the beach all night. Come Sunday morning, they flooded the walkways and promenades, laughing gaily, listening to a brass band, and enjoying life—if only for a few hours—before returning to their grimy streets and another week of hard physical labor.

The days of the Victorian day-trippers were long gone, yet the promenade and pier remained popular attractions. Only now the visitors were often retired middle-class women, aged and infirm and often widowed, enjoying their sunset years. In contrast to these genteel ladies, there had been in recent times an influx of young men and women, economic migrants from Eastern Europe seeking jobs and a better way of life in the United Kingdom. Foreign tongues were now regularly seen and heard along the streets of the town and in its hotels and pubs.

The Bentons' move to Penrhos Bay was largely uneventful, with no major mishaps. Their few personal belongings and secondhand furniture arrived on schedule in a small van, and the movers took less than an hour to carry the couple's things up the narrow path and into their new home. The young couple had elected to walk from the train station to save the taxi fare and take in the sights of their new home town. The spring morning was beautiful, the air crisp and cool, and the sun warmed their bright faces.

Richard wanted to carry Sarah over the threshold, but she ran away from him, laughing up the front path. She pushed the door open, but before her eyes could adjust to the darkness inside, she turned back face her husband. "Oh, Richard, I feel so happy! I'm sure that this move is the best thing that could ever have happened to us."

Richard grinned and went inside first. Sarah followed, holding his hand, and neither spoke. They were in awe as if entering a sacred place, and it seemed already that this new home was to be a haven of peace, a place where their love could flourish.

Ascending the small staircase, they found an uncarpeted landing that led to two small bedrooms and a tiny bathroom. Both the bedrooms had their original black-iron coal fireplaces. Sarah was imagining the happy romantic times they would spend here, tenderly locked in each other's arms, enjoying the warmth of a fire.

The bedroom with the double-bed was sparsely furnished but would be comfortable enough. Sarah went to the small window and looked out.

"Which room shall be ours?" Richard asked, leaving it to his wife to choose.

"Oh, Richard, this room, please! It has a wonderful view of the sea. I can even see the cliffs on the other side of the bay! It'll be lovely to wake up to every day."

"Even on gloomy winter days?"

"Every morning here is going to be gorgeous," she declared, with a thrill in her voice.

Richard laughed and put his arms around her, pulling her close to him. He swung her gently around, and they collapsed on the bed.

Later, Sarah unpacked a few boxes downstairs, filling the cupboards with crockery and tins of food, while Richard spent time in the bedroom, stuffing clothes into the wardrobe and the high chest of drawers.

Sarah came to the foot of the stairs and shouted up, "Come down! I've made some tea, and I have some nice cookies."

They sat across from one another at the little kitchen table, sipping their tea and smiling. They were content, even blissfully happy.

"Oh! What time is it?" Sarah said suddenly. "We mustn't be late for our meeting with Reverend Stannard."

Richard looked at her with amusement. "We've plenty of time. And anyway, it's not as if he's a bishop."

Richard and Sarah met Reverend Stannard at the rectory for a late-afternoon tea. He made them feel welcome and seemed a kind soul, if a bit aloof in his manner. The vicar explained that Richard's duties at the church would not be too onerous and that they would indeed be made lighter if Sarah would be willing to help out now and again. Sarah said she would be only too happy to help and was looking forward to that side of their life at St. David's. Stannard elaborated, explaining that he himself had never married, instead choosing to be wedded to the church, muttering something about St. Paul's admonition in the New Testament. Yet some of the problems he had been asked to tackle in times past were, he thought, not suited to a man. He added that the previous incumbent, also a bachelor, was not especially gifted in the delicate business of ministering to women.

Richard, accepting a proffered ginger cookie, tentatively inquired about the former curate. However, Reverend Stannard was not forthcoming, merely expressing his regret and sorrow at the unfortunate death of the young man, saying, "The Lord's will be done." He then indicated with a sweeping gesture of his hand that this particular subject was closed and that he did not want to discuss the matter further.

After the formalities of tea were dispensed with, Stannard gave the Bentons a tour of the church. There was a small hall used by the Mothers' Union on Tuesdays. A small Bible study group made up mostly of older women had met in the hall on Wednesday evenings, but this particular gathering had been disbanded after the death of the late curate. Stannard suggested that perhaps Richard could reconvene the group. The ladies did not expect deep teaching—simple spiritual homilies would suffice. Their real motive for attending was for tea and cake and to catch up on the local gossip. The vicar said, "All you have to do is stay for one cup of tea after the lesson and then nip off. The ladies won't even notice you're gone, and they will lock up the hall."

A neat and well-equipped kitchen was the next stop on the tour. They exited the kitchen into the back hall, which was surprisingly cold. Stannard beckoned to Richard and Sarah to follow him up a winding, bare-timber staircase to an upper room with a couple of toilets. A grubby towel hung loose on a wooden roller near the toilets. The room had no floor covering, and the varnished floorboards were dusty and in need of a thorough cleaning. The room was a good size for meetings or even games, but clearly it had not been used for a long, long time. Richard ventured to ask what this room was used for, and Stannard gave a gesture of dismay, saying, "Oh, nothing really.

Health and safety regulations and, I believe, the intricacies of local fire regulations prohibit its use."

They followed Stannard back down the stairs to the cold hall and then through large oak doors into the sanctuary itself. Standing in the nave, Sarah exclaimed with delight that it was indeed an impressive building. She asked if it was very old. The vicar picked up a leaflet from the table of books and handed it to Richard, saying, "This will give you the entire history of the church, et cetera. I wrote it myself."

Richard handed the leaflet to Sarah.

She noticed that the offering box mounted on one of the stone columns had been broken, and she went to inspect it more closely. Before she could ask, Stannard said, "Yes, dreadful incident. It was broken into a couple of months ago. The thief made a mess of the box with a hammer and chisel, I should think. Inexplicably, the money was left in the box. The thief must have been disturbed by someone, or something, before finishing the job. Mary, my housekeeper, whom you met earlier, noticed the state of the offertory later in the evening when she came to lock up the church." He then said rather gruffly, "If I had my way, I'd keep the building shut and open it only for services."

Richard exchanged a glance with Sarah.

They walked up the aisle together, and Stannard and Richard genuflected in front of the altar. The vicar indicated the main features, including the vestry and a small chapel off the south transept. Stepping through the "devil's door" situated on the north side of the church building, they walked outside. The streetlights were just coming on as the sun began to set. Outside the church, Richard noted, was a neatly cut lawn and, most surprisingly, a pay-to-park lot with several notices prominently displayed warning that any unauthorized vehicles left without proof of payment would be booted and the car's owner charged a release fee of £100.

Richard asked how it was that there was a public car park on the church grounds.

"A simple explanation. It's one of my fund-raising schemes. The church charges the townspeople for the privilege of parking their vehicles here. We're near the centre of town and very close to the shops. I get a very good return, which comes in handy for odd expenses here and there. Another of my schemes, which unfortunately is in abeyance until the bishop gets around to approving it, is to allow a mobile phone company to erect a mast on top of the tower."

Another glance of surprise passed between husband and wife.

"Wouldn't the local planning commission object?" Richard asked.

"As far as the town planners are concerned, the church is for all practical purposes exempt from planning laws, and this gives me free rein to do almost anything."

Walking past the north corner of the church, they came to the spot where Maynard Jones had fallen, ending his all-too-brief life. Stannard hesitated at the place, looking down for an instant, then hurried on, stepping around the accursed spot.

When they arrived at the main gate to the church grounds, Stannard expressed hope that they had enjoyed the tour. He pointed toward High Street. "That's the best way back. I am sure you have many things to sort out at your new home. Take the weekend off and come and see me in my office on Monday morning around ten. That will suit me, and we will go over your duties in more detail then."

Richard and Sarah felt as if they were children being dismissed.

"Shall we not come to church on Sunday?" Richard said. "I mean surely—"

"No, no. Please, there is no need. Enjoy your new surroundings. Take a walk on the pier. People do say it's good for one's health. Myself, I rarely have time for such excursions. On Monday, then. Goodbye." And with that, the vicar walked briskly in the direction of the rectory.

Richard and Sarah looked at each other with some consternation.

"What a strange man," Sarah said.

"Harmless enough, I should think," Richard replied.

"Well, I think we should enjoy our weekend off to the full. We'll wrap up warm and watch the fireworks on Saturday evening. Then on Sunday we can trek up the Ulm. We'll have our very own church service at the top of the hill with the sheep and goats as our first congregation." Linking her arm in his, Sarah drew her dazed and bewildered husband onto the busy High Street, and they headed for home.

TWELVE

It didn't take long for Richard to learn that the bishop was correct about Stannard not standing over his curate's shoulder. Richard didn't see much of Stannard, and the vicar clearly had little interest in spending time with his curate. Over the next few months, Richard found his duties to be light indeed and consisted mainly of shepherding community activities and visiting shut-ins and the local hospital to offer words of support and comfort.

Soon after their arrival, Richard and Sarah had been invited to an ecumenical supper at the United Reformed Church, and it was there that they learned about the strange circumstances surrounding the death of the former curate. They were also shocked to learn what the local clergy thought about Stannard.

While Richard settled into his new job, Sarah was enjoying "prettifying" the cottage. She had taken down the old dusty curtains, bought some material from the charity shop in town, and made attractive new drapes. She cleaned the windows inside and out, swept the path, clipped the rose bushes, and trimmed the small lawn until the place began to feel like home. A thorough clean of the kitchen was still needed, however. Even though the cottage had supposedly been cleaned before they moved in, there was grime upon grime inside the oven, and Sarah was certain that the previous tenant had rarely bothered to do any cleaning at all.

One afternoon, she was busy vacuuming when the head of the vacuum cleaner banged against an object under the bed. She got down on her hands and knees to investigate and found a wooden box of some sort. She reached under the bed and tugged at the heavy container until she at last managed to pull it out.

It was quite a large box, about two feet square and twelve inches high and made of sturdy varnished wood. The box looked old and had obviously seen a lot of use, given the proliferation of dents and chips on the surface. Inscribed on the top were the initials M. J. in block lettering. The box was secured with a small metal lock. Sarah remembered a small brass key she had found when cleaning the kitchen drawers. She had left it in the drawer along with a few other odds and ends, just in case. She went downstairs and retrieved the key.

The key did indeed fit the lock, and the latch clicked open easily. But before raising the lid of the box, Sarah hesitated. Did she have the right to open the box? She reasoned that perhaps she should find out who it belonged to, and then she could return it to the owner. Or it might have belonged to the late curate, in which case Richard should be there to examine its contents. She finally decided her curiosity would have to wait. She closed the latch and secured the box once more. Then she stood and placed the key on the dressing table and carried on with her chores.

Samuel did not care for the sound of the vacuum cleaner, so as soon as he saw Sarah set up the contraption, he had gone outside to sit on the roof and spend time meditating on the Lord. When he heard the cleaner stop humming below, he returned to keep an eye on his charge. He saw Sarah kneeling, and at first he thought she was praying.

Then he saw the box and the key in her hand. He could tell she was thinking about something important because it seemed to distract her from opening the box. When she set the box aside and picked up the nozzle of the vacuum once more, he quickly returned to the roof.

THIRTEEN

"What was the name of the previous curate, the one who died?" Sarah asked.

"Maynard Jones, I think. Why?"

"I've got something to show you. It's upstairs in our bedroom."

In the bedroom, Sarah explained how she had found the box, how her thought had been to open it straight away, before thinking the better of it. They sat on the bed together, staring at the box, as Sarah turned the small key over in her hand.

Richard said, "We should, by rights, hand it over to Stannard. He could forward it on to Jones's next of kin."

"He didn't have any. Don't you remember the vicar saying as much?"

"Yes, I do recall that now, you're right."

"Richard, what shall we do? I think giving it to Stannard would be a mistake. He'd probably chuck it with the garbage."

They sat in silence until finally Richard stood up, held out his hand, and said, "Okay, give me the key. I'll open it. Whatever we find, we'll treat with the respect it deserves. And seeing what is inside, we can more easily decide what to do with it. Agreed?"

Richard placed the box onto the bed and said, pointing at the engraved initials, "'M. J.' Maynard Jones, I presume." He inserted the key and removed the lock, and then lifted the lid to reveal the contents.

The box was filled to the top with all kinds of personal memorabilia, letters, papers, photographs, and small books. They removed the contents carefully and laid them out on the bed. Sarah and Richard both felt rather sheepish and guilty that they were stealing a look into a stranger's private life. The chest contained several books—quite old, judging from their condition, but precious to their owner. One was a small school hymn book. Dog-eared and ink stained, the fly leaf contained an inscription in neat lettering: *Maynard Jones, Form 3B*, and in brackets, *[aged 12]*.

Richard picked up a hardback copy of a children's novel, *Still William* by Richmal Crompton. Inside the cover there was a badly-drawn sketch of the main character with the words *My Hero* written underneath. On the opposite page, in spidery, disjointed letters, was written, *This book belongs to M. Jones Esquire, Finchley, London, England, World, Universe.*

Other children's books and comics had also been preserved in the case. Jones had apparently been keen to hang onto his childhood or at least remember it with affection. There were also some postcards in the box and holiday photos presumably depicting Jones's parents and relatives. One small black-and-white photo showed a couple standing against the iron railings of a seaside pier. Sarah looked at it more closely and said excitedly, "Look! Richard, if I am not mistaken, that's Penrhos Bay Pier. It is! You can see the Grand Hotel in the background!"

"So maybe he came here as a child on school vacations?"

Among the contents of the box was a small plastic container with a medal inside. Richard removed it and showed it to Sarah. The medal was engraved with Jones's name and the date and had been awarded for winning a cup in a school rugby competition.

"I wonder what position he played?" Richard said absently.

Sifting through the papers, Sarah found a photograph of Jones's rugby team in full kit—shirts, boots, and all. The front row of boys crouched on one knee, the boy at the centre holding a large silver cup. A short stocky man, probably their coach, stood to one side, smiling, obviously proud of his boys' achievement. Flipping the photo over, Sarah saw that the young Jones had written in pencil the names of his fellow players, in order, from top to bottom and left to right. The third person in the top row was identified simply as *Me*. The name *Roger* had been circled.

Sarah turned the photo over and traced her finger along to a tall, blond-haired boy with both arms crossed. "Look, Richard. This one here is Maynard Jones." She held her finger against the picture pointing to Jones. "And the boy beside him is Roger. His name is circled on the back."

"I suppose they were probably close friends." Richard gazed at the figure of Jones intently. "Seems a fit and healthy boy. Tall for his age. Strange to imagine he died young from illness."

They carried on looking through Jones's personal effects. There were bundles of letters that both agreed they would not read. More photographs of unknown friends, happy, smiling students enjoying halcyon days. There was a city guide and map of Barcelona and a ticket to the *Sagrada Familia*, the famously whimsical but unfinished church by the Spanish architect Antoni Gaudí.

At the bottom of the box was a black leather-bound book. Richard opened it to the first page. There was written, *This is the Journal of Maynard Jones, Curate of St. David's Church, Penrhos Bay*. It was dated two years earlier. The text was written in a neat script in black pen, and each page was headed by a date. Leafing through the journal, Richard saw that the curate had not kept up his writing every day, and often the gaps were several days in length.

Richard silently read the first few pages. As Sarah watched her husband's face, she saw it darken and grow sad. Then Richard carefully and slowly closed the book.

"Let's put his things back in the box," he said.

Sarah picked up those items closest to her and placed them back in the wooden box.

Richard did the same but left the journal on the bed.

"Sarah, after dinner I think I shall spend some time in prayer, and then I aim to read the journal. I feel we are meant to know what it holds."

Sarah knew by Richard's manner and tone of voice his mind was made up. She rose from the bed, bent low to kiss him on the top of his head, and quietly went downstairs.

The early pages of the journal were written in a remarkably neat hand that enjoyed the use of flourishes and curlicues. Maynard Jones had obviously taken great care in forming the words on each page. The margins were littered with clever little drawings of various things mentioned in the text. The journal was dated from the time Jones was made curate of St. David's, when he had moved to Penhros Bay from London.

Various entries described the little cottage on the hill and how delighted Jones had been in being billeted there. There were sketches of flowers and birds and one very good drawing of the head of a goat with large horns and devilish eyes. The accompanying notes detailed walks taken on the Great Ulm or on the beach at West Shore. Life, it seemed, was to be enjoyed, and it was clear from the entries that Maynard Jones had been sensitive, thoughtful, and a kindly soul.

Later in the journal, Richard found comments on passages from the Old and New Testaments. Jones's considerations of the verses did not reflect deep revelations of spiritual truth, but his commentary certainly showed a thorough knowledge of scripture and its application for modern man. Jones was fond of using abbreviations, and Richard soon began to pick up the meanings of some of these. *STD* apparently referred to Reverend Stannard. *RG* was Jones's friend Roger, who lived in London. *SD* was St. David's Church, and *TO* was short for "time off," which was always followed by an exclamation point. The one abbreviation whose meaning eluded Richard was *A*. In the latter pages of the diary, Jones made several single statements of which the following were typical:

> *A not here today, thank God.*
> *A here again, a most unwelcome visitor.*
> *A visited me during the night—worse than a demon!*
> *Talked to STD about A but got little sympathy from the white-walled sepulcher.*

Under this last entry, Jones had written, *I am coming to believe that STD actually despises me!*

During his final months, Jones had begun to write more and more about his growing feelings of despondency, reminding Richard of his days in Helmsbridge and his own pain and disillusion.

The comments on daily Bible reading became scarce in these pages, replaced by Jones's musings regarding his spiritual state. There were scraps about unanswered prayers and notes referring to "unfinished tasks" presumably set for him by Stannard. Little by little, the journal charted the demise of the man, not just spiritually, but mentally and physically.

On one page Jones had written a single entry in large separated capital letters:

> *RESULTS CONFIRMED—A IS HERE TO STAY!*

The entry was underlined several times in an erratic way that spoke of extreme emotional conflict. Richard could almost feel the pressure of the pen on the page.

A again. Who was he? Or she?

It was Sarah who supplied the answer as they talked about the journal later. "Richard, I think the poor man had AIDS. He was dying a slow, painful death!"

Richard scanned the other entries on the previous pages where *A* appeared. "I think you may be right. That would explain so much."

"It would surely explain Jones's comments about Stannard."

"Then I guess he was a practicing homosexual," Richard said sadly.

"And Roger, I suppose, was his partner. Their friendship seemed to survive long past their school days," Sarah conjectured.

Richard had a strange, bemused expression on his face. "In that case, how did Jones make it all the way through Bible college? And how is it he was appointed curate in the first place?"

"Richard, you are a trifle naïve. Didn't you meet any gay students at Oxford?"

"What, in the college?"

Sarah raised her eyebrows as if to say yes.

"No, I don't believe I did," said Richard, a bit peeved. "What about church teaching? Its proscription against homosexuality?"

"What about it? Do you think the church's stance stops anyone from loving Christ, even gay people?" she said with some passion. "This is the twenty-first century, after all. The church doesn't burn anyone at the stake anymore. God's grace is the answer."

Richard was pensive and silent.

Then Sarah asked, "What about that guy from Exeter? Paul whathisname? He used to hang around with Giles. You remember Giles, surely?"

"Yes, I remember Giles. We did a workshop together on needs in the community. Nice guy, very bright."

"Yes. Paul and Giles?"

"Come on, they were just good friends, right?"

Sarah smiled.

He had been painted into a corner, as usual, by his clever wife. "Wow, I am a bit naïve, aren't I?"

"Just a bit, Darling, but it's an attractive quality in you."

Sarah returned to her own reading. Richard set down the journal and began to think about its contents in a new light. After a few moments of silence, he said to no one in particular, "He could have helped the man in his desperate hour of need."

Sarah looked up from her book.

"Stannard I mean," said Richard.

"Yes, he should have. Aren't we to hate the sin but help the sinner?" Then Sarah added thoughtfully, "I'm becoming very worried about our vicar."

During the next few days Richard read the journal again with newly enlightened eyes, and he began to understand the sad life of Maynard Jones. The man had loved God, had been a devout believer once. Plagued and hounded by his own feelings of guilt, he had lost his way and given in to despair.

Richard could see from the entries that many of Jones's problems had originated in boyhood, in particular the time he spent at boarding schools, away from his family. Cruel regimes had been the norm at these places. Indeed, all English boarding schools were founded upon the principle 'spare the rod and you spoil the child,' but the rod had been cruelly administered without compassion in those days. One of Jones's entries, in which he reminisced about his friend Roger, read, *The lives of young boys at public schools are, for the most part, unholy and filled with cruelty. The whole sorry mess should be done away with.*

The final entries in the journal were mere caricatures of the earlier pages. Words hastily scrawled became an unintelligible scribble so that Richard could not make sense of some of the passages. The meandering style was no longer focused but indicated Jones's chaotic state of mind. Richard thought it a great pity for a life to end in such a melancholy way, with no one on hand to provide help or comfort. He felt a deep sympathy for Jones and was sorry not to have known him. Perhaps they could have been friends.

One of the final entries read:

Surprisingly lucid today, despite feeling wretched. Have read my Bible and prayed and experienced a peace not felt for a long time. Have come to a conclusion regarding my spiritual state, and all now seems much clearer to me. I was thrown into despicable situations as a child, particularly at Chiltern's Boys School. Had it not been for Roger and his courageous love, I think I would have happily jumped from the rooftop. I can see now I have long had a certain proclivity, but whether this was nature or nurture I don't believe matters. The absence of my mother for most of my life, the male-only schools, even graduation to university life and the clergy all cemented in me a particular bent, like a brick set into a wall. The die was cast for me.

Roger and I enjoyed happy times living together in London, though I was aware that adulthood could never compare with the pure, sublime joy of childhood companionship. The essence of true love and affection was lost in my manhood amidst the sordid trappings of desire and lust. I began to believe purity could never be regained or revisited. We can never turn back the clock. When I shared these thoughts with Roger, he became moody and offish, so I didn't talk about it anymore, and we began to grow apart.

That is why I came here, to get away and to find myself again. I can't remember which holy saint said that truth can only come out of deep suffering and total surrender to God. I am beginning to understand this. I know now what true love is. The desires of the flesh can only inhibit and bar the way to true love, to knowing Christ infallibly. The human spirit must break free from these earthly entrapments.

I fully comprehend now what St. Paul meant when he said he would prefer that disciples of Christ should not marry. I have read and reread the epistles to get to the heart of the truth. I know the pain will return, but I am not afraid anymore. I have purchased the field and hold the pearl in my hand. Thank God, I have emerged from the clouds of obscurity and can see my way forward. I know there is no cure for my unhealthy state—there will never be a return to normal life for me. This dreadful disease will soon reduce me to a pitiable condition. In some ways, I feel, the suffering will cleanse me. But still, I would have these final hours of torment taken from me. My flesh is afraid, but my spirit is strong. I pray the Lord to take my soul and spare me from this agonizing death.

The only way for me to truly live is to shed this body and release my spirit into the hands of God. There I shall be free of disease, free of the petty vanities of love, and where I may know the peace and joy that passes all understanding. I know my Lord understands me and that He will forgive this prodigal son, soon to return home.

Richard lay the journal down, picturing in his mind the Father waiting patiently at the gate for His prodigal son. Richard closed his eyes and prayed that Maynard Jones was indeed at rest with the Lord Jesus in Heaven.

FOURTEEN

The days had grown shorter now that autumn was well underway. The time was just past midnight, and gray clouds scudded across the bright half-moon. The wind howled and moaned among the rafters of the old deconsecrated church, and the air in the building was ice cold. The gorgeous stained-glass windows depicted scenes from Jesus' parables and His ministry. The windows had been made in a time when most of the laity could not read and were meant to inform the righteous and the unrighteous how they should live in order to glorify God. One window showed a traveler bent low over a beaten and unconscious man, whilst another man in priestly garb hurried by on the other side of the road. Another portrayed Jesus, robed in luminous white robes, raising a child from her death bed. At the far end of the nave was a magnificent arched window illustrating the feeding of the five thousand. Every picture told the same story: Trust in Almighty God and salvation is yours for the asking.

During the daylight hours, visitors from near and far crossed the threshold of the former church to find peace, wisdom, and the meaning of life. But the last time a searching soul had offered a prayer of thanksgiving to the living God was long past. The old building was now a New Age centre, where all kinds of necromantic devices and objects were sold, from the ancient magic of the druids to Wicca and witchcraft, the occult, and the dark arts. All visitors, whether naïve or learned, were encouraged to purchase these seemingly innocent objects. Some were proselytized and persuaded to become members of dark societies. Séances, tarot readings, spiritualism—you could buy almost any sort of divination at the centre. The main sponsor of this enterprise was Lucifer himself, and Rimmon made sure it thrived.

At this hour, at the back of the shop where the owner gave private readings, an elite circle of confederates sat in conference. Rimmon, Ganymede, and Gathan were planning for the upcoming All Hallows' Eve.

"There is a wonderful atmosphere of defeat in this place, which was once sacred and is now ours," Rimmon mused. He gestured at the stained-glass images that were devoid of meaning to the souls that passed through this establishment. "There is a delicious irony that we are the only ones in this place who truly comprehend these images of myth."

Ganymede burst into a profane laughter. "Sire, you are so clever!"

Rimmon allowed a condescending smile to pass over his lips at the compliment. But Gathan merely looked on in silence, for he did not like to be in Ganymede's company.

Rimmon continued. "So with Halloween nearly upon us, I have elected to give our soldiers free reign to do as they please. Each may dream up his own brand of mischief and create havoc in the town to his heart's content. So let me have your best suggestions. I am in a mood to grant wishes."

It was now Gathan's turn to utter a chuckle of glee. Rimmon was talking his kind of language. "Master, I recall fondly the days when some of our followers on this night inserted pins and razor blades in caramel-covered apples, while others put poisonous concoctions in fizzy drinks and deadly sweets for the little ones."

"You have my blessing to revive these paraphernalia." Rimmon held out his hand, and Gathan dutifully kissed the master's jeweled ring.

Ganymede looked away in disgust as the fawning demon genuflected in front of Rimmon. "That all sounds a bit crude," he said. "I mean, razor blades in toffee apples? Where can you obtain razors in this day and age?"

"We could use broken glass instead," Gathan said testily.

Ganymede ignored the retort. "I suggest something a little more subtle and a bit more sophisticated. Let's come up with something that will be remembered, something so devious, so iniquitous that word of this night will reach the ears of our father below. We certainly won't be mentioned in dispatches by carrying out childish japes and games."

Rimmon stared at Ganymede thoughtfully. "Yes, I see what you mean."

Ganymede, seizing the moment, stood up, purposefully blocking Gathan from Rimmon's line of sight. Bending low he spoke to Rimmon in a whisper, "You have two options, lord. We can be vilified for instructing base-minded devils to have free-for-all, which may end in disaster for all of us. Or . . ." Here he paused.

Rimmon leant eagerly forward. "Yes?"

"Or we devise a plan that will not only create chaos among the poor souls of this town, but will also plague the Christians and send their heavenly helpers into turmoil! I suggest we marshal our best forces in strong phalanxes, careful to keep them hidden in the caves above the town, whilst our inferior brothers create pandemonium below, thus certainly causing the enemy to attack. Then, just when they are weary yet confident of victory, we shall swoop down and vanquish them with ease! Then we send glad tidings to our lord and wait with expectation of our just rewards."

"Ganymede, when I am congratulated and rewarded by Satan, I will make sure you are suitably commended."

Rimmon sat back with an expression of pure joy on his countenance, his eyes closed. He was already basking in anticipated glory. He then opened his eyes and said, "Your suggestion has merit

but lacks detail. We shall all meet here again tomorrow night, and you
will present a comprehensive plan."

Ganymede wondered whether in the future he should keep his
mouth firmly shut.

The following night, at the appointed hour, the three demons gathered
once more, but this time they were not alone. In the basement of
the building, several women were congregated about a round table,
eagerly intent on what was about to happen. They looked to their
leader, who sat in an ornate carved wooden chair. Madame Jezebel
James was in her late forties but maintained a voluptuous body that
still retained some of its former beauty. She wore an extravagant rich
robe of the deepest black velvet embroidered with red, green, and blue
astrological signs, gold stars, and silver moons. Upon her head, she
wore a strange contraption that couldn't truly be called a hat. It was
a pointed piece of metal that spiraled upward, glowing and changing
hue every few seconds.

Upon the tabletop were engraved the signs and symbols of
Madame Jezebel's dark art. At the centre of the table there burned an
incense stick that protruded from the mouth of a dragon statuette. The
woman in the robe clapped her hands above her head ceremoniously,
and the lights in the chamber dimmed. The other women gasped at
this bit of trickery.

"Ladies, let me warn you from the outset that we may be in touch
with the powerful and playful spirits of the dead tonight. Please, *please*,
do not break the circle at any time during the proceedings. You do so
at pain of death. If any of you wish to depart, then I advise you to do
so now."

Madame Jezebel scanned each one in turn, letting her flaming eyes
rest upon each one. No one moved to leave. "Then let us begin by
joining hands. Now close your eyes to protect yourself from sights no
mortal should see."

Her voice boomed theatrically with sensuous resonance, and the women, breathing in the potent incense, began to feel intoxicated with a mixture of excitement and fear.

"I shall call upon my faithful spirit guide, but before I do, I must warn you that he is, or was in earthly life, a great barbarian warrior who ravaged and pillaged his way across the steppes of Mongolia many hundreds of years ago. He was a man among men, a warrior's warrior, and he had many wives and hundreds of children. He was slain by a band of fifty renegades, shot through with arrows. Yet he stood valiantly with sword erect until sweet death carried his mighty spirit into the depths of Hades."

The ladies trembled at the thought of encountering such a creature.

"You will find his manliness irresistible, his powerful presence terrifying! His voice is as a hundred waterfalls, and you may drown in its torrents if he addresses you."

Rimmon and Ganymede were enchanted by this woman's skills. Gathan looked on expectantly, fidgeting to and fro, jumping wildly from one foot to the other.

"Shall I summon Gathan the Great?" Her voice bellowed out and reverberated around the room.

The women all cried out, "Yes, yes. Yes!"

Madame Jezebel cried out, "Gathan, come forth!"

Ganymede turned to Gathan. "I think that's your cue, 'Gathan the Great.' Do your bit for these fine ladies!"

Gathan leapt from his perch and landed at the centre of the table, which shook and rattled as he materialized in their midst.

The women screamed, but Madame Jezebel merely smiled and bowed her head.

"Welcome, my lord!"

The smoldering light and smoke from the incense tantalizingly outlined the muscled and hairy body that Gathan exhibited during these séances. The odor of earthy, musty sweat combined with the incense, creating a strong, intoxicating aroma.

Madame Jezebel chanted the words of ancient incantations that she thought held Gathan the Great in her power. Meanwhile, Gathan amused himself by blowing onto the frightened faces of the women. Each screamed with fear and delight as she felt his warm breath upon their skin. Leaping from the table and carousing behind them, he went from one to the next, sinking his teeth gently into their necks and fondling their flesh. The women were beside themselves, some to the point of fainting.

Gathan's companions watched, hardly able to contain their laughter.

Rimmon at last turned to Ganymede and said, "That should keep him entertained for a few hours at least. Shall we continue with our business? Come, the night wanes too fast for my liking."

Ganymede was happy to oblige. "My Lord, I have concocted a marvelous menu of amusements for All Hallows' Eve. You will be delighted and amazed at my ingenuity, I promise you. I have even given it a name! 'A Night of Fear and Fun.' Fear for the mortals and fun for us. The night will be filled with the most atrocious, indecent and frightful acts to keep our henchmen—and our enemy—fully occupied. I have written it all down so that you may read it at your leisure." Ganymede unrolled a scroll of parchment and handed it to Rimmon.

Rimmon held it in both hands and quickly scanned the list of activities that his subordinate had devised.

"As you will discover, I have conceived a marvelous high point involving these dear ladies."

They both turned to where Gathan was continuing with his debauchery.

"The *pièce-de-résistance* will confound our enemy and place Madame Jezebel and her so-called occult arts in high regard. We shall rule this place with ease thereafter. And what's more, the Christian remnant will be deliciously discredited for good."

"Well done, Ganymede!" said Rimmon, clapping his hands together. "I knew you would not let me down."

FIFTEEN

Detective Inspector Stewart's flat overlooked the sea at West Shore. It was a cheap one-bedroom apartment. No garden, no balcony, no frills. But it suited his lifestyle. Divorced for more than six years, Stewart had become set in his ways. He didn't want a roommate either. And to be honest, he had learned to do without female companionship. Every time he thought about dating, he shuddered. He told himself he was past all that stuff.

This had been Stewart's day off, but as every cop knows, a policeman never stops working. If he is off duty and walking down the street, going to the cinema, or at a football game, his eyes are always scanning the people, watching any suspicious-looking individuals and wondering what they're up to. Stewart was no exception. He couldn't just switch it off. At night, he would often lay awake for hours, turning over in his mind all of the significant and insignificant details of an unsolved case. Sometimes the breakthrough came suddenly in a "eureka" moment. This didn't necessarily require a great leap in imagination or a cataclysmic revelation, but rather, just a little tweak of something, a seemingly unimportant scrap of information that shed light on the dark details. Other times it meant making a connection between the unlikeliest of partners that proved to be the key.

The curate's death was something else, though. Although the case was now six months old, the threads stubbornly refused to untangle, and no logical solutions presented themselves. He had been obsessing about the case all day. It was now around six o'clock and dark outside. Stewart sat in the kitchen nursing a mug of tea. He was unshaven and still in the underpants and vest he had slept in the night before. He watched the smoke from the cigarette in the ashtray spiral toward the ceiling. From the living room came the sounds of the television he had switched on earlier before being becoming distracted by his thoughts. Unwashed pans, cutlery, and dishes were piled up in the sink, left over from last night's supper and this morning's breakfast. Lunch had been coffee, several biscuits, and three cigarettes. A can of beans was sitting on the kitchen counter, waiting to be heated up for his evening meal. To that, he would add a couple of fried eggs and two slices of bread, washed down with a can of beer and followed by more a few more smokes.

He doodled with a ballpoint pen on a pad of ruled paper, trying without success to make sense of the facts surrounding Jones's death. He was hoping to find some correlation between the words he had used to abbreviate the main points of the case, some link that might spark and give him a lead to follow. All the clues so far had taken him down cul-de-sacs that led precisely nowhere.

The cigarette finally burned down to the filter. He pulled another from the packet, lit it, and took a deep drag. The smoke disappeared deep inside his body and emerged seconds later from his nostrils. He studied the paper again, drawing imaginary lines between the words, pairing up in his mind ideas that appeared to be in diametric opposition to one another. A rough sketch of the church tower adorned the centre of the page, and beside it, circled several times in black ink, was the sergeant's measurement of *20 feet*. He tapped the figures and then threw the pen down angrily and cursed aloud.

Twenty feet. Just over six meters.

If it weren't for that one fact, this would have been an open-and-shut case of suicide.

Picking up the pen, Stewart began to methodically cross out the notes he had made. One by one, he eliminated them from the equation. He looked in dismay at what was left: *20 feet.*

He sighed and took another puff on the cigarette, this time leaving it dangling from his lips. He once again made rings around the number *20.*

Then he stood and tried reasoning it out aloud while pacing.

"First point: Is there a murder here? Maybe not. There is simply no proof that another person—or persons—was connected with the incident. The forensics people have confirmed, there's no evidence of violence or signs of a struggle. Not in the church, on the tower, or on the ground. Yet my innards tell me different.

"Second point: Jones's physician reported to the coroner that Jones was suffering from AIDS and that the illness was incurable. In fact, if Jones hadn't killed himself, he would have died within week, perhaps even days. He obviously knew that his condition was deteriorating rapidly and that he would soon be hospitalized. There was no wonder treatment in the offing. The only alternative was palliative care, which the doctor said at the inquest that Jones had refused. He would accept only painkillers and sleeping pills. *Ipso facto*, the curate killed himself."

Indeed, the coroner had ruled death by suicide. The matter of the position of the body had to be discounted, as there were no corroborating facts to explain its unusual placement.

"Maybe a big, bloody wind carried him twenty feet," Stewart muttered.

He removed the cigarette from his mouth and took a sip of cold tea.

"And what about the vicar? What about him, eh?"

Stewart disliked the Reverend Stannard immensely but honestly couldn't imagine that he was in some way directly responsible for the curate's death. The vicar had certainly felt a fair amount of animosity toward his curate, but not enough to be a motive for murder. Stannard might be an offensive oaf, but he was not a homicidal maniac. After all, he was a clergyman. That should count for something, shouldn't it? Stannard and Jones were supposed to be holy men. Weren't they supposed to represent the best of humanity's, serving God and man? Wasn't that how it worked?

Stewart's own experience of church was limited to his time in the scouts as a boy. He had sometimes attended Sunday morning services with the troop. However, that was more spit and polish and uniforms than anything to do with God or Jesus. To tell the truth, he had never given any credence to such matters. His parents certainly hadn't bothered with all that. They had been too busy making ends meet to go to church on Sunday or any other day. And so for Detective Inspector Stewart, the church was just another building on High Street. Church was fine for christenings, weddings, and funerals, but it was surplus to requirements, as far as he was concerned. Yes, he'd met well-meaning individuals who claimed to know Jesus Christ, but they were not the kind of people with whom he wanted to associate.

As a cop, he had seen enough tragedy and strife and, for that matter, meaningless and pointless death. Where was God Almighty in those situations? Even if Stewart were to give religion a second thought, he would probably agree with millions of others that in this world the very idea, let alone the existence, of a loving God was just a story. He was likely no more than a helpful delusion, a fiction created by people who couldn't face the grim reality of life. As for these two so-called ministers, well, who would want to go to Stannard's church? The man was a walking contradiction. Stewart would rather attend an atheist church, if there was such a thing. He'd probably get more tea and sympathy there than at St. David's. As for Jones, he didn't know the man, but surely it couldn't be right that a practicing homosexual should be a priest.

He shrugged. His thoughts returned to the case. As far as everyone else was concerned, the case was in fact closed. Stewart had officially archived the file on his PC, and weeks ago he had dropped the case folder in the out-tray on his desk. Inside the cover he had stuck a small yellow Post-It note bearing a large question mark in red ink and, beneath it, the words "Not solved!"

To his mind this was a suspicious death. However, no crime could be proved, and there were no culprits to arrest. There was good reason to accept the curate's death as a suicide. It all sounded perfectly reasonable—except for the location of the body.

A riddle wrapped in a mystery.

He stubbed out the cigarette in the bottom of the ashtray and tried to push the whole sorry episode to the back of his brain, trying to let it go. One day, he figured, the answer would just come to him.

He went to the living room, slumped on the sofa, picked up the remote, and started flipping channels. In the end, he settled on an old film, one that he had seen before many times.

He was wakened by the sound of his mobile phone. The television was still on, but a different movie was now showing. Stewart glanced at his watch. Nearly 2:30 in the morning. The ringing persisted. He picked up the phone, shook the cobwebs from his brain, and pressed the green key but said nothing.

The station superintendent said, "Stewart? Are you there? Sorry to wake you. I know it's your weekend off, but duty calls. There's a body on the beach opposite the war memorial. Dr. Padelski is already there. Get down there now."

"Will do, sir. I'm on my way."

Stewart cursed as he put the phone down. He struggled off the sofa and made his way to the bedroom to find some clothes to put on.

SIXTEEN

Detective Inspector Stewart stood on the promenade, looking down at the activity on the beach. A cold wind drove angry waves onto the shore. Several people were clustered around a body in the sand illuminated by mobile floodlights. Electric cables trailed past Stewart's feet to where a petrol-powered generator chugged away loudly behind him. A shaft of lightning briefly lit up the sky as the inspector stepped off the concrete and made his way down to the crime scene.

Dr. Rosina Padelski, the woman from forensics, was on her knees, bent low over what was left of a human body. She had a scalpel in her hand and was delicately teasing out a tiny object from the mutilated flesh and bone.

"Hello, Doctor. How are you?"

"You ask the funniest of questions, Inspector. Does it look like I'm all right? It's half past two, it's 'bloody freezing cold,' as you English say, and I am picking through a cadaver."

Stewart was beginning to appreciate her wit. He found it very attractive.

"I'm just about done," she said. "There's nothing more for me to do here. It's like searching for a needle in a hay house."

"Haystack," he corrected her.

She hadn't looked up in all this time, but standing, she said, "What?"

"It's *haystack*, not *hay house*."

"Oh, thank you. I like to be admonished when my English is wrong."

He replied by saying "You are welcome" in Polish. "*Wy jestescie pozadani.*"

"Why, Inspector, do you speak Polish?" She looked up, surprised.

"No, not really. I had a Polish girlfriend when I was younger, and she taught me a few words and phrases."

"Very good that you remembered this from so long ago, but your pronunciation is poor. Was she pretty? All Polish girls are pretty," she said with passion.

"As it happens, she was far too beautiful for me. It didn't last long. She met a French fellow. I never saw her again."

"I am sorry. French, eh?"

She turned to her assistant and gave instructions about bagging up the remains. Then she stepped out of the circle of light to cross over to where Stewart stood. She held out her hand. Her touch was warm to his very cold hand. He couldn't suppress a thought about where that hand had been just moments ago.

"You are cold, Inspector. Come, I have coffee in my car. I can tell you all about the corpse on the way. At least, what I know."

They walked up the beach together, the sand granules crunching under their feet. At the entrance to the promenade, a couple of uniformed officers were talking to a disheveled white-haired man who appeared to be frightened. From the look of his clothes, he was a vagrant or a wino. Someone had kindly draped a thick woolen blanket around his shoulders. The old man was shivering and sipping a hot drink from a plastic container held tightly in his cupped hands.

Stewart motioned toward the group. "What's going on there?" he asked.

"You can interrogate him later. Have some coffee first. I have heard something of his testimony already from your colleagues. Very interesting. The man is quite frightened by what he saw—or claims he saw."

She raised the door of her hatchback, pulled off her white plastic coveralls, and placed the suit carefully, along with her overshoes and gloves, into a black bag. She tied the bag off and threw it into the well of the boot. Then she removed a thick-lined coat, pulled it on, and zipped it up tight against the bitterly cold night air. She shook her head to free her hair from the collar.

Stewart looked at her intently. He could see now that Dr. Padelski was a very attractive woman, and he wished he was thirty years younger. She was about five-nine, he guessed, with rich, brown curly hair that fell lazily onto her shoulders. She looked fit and enormously healthy. She made him feel old.

"Sit here, Inspector, beside me." She patted the metal at the back of the car. She deftly unscrewed an aluminum flask and handed him a cup of steaming coffee. "No milk, no sugar, I'm afraid."

He accepted the cup with a smile. She poured one for herself.

"Now tell me, Inspector, all about your Polish girlfriend."

He laughed. "Shall we talk about the body on the beach first?"

"Okay. Business before pleasure. But I'm not letting you go until you tell me, yes?"

"It's a deal."

"Okay, when I arrived, there were several police and an old man. That one there." She pointed to the man in the blanket. "He was having a fit, trembling and shouting. And swearing—awful, terrible words. He said that his mate had been eaten by dragons."

"Dragons?"

"Yes, he clearly said dragons." She paused a moment and a broad grin stretched across her face. "Welsh dragons, yes?"

Stewart looked at her with some amazement but said nothing.

"Inspector, you didn't find my joke funny? I thought Englishmen lived for humor."

Stewart looked at her with undisguised affection. He was beginning to like this girl.

"Very good, Doctor Padelski."

"Please, call me Rosina. What is your first name?"

"It's Paul."

She took a sip of coffee.

"So, Paul, I went to examine the body. It was lying half in the sea, which means that much, if not all, of the forensic evidence had been washed away. The body was a sight. A horrible way for anyone to die. I hope he died from fright, because if he didn't, he would have suffered a slow, terrifying death. So many bites."

"Bites?" he said incredulously. "You mean he was attacked by an animal? That seems unlikely."

"I agree. What animals do you have here that could do such harm?"

"None that I know of. We don't have sharks in these waters."

"I can rule out sharks. A shark bite would have broken the bones, and they are all intact."

"There is a zoo a bit farther up the coast, but surely we'd have heard if a dangerous animal had escaped." Stewart pulled a pack of cigarettes from his pocket and offered her one, immediately regretting it.

She stood and said, "You'll end up like that poor man on the beach—all chewed up inside. If you are going to smoke, let's walk."

She locked the car, and they walked back to where the policemen still stood with the old man. Stewart stayed downwind of Rosina so that the smoke from his cigarette didn't blow into her face.

He recognized the officers and nodded in greeting. He saw that the witness was now holding an empty cup, and he said, "Owen, can you rustle up another cup of tea?"

The old man stared at Stewart with eyes hollowed by shock and horror. His frail body was shivering, despite the blanket. The man's breath smelled of cheap alcohol, and Stewart drew back instinctively.

"You okay, old-timer? You're safe with us. We'll get you fixed up in a nice warm bed for the night. You can look forward to a good

English breakfast in the morning. How's that sound?" Stewart tried to sound chummy but not patronizing.

At first, the man looked at him as if he were speaking gibberish. Then he blurted out, "He only went down there for a slash!" Rosina looked at him blankly, not understanding. "You know—a whiz. He didn't want anyone to see him doing it. He's a gentleman, our Dan. I could hear 'im singing as he walked away, then he disappeared into the darkness down by the beach. Then all of a sudden I 'ear 'im screaming and crying out for help. I thought he was having a lark. He's bit of a joker, our Danny. So I shouted, 'Pull the other leg, Danny Boy!' But he didn't stop. So I started down the beach, but I couldn't see anything in the black of night." He wiped his lips with the back of his hand, and the blanket slipped off his shoulder. Stewart reached out and put it back.

"Then there was this almighty lightning bolt. Lit up the whole beach. And I saw . . . it was horrible . . . they were *eating* him. Four or five dragons tearing at his flesh! He was still alive . . . horrible. And then one of those things looked straight at me. I tell you, I froze on the spot. Its eyes burned bright red, and in its teeth I could see bits of Danny. I turned and ran, but I could still hear the screams. Then it stopped, sudden-like, and all I could do was pray, *Dear God, let him be dead.*"

The old man broke down and sobbed. His whole body convulsed and shook.

Stewart put his arm around the man and called to one of the policemen nearby. "Take him back to the station and see that he's sorted out. Properly, mind you."

The young officer led him away.

Down on the beach, a police photographer was at work. The flashes went off every few seconds, lighting up the gloom.

Rosina looked at Stewart sympathetically. She hadn't ever seen this tender side of the inspector. "Well, Paul, what do you make of that?"

"I don't know. Halloween is next week. It could be some sort of sick, twisted joke. The old fella was obviously drunk when it all happened, even if he seems sober now. Maybe the DTs."

"DTs?"

"Sorry. *Delirium tremens.* Too much drink and you begin to see pink elephants or . . ."

"Dragons."

"Yes."

"You know, in some countries, good people don't go out on All Hallows' Eve for fear of demons that walk the streets after midnight. All the doors are bolted and windows shuttered until daylight the next morning."

"Come on now, that's just superstitious nonsense."

"No, Paul. Our priest would stay in the church all night praying for the village and its people."

"You a religious person, then?"

"No, not religious. But I have a belief in God. Don't you?"

Stewart was silent for a moment. "No. I guess I don't."

Rosina was surprised. "You don't believe in God, you smoke, and you don't have a woman in your life. All in all, you're not in very good shape."

For a moment he felt sorry that his credibility was so low in her eyes.

Then she smiled at him and, taking his arm, said kindly, "I can see I am going to have to look after you. Maybe teach you a few things."

Stewart liked the sound of that.

SEVENTEEN

Sarah struggled up the hill with her shopping bags. Several times she had to stop to catch her breath before continuing her climb.

Richard had gone to Chester for a church meeting and wouldn't be home until late, which gave Sarah plenty of time to prepare a special dinner. She had bought some candles, two steaks, and some rather pricey truffles. Not that they could afford these luxuries, but they had been so happy as of late that she felt they should celebrate. Despite the vicar's odd ideas of running a church and parish, she and Richard had much to thank God for.

As Sarah arrived at the front gate of the cottage, the old woman who lived next door peered out through the curtains of her front room. Sarah set down the bags to find her house key, and the old woman came outside.

"Hello, Mrs. Williams! How are you today?" Sarah said.

"Well enough, my dear. I just came out to tell you that you had a visitor today."

"Oh? Probably someone for Richard, I should imagine."

The old woman grinned. "No. He made a point of asking for you—except he called you 'Sarah Finchley.'"

The use of her maiden name surprised Sarah.

"I said I knew of no Sarah Finchley in these whereabouts. I told him your name is Benton, Mrs. Sarah Benton, married to the local curate."

"What did he want? Did he give a name or a message?"

"No. But I didn't like the look of him, to be honest. We don't get many of his type around here."

"His type? What do you mean, Mrs. Williams?"

"Oh, I don't mean to be offensive. It's just that colored people aren't so very common in this area. Anyway, I told him that if he wanted to talk to Mr. Benton, he should call at the church. I gave him directions."

Sarah had to grab the wall to steady herself as she felt a rush of blood go to her head.

The older woman saw her reaction. "Is something wrong, my dear? Not bad news, I hope?" she asked, hoping to glean more information about the strange visitor.

"No, I'm just out of breath from climbing the hill."

Mrs. Williams stood waiting.

"Well, thank you for letting me know. I suppose he'll return if it's important."

"Is Finchley your maiden name, then?"

Sarah didn't answer. She turned the key in the door and pushed it open with her foot. She then collected the bags and stepped quickly inside, shutting the door behind her. A few moments later, she heard Mrs. Williams's door slam shut.

Now Sarah began to tremble. Her head was spinning, and she thought she might faint. She knew full well who the visitor had been—it couldn't be anyone else. She had been so happy a few minutes ago, and now she felt as if her whole world was about to collapse. Tears began to form in her eyes, and it wasn't long before she was crying and sobbing uncontrollably.

The tall stranger entered the church by the side door. Pinned to the wall outside was a sign that read, *Coffee Morning & Afternoon—All Welcome*. As he pushed the door open, he heard voices coming from off to the right. When he stepped into the hall, the women gathered there at tables stopped talking and stared at him. The man was an odd sight to their rheumy eyes. Normally, no one under sixty attended the afternoon coffee assembly, so to see a young man there was indeed a surprise. After the momentary silence, there erupted a collective murmuring as the ladies speculated as to the identity of the stranger.

He was obviously in the wrong place, and was about to make a smart exit when a two of the ladies stepped forward to greet him.

"I expect you'll want a cup of tea, young man," said the first.

"Or coffee," said the second.

They took his arm and led him to an empty seat at their table. The other women continued their staring and chattering.

"I expect you'd like some of our homemade Victoria sponge, too."

One of the ladies left and then returned with a mug of hot coffee and a generous slab of cake. "Now, you tuck in, young man. Don't mind us. We don't stand on ceremony here, do we, Ethel?"

"No, of course not, Edith!"

Putting the cup to his lips and smelling the aroma of fresh coffee, he suddenly became very hungry and thirsty, too. He drank the coffee down in a few long gulps and ate the cake almost as quickly. He glanced up to see everyone watching him. "My apologies, ladies, for my manners. I did not know I was so hungry. The cake is delicious."

Edith looked at Ethel. "Hungry young men need feeding, Ethel. Fetch him another round of cake."

Before he could protest, Ethel had disappeared into the kitchen, and within seconds had returned with more cake and another steaming mug of coffee.

He noticed a rather large woman sitting behind a single trestle table where she appeared to be collecting money. "How much do I owe you for the refreshments?" he asked.

Edith looked shocked in a playfully mocking way. "Sir, we are here to help the needy. And today you are one of our needy! Isn't that right, Ethel?"

"Yes, that's right," replied Ethel.

They both beamed at their young guest as he finished off his second helping.

Wiping the crumbs from his mouth, he said, "You might be able to help me. I came here to find the vicar's wife—and Mr. Benton, too, of course. I was told I might find him here."

"Oh bless you, *he's* not the vicar," Ethel said. "That would be Reverend Stannard. Mr. Benton is the curate of St. David's."

"Yes, of course. So where would I find them, the curate and his wife, that is?"

"He's not here today. Gone to Chester for a conference, I think. He is usually here to give us a reading from the Scriptures, and then we all pray and have tea."

Ethel asked, "You're not here to give the reading instead, are you?"

"No, definitely not. Not my cup of tea—or coffee, you might say." He laughed, holding up his mug.

Edith leaned forward to speak to the young man. "But I dare say you'll find Reverend Stannard in the rectory just around the corner. You'll not miss it. It's a large old house. Too large for one man, we all say."

Ethel frowned as she gave him a piece of advice. "Please excuse me for being blunt, young man, but don't expect a warm welcome. The reverend is not fond of . . . of foreigners like yourself."

Edith looked shocked. "Ethel, really! How can you say such a thing? This young man might have been born in Bangor."

He stood up. "No offense taken, ladies. Ethel is right. I was born in Ghana. Thank you for the advice. I appreciate it." The young man shook hands warmly with them both.

"But we don't know your name," they said in perfect unison.

"It is Morgan. Morgan Enenoah at your service." He made a theatrical bow.

As the door to the hall closed, the voices inside rose to a deafening crescendo, and several women rushed over to Edith and Ethel to hear news of the tall stranger.

EIGHTEEN

Edith had been correct. Morgan had no trouble finding the rectory. He walked straight up to the door and pressed the doorbell, and he heard it ring from somewhere deep inside the house.

Stannard was in his study poring over his stamp collection and searching the Internet for the best price he could obtain for his latest acquisitions. He heard the doorbell but carried on examining the stamps. The bell rang again. Jusach, the vicar's personal demon, was reclining on the sofa, taking a nap.

"Mary! Mary!" Stannard hollered. "Answer the door, if you please!"

The bell sounded once more before Stannard remembered it was Mary's afternoon off. "Who in the blazes can that be?"

He got up from his desk and made his way to the front entry. When he opened the door, Stannard did not take the trouble to disguise his displeasure at being disturbed. He also made no attempt to hide his reaction at seeing a black face staring at him from the doorstep.

"Yes? What is it?" he said rudely.

"Good afternoon, sir. I wonder if you could help me. I am trying to find a friend of mine—someone I have not seen for a number of years."

Now thoroughly annoyed, Stannard was just about to shut the door in Morgan's face when he remembered that he was still wearing his collar. "Well, young man, it may surprise you to know that I am not here to assist in the recovery of displaced persons," he said with heavy sarcasm.

"No. I mean to say, well, I think the person I am looking for is the wife of your curate. Sarah Finchley was her maiden name."

For a moment, Stannard again considered closing the door, but a second thought entered his mind, sown there by Jusach, who was curious about this odd person.

"You are an old friend of Sarah's. Not a relative, then?" he said squinting his eyes at Morgan.

"No, not a relation. Sarah and I were friends once, several years ago."

Jusach, the stunted demon, was at the vicar's side. He whispered again into Stannard's ear, "Find out what this is all about. I smell something amiss here."

Stannard opened the door wider and stood back. "Perhaps you had better come in. I may be able to help you in your quest."

Taking a seat in the vicar's study, Morgan surveyed the room. These kinds of Old World furnishings were quite foreign to him. He'd spent most of his working life aboard ocean-going ships as an able-bodied seaman.

Stannard sat down behind his desk. "Would like some tea, Mr. . . .? I'm sorry you didn't give me your name."

"My family name is Enenoah. I am Morgan Enenoah. As for the offer of tea, no, thank you. I have just had coffee with some kind ladies at your church hall."

"Have you now? So how may I help you?"

"Well, I am looking for Sarah Finchley. Rather, that used to be her name. I understand she is married to your assistant."

"Yes, that is correct," said the vicar patiently.

"I was told I might find her at the church with her husband."

"Please forgive me for asking, but as vicar, I must abide by certain rules of confidentiality, you understand."

Morgan nodded.

"Were you *close* friends?" Stannard emphasized the word, insinuating an intimate relationship.

"Well, sir, yes. I suppose we were for a short time. And then I had to leave on a ship to South America. I am a seaman serving in the British navy. Then one thing led to another, and my job kept me away from the UK. I lost touch with Sarah, but I promised myself that I would look her up upon my return to Great Britain."

"So this is just a social visit. Nothing . . . untoward?" said Stannard, apparently disappointed.

Jusach poked the vicar in the side of his head to prod him to pursue the subject. Stannard instinctively scratched at the place where the demon's long fingernails had pierced him.

"Untoward, sir? I am sorry, but I do not understand the word."

"Quite. You are not the bearer of bad tidings, I hope? I may assume you have benign intentions toward Richard and Sarah?"

"Oh, y-yes," Morgan stammered. "I just wanted to see Sarah again. I know she is married, but I . . ." There followed an awkward silence.

Stannard was clever enough to understand much from the silence.

"Do they have any children?" Morgan asked.

"Richard and Sarah? No, they don't. My advice to Richard has been to leave that sort of thing for much later in his career."

Stannard was now feeling quite satisfied with the conversation. He felt there may be something here he might use to his advantage at such a time when he needed Richard to do something discreet for him.

Jusach moved to where Morgan was sitting and studied him intensely, trying hard to read the young man's mind but without success. Nevertheless, he was sure there was more to this man than met the eye, even the eye of an old demon. Jusach considered abandoning his watch on the vicar to follow the young man, but he hesitated to act. If he was wrong and could not justify his actions, he would be charged with dereliction of duty and would face the wrath of Rimmon.

Morgan held out his hand to Stannard, but the vicar ignored him and showed him to the door. "If you come back on Sunday to the morning church service, you will certainly find both Richard and Sarah in attendance."

Before Morgan got a chance to express his gratitude, Stannard had closed the door.

Nineteen

Sarah looked at her watch. Just past eight. Richard ought to have been home by now. She thought of calling him on his cell phone and was about to dial the number when a new wave of fear washed over her. She was certain her voice would betray her, letting him know that something was wrong. She set her phone down on the kitchen table. It was dark outside now, and the shopping bags lay on the floor, the groceries still inside.

It had happened so long ago. She was only sixteen when she met Morgan, and she had been immediately infatuated with him. He was handsome and exciting and older than her by five years. He seemed so sophisticated, and she had been smitten with his warm, friendly manner and his strange, charming accent. They had met at the youth club in the village. He was a friend of Matt, one of the youth club's leaders.

Until then she had led a pretty sheltered life. She was an only child, and her parents had certainly cared for her with love, but it was always tempered by strict discipline. Whereas her classmates were given more freedom as teenagers, she had been given less. Her parents' overwhelming desire was to see her go to university and get a degree. Sarah appreciated their hopes and wishes, and she did not disobey them. But inside were growing desires of her own, and some of these were physical and emotional. She had never had a boyfriend, and at age sixteen, she felt a strong urge to find out what that was like. That's when Morgan had literally walked into her life.

She had been sitting in the youth club kitchen with the other assistant leaders, sipping hot chocolate, when Matt waltzed in, dragging Morgan with him, and introduced him to everyone as his best mate. Sarah had never had a conversation with a black man before, and she was embarrassed to find she couldn't take her eyes off him. Morgan had noticed her staring and was stricken by the fresh-faced country girl. She had shoulder-length blonde hair and freckles, her blue eyes were bright and young, and she wore no makeup to detract from her milk-white complexion. He had been captivated by her, and she by him.

By the end of the evening, they had spent the best part of two hours talking, but more than words were being exchanged. Sarah's father arrived to pick her up in his car as he did every week, not allowing her to walk home with her friends, but she was reluctant to leave that night. Morgan made it very clear that he wanted to see her again soon.

By chance, they did meet again before the next club night. Sarah had been doing some study work in the Town Centre Library when she spotted Morgan in one of the aisles, his head buried deep in an atlas. She crept up behind and surprised him. They sat down at a table, and he told her he'd been reading up on South America, where his next deployment in the navy was taking him. They talked and talked, about nothing really, and before long they were holding hands under the table.

Over the next few days, all of Sarah's thoughts and dreams had been about Morgan, and she knew that if her parents found out they would stop her from going to the youth club. At the next meeting, Morgan arrived early to see her. Matt was aware of the budding romance, so he gave Sarah freedom that evening to spend time with his friend. After dark had set in, the two of them walked down the lane to the edge of the woods, and they kissed under the moonlight. It was Sarah's first. The feelings stirred by the kiss surprised and excited her, and though young himself, Morgan knew enough about girls to fan the flames of her ardor.

The following weekend, Matt would be out of town at youth leaders' training, and his small flat was free for Morgan to use as he wanted. When Morgan suggested to Sarah she stay over on Saturday night, she had been shocked at first. This was dead against everything she had been brought up to believe. It would mean lying to her parents, and to stay with Morgan meant sleeping with him, which until now she had not seriously considered. Her knowledge and upbringing said no, but her heart and body screamed yes. And she succumbed.

In the days after their night together, both Sarah and Morgan began to feel the pain of impending separation. Morgan declared he would resign and stay with her. They could talk to her parents, he said, bring the affair out into the open and plan for a future together. He was like a kid with a new dream, and Sarah loved him for it. But Sarah knew her parents would never allow the relationship to continue. In the end, they pledged to wait. She would finish her studies, and they would be together when he returned from the navy. With many tears and declarations of love, he finally departed, and there followed many sad days for young Sarah.

Her parents still knew nothing. They noticed the change in her moods but could not elicit the truth from her. After a while, they had chalked it up to a teenager's hormones and nothing more.

Instead of going straight home that evening, Richard had headed for the rectory. The whole business of Maynard Jones's demise and the awful truth about Stannard's lack of compassion had angered Richard to the point that he'd decided to confront the vicar. He banged several times on the front door impatiently with his clenched fist. He waited but no one came. He banged louder this time, and then he heard Stannard shouting, "All right, I'm coming!"

The vicar opened the door, and without waiting to be invited, Richard brushed past Stannard and went into the hall. "I need to speak to you right now, sir, and it cannot wait." Richard's whole body was shaking with righteous anger. Stannard still stood holding the door open. Richard shoved the door shut with a loud thud. The vicar looked at him as if he had gone mad.

"How dare you burst into my home like this? What on earth do you think you are doing?"

Richard ignored the vicar's question and held up Maynard Jones's journal. *"This* is what I am doing. This journal belonged to your previous curate. Sarah found it in the cottage, hidden from prying eyes. It tells of a man in desperate need of spiritual and physical help—"

It was Stannard who now pushed past Richard, disappearing into his study and taking refuge behind his desk.

Richard followed him while continuing his tirade. "—a desperate man in need of *your* help, Stannard. He was gravely ill, confused, and in spiritual torment, and it was your place to show him support, sympathy, and kindness."

The vicar slumped into his chair and fixed a pair of frightened eyes on Richard.

Richard faced him across the desk and scoffed at him, "But you had none to give him. Even when he was dying, he called you for help to get him a doctor, but you cut him off." Richard raised the journal and said, "It's all in here. The poor man chronicled not only his own abject fears and trepidations, but he describes in detail your cold-hearted attitude and behavior. Stannard, the man was your curate. He was your responsibility! Doesn't it say somewhere in your oath as a minister ordained of God that no one of Christ's family shall 'take any hurt or hindrance by reason of your negligence'?" Richard was shouting now.

"Look at you!" Richard pointed to the books and albums of stamps spread out on the desk. "You're more interested in your bloody stamps than in the souls of men. You don't have the love of God in your heart! Why carry on with this masquerade? Why don't you resign and be done with it!"

Richard was beside himself, but as he looked down upon this pathetic creature, this caricature of a man of God seated behind the desk, Richard began to feel pity.

The brief silence gave Stannard an opening to muster a defense, and Jusach, his unseen companion, was filling him with all sorts of lies and barbs to fire back at the curate.

Richard had bowed his head and was now feeling weary and crestfallen. He had thought that by confronting Stannard with the truth, the vicar's hypocrisy would be exposed and perhaps he would be shamed into a state of contrition. He had been mistaken.

Stannard stood up slowly and with rage building in his countenance, said, "How *dare* you lecture me on my oaths to God and my vocation? What do *you* know of life? You're still wet behind the ears. Maynard Jones deserved all he got, for he brought it upon himself. He was a homosexual, a disgrace to the church. He signed his own death warrant by partaking in activities abominable to God. The man had *AIDS!* And if that disease wasn't sent by God Himself to rid the world of these people . . ." The vicar began to splutter and shout, and waving his bony fingers at Richard, he cried, "Remember Sodom and Gomorrah? The Lord gave no quarter there. He wiped their kind off the face of the earth. When I saw Jones's mangled body in the morgue, I felt no sympathy for him. He is welcome to rot in hell forever. He can get his sympathy from the devil, for all I care. And there are many of my clerical brothers who would stand by me in this. Now *get out!* And don't think I shall not write to the bishop about this outrage. Get out, I say—*this instant!*"

Richard looked at Stannard with real pity in his eyes. "You are far sicker than Maynard Jones ever was." Richard tossed the journal on the desk. "Read it if you dare! Read his journal and pray that God will forgive you."

Richard turned and walked briskly out of the study. He flung open the front door and stalked out, leaving the door standing open. Stannard shouted at him from the doorway, "You think you are so holy and righteous, Benton? Try asking your wife if she had a visitor this afternoon!"

Richard slowed and turned back, only to see Stannard slam the front door shut. He wondered what the vicar had meant.

TWENTY

Sarah was drowning in shame and guilt. She now wished she had told Richard all about Morgan long ago, or at least before they were married. She thought to herself, *The Word of God is true when it says your sins will find you out one day, even if it is years later.*

She was in abject fear of losing her husband over a wrong she had committed as a teenager. Yet surely she could not be held accountable— she had been so young, barely an adolescent. She hadn't loved Morgan. She knew now her feelings had been little more than infatuation and curiosity and a longing to know about the forbidden things of love and romance. She paced up and down the hall in the cottage, looking anxiously at the front door, expecting Richard at any moment.

What would she say to him? She had to tell him the truth. It was no good thinking she could hide this from him. Her head ached as she turned the matter over and over in her mind. What if she could keep Morgan away? Maybe he wouldn't return, but what if he went to the church and told others? Told Stannard? Oh God, no, please not him. The tears began to flow again. Her face was blotchy from crying, her eyes shot through with red.

Then the door opened and Richard strode in, obviously angry and upset. She thought he must already know, and she ran to him, sobbing, "Oh, Richard, please forgive me. I am so ashamed of myself. I ought to have told you. Only don't leave me, *please.*"

Richard, shocked at her behavior, pushed her away so he could see her face while still holding her. "What on earth is the matter? Sarah, why are you crying?"

She raised her eyes to his. "I— I . . . You don't know? Oh, Richard, I am so sorry, so very sorry."

"Come, you had better sit down and tell me what this is all about." He guided her into the living room and sat down beside her on the sofa. "Now, why are you so upset? And why are you apologizing to me?" he asked gently, momentarily forgetting the incident with Stannard.

The angel Samuel stood unseen in the corner of the room watching them intently. His heart was troubled.

She dried her face with a tissue, dabbing at her eyes as she spoke. "You— you came in so angry. I thought it was because of me. I became frightened."

"I was angry because I just had a blazing row with Stannard over his treatment of Maynard Jones. I thought it was about time sometime told him what a cruel man he really is, and I purposefully didn't call you beforehand because I knew you'd try to dissuade me from going."

"Oh, I see. I didn't realize," she said in a subdued voice, trying hard not to sob.

Richard put his arm around her and looked at her tenderly. "Now, what is this all about? Sarah, I think you should confide in me. I am a clergyman, after all." He smiled.

"Richard, it's not a joke, and I do have a confession. Something I should have spoken to you about when we first met, when we began to fall in love. But I thought the past was over and done with, that I could put it behind me forever." She took a deep breath before continuing. "I apparently had a visitor this afternoon. Mrs. Williams from next door spoke with him, though I did not. But from her description, I know who it was."

Richard was now beginning to look worried.

"It's someone I knew when I was sixteen. A man." Sarah was speaking very slowly, and her breath was becoming labored. Biting her lip, she went on. "I don't know how to say this."

The worry on Richard's face was giving way to deep anxiety. He withdrew his arm from her shoulder.

"It was all stupid," she blurted. "I was young and naïve. I didn't really know what I was doing." With tears falling onto her cheeks, she related the story of her affair with Morgan, leaving the worst for last.

"After Morgan had gone back to sea, I found out I was pregnant with his child. We only made love the one time."

Richard stood up suddenly and looked down at her. "So what happened? Where is the child now? My God, the child must be ten years old at least. Was it a boy or a girl? And is the child black or white?" Anger had crept into his words.

Sarah began to sob again, her body heaving with shame. "There is no child. I miscarried at six months. The child was stillborn."

Richard immediately regretted at what he had said in anger. "What happened then with the man? Did you continue to see him?"

"No, I swear, I haven't seen Morgan since. He went away, and I never heard from him again."

"Until now, that is!" Richard turned his back on Sarah. "Is he expected back? Have you agreed to meet him?"

"No, Richard. I don't want to see him. I love *you!*" She rose from the sofa and tried to put her arms around him, but he pushed her away somewhat brusquely.

"Don't, please," he said. "I need space to think this over. You have lied to me."

Horrified, she stared at the husband who now seemed so distant from her. Samuel instinctively moved beside her to let his warmth comfort her. He could see that she was repentant and full of regret. Her soul was clean. All that her husband had to do now was find it in his heart to forgive her, especially as this had all occurred before they ever met.

Grabbing his coat from the hall, Richard headed for the door.

"Richard, please don't leave me. Don't go," she pleaded.

The door slammed behind him as he ran down the path and disappeared into the darkness.

Samuel had been charged with watching over both Richard and Sarah, but he now had to make a decision. Should he stay with Sarah or follow Richard? The man appeared to need his help now more than the woman, and Samuel made his choice. He rushed alongside Richard as the young man ran toward the promenade.

TWENTY-ONE

The sky was darkening, the last rays of sunlight outlining the clouds on the horizon. Richard slowed and walked, out of breath, along the promenade, going nowhere in particular. His mind raced with all kinds of questions that had no easy answers. Sarah's confession that she had been pregnant at sixteen went against everything Richard thought he knew about her. If she had been unable to tell him about such an important episode in her life, how could he ever again believe anything she told him? She had hidden the truth from him all this time, and he had been raised to believe that was the same as lying.

He realized with some pain that her parents, too, were culpable in this deception. They had known about it and still did not say anything to him before the wedding. *I suppose,* he thought, *they were glad to be rid of her.* His conscience chided him, *No, that can't be true. They supported her to go to university. What am I thinking? She's my wife, and I love her, but . . . why did she lie to me?*

Leaving the promenade, Richard struck out along the shoreline until he came to a place where the waves of the sea crashed against the bottom of the cliffs and he could go no further. He sat down in the sand and for hours wept tears of anger, frustration, and disappointment. The same question kept repeating itself over and over again in his mind until the words had lost their meaning and, becoming abstract, simply dissolved into searing pain. Why had she kept this terrible secret from him all these years?

The onrushing sea crashed against the rocks, and with each surge the waves crept nearer to his feet. The tide was coming in fast. Richard shivered as the frigid night air seeped into his bones. Pulling himself up, he perfunctorily brushed the sand off his trousers and started walking back toward the promenade. His legs moved as if made of lead, as if he was a robot, a mindless automaton on a mechanical journey to nowhere. He slipped and tripped as his feet encountered the raised timber step of the old pier. The hour was late now, and there was no one else about. The small shops, booths, and amusements were all boarded up. Everyone had gone home long ago, leaving windblown litter as the only evidence of their having been there. Fish-and-chip bags, empty soda cans, and cigarette butts—slowly, everything was swept into the waters below.

Reaching the end of the pier, Richard halted and looked absently at the sea. The waves violently churned against the rusted stanchions that held up the timber deck. Overhead, gulls squawked loudly, diving fast and swooping low over the waves in search of morsels of floating food. Richard could see in the distance the lights of a ferry bound for Liverpool, but the lights were suddenly extinguished by a dark sheet of rain moving in on the leading edge of a storm. Soon the rain rushed onshore with the wind and lashed at Richard's unprotected face.

He turned his face away and drew the collar of his thin jacket up around his ears to ward off the shock of the cold rain. Spotting a shelter nearby, he pushed himself into a corner on the lee side, and closing his eyes, wrapped his arms around himself in an effort to stay warm. His mind was numb and his body weary, and it was not long before the strain of the past few hours became too much. Exhaustion set in, and Richard fell into a deep sleep.

The angel Samuel stood guard over the despondent young man. Hours had passed when suddenly a bright light began to shine before him and illuminate the pier. Samuel knew instantly this was the Shekinah, the glory of God's presence. Only one such emanation in the universe that manifested in this way: the Spirit of God. Samuel fell to his knees and bowed low, his forehead touching the planks of wood.

"Samuel, Samuel." The voice of Yahweh shook the pier.

Samuel dared not raise his eyes to look upon the Spirit of God, but the words flowed through his very being, strengthening and emboldening him.

"Speak, Lord, for your servant listens."

"My good and faithful servant, I give you a command. The man you protect this night is to be used mightily in My plans. I shall do a work in this place that will cause reverberations around the world. I charge you this night to stand against Satan and his dark angels. I give you a sword of truth that when plunged into the heart of a demon will banish it to the fiery pit until Judgment Day. Guard this weapon well, for with it you shall witness a glorious victory over the rebellious hordes. I, Yahweh Sabaoth, the Lord of hosts, have commanded you this night."

The light vanished, leaving only a profound silence. Samuel did not move nor open his eyes for some time. He trembled still as he felt the residual power of the Lord coursing through him.

Finally, the angel stood, raised his arms to the heavens, and exclaimed with joy, "Praise the Almighty One, the Living God of Heaven and Earth! Hallelujah! He is Lord!"

Richard now stirred from his slumber. He felt oddly refreshed in a way he had never experienced before. New life and new strength coursed through his veins.

He sprang forward and began to run along the pier, heading for home. As he ran, he shouted at the top of his lungs, "Father, forgive me! I have been a fool. I am sorry for the pain I must have caused Sarah this day. Forgive me, Lord!"

The angel Samuel laughed as he ran beside Richard. They praised God, angel and man in unity.

Sarah was waiting at the door when Richard arrived, and she ran straight into his arms. "Oh, Darling, I have been so worried about you! You've been gone hours, and you didn't answer your phone . . . I wanted to say—"

Before she could say another word, Richard placed his hand gently over her mouth to stop her. "Never mind all that. I am the one who should apologize. I have been such a fool."

They walked arm in arm into the cottage, and with his foot Richard shut the door behind him.

Sarah looked into his eyes. She could see that something had happened to her husband. His eyes sparkled, and his face shone. Even his smile was somehow magnified.

He kissed her on her lips, pulled her close and told her he loved her deeply. She felt his ardor, the passion of his desire for her. With abandon she pulled him toward the stairs and up to the bedroom. It took only seconds for them to completely disrobe and fall onto the bed, wrapped in each other's arms. The night air was cold, but they were oblivious to it. Together they found a new closeness that night, an intimacy they had never known.

The angel Samuel hovered over them, delighted to see this reunion, but he was perplexed, never having witnessed this miracle of human love firsthand. He found himself overwhelmed by this episode, and rising up through the roof, Samuel flew into the brightly starred heavens, singing and praising until he could sing no more.

Afterward, Richard and Sarah lay beside each other, enveloped in the soft darkness, perfectly satisfied and content.

"Richard," Sarah said softly, "do you believe in angels?"

"Well, yes, I suppose I do, as they are mentioned several times in the Scriptures."

"I don't mean in the Bible. I mean here and now. Do you believe they are sent to protect us?"

"Hmm . . . I don't really know. Why?"

"It's just that over the last few days, I have felt the presence of someone with us. Even tonight, in this room. I think an angel was here, sharing our moment of joy."

TWENTY-TWO

Morgan walked up the cottage path to find the smiling faces of Richard and Sarah Benton waiting for him at the door. Richard stepped forward and offered his hand. "Welcome. You must be Morgan. Please come in."

The three of them stood awkwardly facing each in the small living room of the cottage.

"Can I get you a tea or coffee?" Sarah asked brightly.

"Yes, thank you." Morgan had expected a different kind of welcome, and he had hoped to be free to talk to Sarah alone.

Richard motioned to a chair. "Please sit, Morgan. I know this must be difficult for you, and believe me when I say I think I understand your feelings. Sarah and I have talked and prayed about the time she spent with you when she was younger, and well . . . I think it's best if you and Sarah talk it over alone. I know she has a lot to tell you—some of it pretty important. She has gone through great distress these last few days, and my only request, Morgan, is that you treat her with respect and understand what she suffered all those years ago."

Richard stood up and offered his hand again to his visitor. Morgan rose from the chair and shook Richard's hand warmly. He said, "You can trust me. I am not here to cause any trouble. I just wanted to put things straight. I heard so many rumors when I returned to Britain that I didn't know what to believe."

As Sarah passed Richard in the hallway, he kissed her on the cheek. "I'll go for a ramble on the Ulm. Call me when you are ready. No need to rush." Richard pulled on his coat, hat, and scarf and left them alone together.

Sarah handed a mug of coffee to Morgan, who said, "He seems a good man. But I suppose being a curate, he ought to be, eh?"

"Being a clergyman is no guarantee of good character," she said, thinking of Stannard.

Morgan nodded. "I believe I understand. I met your vicar yesterday."

Braving the icy wind, Richard climbed the steep winding path that seemed to wander all over the great rocky hill. From here he could see the funicular, the cable car carrying hardy tourists from the bottom to the top of the Great Ulm and vice versa. He promised himself that as reward for his exertions he would buy a hot chocolate and an iced bun at the Summit Café before setting out on the downward trek.

Once he reached the summit, Richard energetically strode across the car park and jumped over the low stone wall that stopped cars from going over the edge. Carrying on a few yards more, he stood at the brink of a steep incline that descended all the way to the sea far below. To the west, he could see Anglesey and the famous Puffin Island, and in between the bits of land he could just make out the tall striped lighthouse whose bell clanged every thirty seconds, day and night, to guide passing ships away from the rocks. To the north was just a great expanse of sea all the way to the Isle of Man and beyond.

Richard loved this spot. Compared to other places he had known this was heaven on earth. The sea and the rocks spoke of timelessness, and he always felt nearer to God here. He often came to this spot to pray. He recalled when he and Sarah had come up here after dark one night to watch the stars. The night had been cold but dry, and they lay upon the grass for hours, holding hands and talking about nothing particular. They had stared at brilliant stars shimmering in the cloudless sky, in awe of the beauty of God's creation. Richard had recited from Psalm 8, one of his favorites: "When I consider Your heavens, the work of Your fingers, the moon and the stars, which You have ordained, what is man that You are mindful of him?"

Sarah had turned to him and kissed him, saying, "Darling, I love you so very, very much." Then, in the next moment, she had exclaimed, "But you know what infuriates me the most about you?"

Richard had been taken aback, his mouth agape.

Sarah said, "Every time we do this—looking up at the night sky—you say, 'Wow, did you see that shooting star?' And by the time I turn my head to see it, it's already vanished."

To Sarah's surprise, Richard had jumped to his feet. Standing tall, and theatrically throwing his arms aloft, he cried out, "Lord! We want to see the most amazing shooting star cross the sky right there." He pointed to a high point in the western sky. "And we want it within the next thirty seconds."

Sarah had scrambled to her feet and was standing expectantly at his side as he started to count aloud. "One, two, three, four . . ."

He got as far as fifteen when a light suddenly appeared above the horizon, flaming brightly, streaking across the night sky, accompanied by a sound like the roar of a great wind. *Whoosh!*

After the shooting star had faded from view, Richard and Sarah simply stared at each other with their mouths open in wonder. They stayed like this, transfixed, for several moments until Sarah cried, "Richard, that was amazing! God heard your prayer and answered it in style!"

Richard smiled as he walked back across the car park to the Summit Café, smiling at the memory of that night when God had come near to both of them. He found an empty seat by the window and, sliding in, ordered a hot chocolate. He didn't bother with the iced bun, although they did look delicious. He had been there for about ten minutes when his phone rang.

"Richard, you can come back home now. Morgan's gone."

"Gone happy?" he asked.

"Well, I don't know really. But he's left wiser than he came. He's a good man."

Richard put the phone back in his pocket and made his way home with a jaunty step in his walk.

TWENTY-THREE

Halloween night began innocently enough. A gang of loud teenage boys wandered around the town centre, dressed in outrageous costumes. A young man dressed as Harry Potter, with a red lightning bolt painted on his forehead, was swigging vodka straight from a bottle. His raucous mates were made up to look like zombies, skeletons, and assorted monsters. Nearby, a group of intoxicated teenage girls, dressed as witches, waltzed arm in arm while singing unintelligible words to a popular song. Most of it was good-natured stuff, and the policemen posted on the corner by the bank only smiled as the revelers passed.

The cold weather had continued. Every now and then, lightning lit up the dark vault of the night, followed by loud cracks of thunder, but no rain fell. Along the rooftops, on spires, masts, and chimneys, sporadic bursts of luminous green electrical light burned bright for a few fiery seconds before moving on, as if searching for a place to rest.

Small bunches of younger children were safely herded by their mothers, moving from house to house, knocking on doors, calling "Trick or treat!" in shrill voices, and collecting sweets in bags and wicker baskets. Many of the kids wore costumes purchased cheaply from the local supermarket. Some wore witches' hats and flowing black plastic capes. A few even sported miniature broomsticks. Others cavorted in red devil outfits with pointed tails and little pitchforks. Monstrous masks glowed eerily in the dark.

All "harmless" fun, but there would be casualties this night.

The previous Sunday, all across town, the priests and pastors and vicars had torn up their sermon notes and preached a message that had been implanted in their hearts. They warned the faithful that Halloween was a celebration of Satan, that the longtime ritual glorified all the worst that is mankind. The pagan religions that existed in these isles before the coming of Christianity had been fostered and sustained by Lucifer's hordes. Even in these modern times, the old religions attracted many devotees who thought them romantic and fascinating, though none of them really understood the ancient evil upon which these beliefs had been founded.

The inspired clergy denounced the frivolities and party atmosphere of All Hallows' Eve. No matter how comic and harmless, the costumes and activities may appear, the festivities paid homage to the lord of Hell. And those who naively partook of these festivities exposed themselves and their children to the bestial influence of Hades. "The Word of God says, *'Resist the devil and he will flee from you.'* So resist him *you must in prayer, in thought, and in deed."*

Such sermons had not been heard in these churches for decades, not since the last great Welsh revival. The message was simple: Lock up your homes and put a sign on your door, as the Israelites smeared blood on the doorposts and lintels of their dwellings to protect them from the Angel of Death. The call had gone out for prayer warriors to gather in homes and in the churches to pray against dark powers and principalities.

In the streets, the demon servants of Prince Rimmon mocked and derided everyone in their path, encouraging the humans all the more to make fools of themselves.

But the angels had their commands: *Stand and watch. Repel any demon that tries to invade any sacred place, including the homes of believers and places of good governance— hospitals, fire services, and police—but under no circumstances take the initiative and engage the enemy. Remember that those humans who have chosen to participate in the festivities are under the influence of the god of this age.*

Bezalel had commanded Samuel to keep his sword of truth sheathed, saying it was not to be used on this night.

On this night, as on every Halloween, emergency facilities and workers were on high alert. Emergency room staff at the local hospital expected a higher-than-normal intake of bruised bodies, broken bones, and as the night wore on, those injured in drunken fights. At the police station, the cells would no doubt become filled with miscreants and petty criminals who would be out to take full advantage of the revelry.

A group of nurses smoking cigarettes outside the entrance to the emergency department noticed the first signs that something was wrong. The parking lot was quickly filling with vehicles and ambulances carrying dozens of young children displaying the same symptoms: repeated vomiting followed by acute diarrhea. Their faces were pale, their limbs slack in their mothers' arms. The waiting room was soon full of crying children and angry parents seeking immediate help from beleaguered nurses and doctors. Local family physicians were called in to offer much-needed assistance.

Outside the hospital, a band of angels stood guard, their faces grim. Nearby, clusters of demons laughed derisively and jeered at the angels, who were bound by orders not to intervene.

In years past, the local constabulary had easily kept public order on Halloween without drafting reinforcements. But tonight they had their hands full. It was as if the town had suddenly gone mad, infected with some strange contagion. At first, a few fights broke out among people drunk on cheap liquor. But before long, shop windows were being broken and goods stolen in full view of police officers. Rampaging youths began smashing car windows and setting vehicles aflame. The police regrouped and moved in with truncheons to restore order, but they were seriously outnumbered.

Meanwhile, in a back alley, a tramp was being kicked and beaten to death by Harry Potter and his friends, who laughed like maniacs as the vagrant was tossed among them like a rag doll. Their last act before speeding off was to set fire to the body.

Unseen by human eyes, a group of grinning devils gathered about the burning man, pretending to warm their hands on the flames and gesticulating crudely to a group of nearby angels.

Twenty-Four

Melanie O'Reilly was a Scouser, a native of Liverpool with an Irish family background. A single parent, Melanie wanted to do right by her four-year-old daughter. She wanted to bring her up good and proper, different from the childhood she herself had experienced. She had been beaten by her alcoholic father, neglected by her mother, and at the age of fifteen, she had received her first conviction for drug abuse. A few months later, she had gotten pregnant. She didn't know who the father was—it could have been any of three or four boys she'd slept with at an all-night binge party. She didn't really care. She had no time for blokes, especially *those* losers.

After the baby was born, Melanie had been offered a flat in Golwyn Sands, a nice seaside town a few miles up the coast from Penrhos Bay. The flat was in a council-owned block full of wayward girls like her, but it wasn't as bad as the hostel. At the end of the day, she could shut the door and have her own private space. The flat came with a condition that once a week she visit a drug rehabilitation clinic run by a Christian charity in town. There she got real help. Now she was off the hard drugs and smoking less than a pack a day—and the odd joint now and again.

Life was good, in fact. Money was scarce, but she intended to get a job at the local superstore when her kid started school in just a few months. And of course, she had Emily.

Melanie had promised her daughter they would go trick-or-treating on Halloween. They had gone to the supermarket to buy her a witch's costume and broom. It would be Emily's first time.

Melanie had intended to go out earlier in the evening, while it was still light out, but she had been held up waiting for her box of groceries to arrive from Food Share, the local charity that helped people who were down on their luck. She had expected the two ladies to compliment her daughter on her Halloween costume, but oddly, they had said nothing.

Melanie and Emily lived close to the centre of town, so they could walk there in just a few minutes. It was nine o'clock by the time they started knocking on doors. In a short time, Emily had collected more sweets than she'd ever seen in her short life. Melanie had to stop her from eating them all at once.

The hour was getting late, and there didn't seem to be any other young children on the streets. Melanie was getting a bit worried because there were many older kids about, screaming and shouting and acting stupid. It seemed that every ten minutes an ambulance rushed past, sirens blaring and blue lights flashing.

Emily said she was feeling a bit sick. Melanie picked her up to comfort her, telling that she had been naughty to have eaten so many sweets so quickly.

Melanie headed across an open park, taking a shortcut back to the flat. Halfway across the park, Emily held up her head and said, "Mummy, do you hear music?"

Melanie stopped. She could hear it. The music was instantly recognizable. It was the calliope of a merry-go-round, like the carousel she had seen at the fair that summer. Mother and daughter could see multicolored lights coming from the other side of a copse of trees.

"Mummy, can we go see it? Pleeease?"

Melanie set Emily down on the grass and clasped her small hand, and together they ran to where the music was coming from.

When they arrived, the carousel was turning full tilt. The grotesquely beautiful painted horses moved up and down in time with the music. There were only a few children on the ride, but they were all laughing and enjoying themselves immensely.

Emily was dazzled by all the noise and lights. She laughed and giggled every time the horses went by in a blur of light and color. She cried out over the noise of the music, "Mummy, can I go on? I so love the horses. Please, can I? Say yes!"

Melanie nodded.

"Mummy, Mummy I like that one! I like the white and gold horse!"

After the ride came to a halt, Melanie helped her daughter up onto the white horse's saddle. For a moment, before she let go, she had second thoughts.

"Will my daughter . . . ? I mean, she's safe, isn't she?" Melanie asked the man operating the ride.

"Sure. I'll slow it down this time, okay? And don't worry, Mum. I'll keep an eye on her."

When she asked how much, he waved her money away. "This one's on me. It's Halloween, after all."

Melanie stepped back. She watched with anxious eyes as the carousel began turning again. Emily disappeared for a few seconds, and then, as the ride came full circle, she came into view. Melanie called out to her, but her daughter was already lost in a magical world of princesses and horses. Melanie relaxed and got her cell phone out to take a photo of Emily when she came around again.

Lightning flashed in the night sky above her, and Melanie worried now that it would rain before they could get home. *Hey*, she thought, *it's only water.* The ride continued turning, and it was then that she noticed that Emily was the only child on the ride. Perhaps they had caught the last ride of the evening, she thought and glanced at her watch. Almost ten o'clock. Every time Emily passed, Melanie waved, trying to catch her eye. At last, the ride began to lose speed. Emily now wore a big frown, sad that the adventure was coming to an end. The carousel finally halted, but it stopped with Emily and her white and gold steed on the opposite side. Melanie waited a few moments, expecting to see Emily come running around the side. The music had stopped, and all was quiet.

Melanie started to walk around the merry-go-round, calling out Emily's name. She thought maybe her daughter needed help to get down. "So much for the guy in charge," she muttered. Arriving at the other side, she saw that the white and gold horse was without a rider. Melanie walked more quickly now, hoping to find Emily waiting for her on the side where they had started. She completed a full circle of the machine, but Emily was nowhere to be seen.

"Emily," she called out. "Emily!"

Melanie felt panic rising from her stomach. Where was the man who operated the ride? A terrible idea began to form in her mind. She tried hard not to think it, but it just grew inside of her. With tears welling in her eyes she cried, "No, no! Please, God, not my baby!"

She looked all about her, hoping to catch a glimpse of the man with Emily. She ran to the edge of the trees. Wildly brushing them aside, she scanned the dense undergrowth.

"Emily! Emily!" she screamed, becoming more frantic by the second.

Finally, when she could not shout anymore, Melanie slumped to her knees. As she sobbed, her body convulsed and shook uncontrollably with the pain and anguish that had enveloped her whole being.

It was some time before the medic and policewoman could calm Melanie down and get her to tell them what was wrong. A few minutes earlier, she had rushed into the police station, screaming and shouting. No one could understand what she was trying to say. At first they thought she was suffering from an intake of bad drugs, her actions were so mad. Her clothes were unkempt and torn from the bushes. Mud coated her shoes and jeans. She was a pitiable sight to the few now gathered around her.

The female cop whispered to the medic that perhaps she'd been raped. The medic shrugged. Just as he was reaching into a bag to get something to quiet her down, Melanie suddenly stopped screaming. Collapsing to the floor in a squatting position, she simply sobbed and whimpered. The woman cop knelt beside her. Putting her hands upon Melanie's shoulders, she said gently, "We need to know what has happened to you. Can't you tell us? Then maybe we can help you."

Melanie wiped tears from her face with her hands. Without looking up, she said in a hoarse voice, "My daughter, Emily . . . she's been taken by a man . . . she's only four!"

The policewoman turned her head to look at the medic and said in a quiet hushed voice, "Lord, no."

TWENTY-FIVE

Jezebel stared in almost disbelief. It was one thing to experience her spiritual mentor through the ether of a séance, but it was quite another to meet him in the flesh. With head bowed low, Jezebel trembled as Gathan stood before her in human form with the child Emily in his arms. He was dressed in gypsy garb.

"Where shall I take her?" he asked brusquely.

"This way, my lord," she said, keeping her head down.

Gathan followed her up a flight of stairs to the suite of rooms that served as her private residence above the New Age shop. Gathan deposited the child on the sofa of a lavishly furnished lounge that bore all the soft and subtle ornaments of a witch of high standing.

"What shall I—" Jezebel's voice shook with fear under Gathan's intense, unblinking gaze.

"Do what I instructed, woman! Keep the child hidden. When the time comes, you will miraculously discover her whereabouts by supernatural means. Your face will be on the front page of every newspaper in the land. This is how I choose to reward you for your faithful service."

Jezebel wondered if she should kneel in gratitude. "Yes, sire. But what do I do with her? What if she tries to get away? I can't—"

"Foolish woman! I have put the child into a coma, a harmless sleep. She will need no sustenance. She will come to no harm, I promise you. Now avert your eyes!"

The command came so strongly and suddenly that Jezebel instinctively hastened to cover her eyes with both hands. After a few seconds, she uncovered her eyes.

He was gone, returned to the unseen netherworld.

She looked down at Emily and smiled. Reaching down, she brushed back the fair locks that had fallen across the child's face. Then Jezebel's smile faded. There was an uneasy feeling in the pit of her stomach, and she began to wonder if her unholy alliance with Gathan was worth what he had promised.

Melanie stood with Detective Inspector Stewart in the park where Emily had vanished. The sky was still dark, but the area was lit up like day from the headlights of several police cars and four-wheel drives.

Her face was full of anguish and stained with tears as she desperately tried to convince Stewart and the other uniformed officers who stood disconsolately around her that what she was describing was true.

"Are you sure this was the spot where the fairground ride was?" Stewart was trying very hard not to sound patronizing.

"I am not lying! It was right here. Why don't you believe me?"

Some of the officers turned away at this, pretending to be busy at some task.

Stewart replied in measured tones. "We do believe you Melanie. But look—there are no vehicle track marks here. Nothing at all. A heavy piece of equipment like a carousel would put down steel legs to ground itself, but there's no evidence of that. Not even impressions in the grass."

Melanie put her hands to her face and shook her head. "I don't understand," she screamed. "This is the place! I know it is!"

Stewart stepped closer to her and tried to comfort her. But it was clumsily done, and she pulled away from him.

Melanie fumbled for something in her coat pocket. "Look, I can prove it." She pulled out her cell phone. "I took a photo of Emily, and it came out all blurry. But you can see the colored lights of the merry-go-round. Look!" She handed the phone to Stewart.

Stewart scrolled through the pictures on the phone. "There's nothing here, ma'am. Just photos of Emily playing with some dolls in what appears to be her bedroom."

Melanie snatched the phone back and frantically searched for the picture she had taken of the carousel. It wasn't there.

She looked at Stewart with such fear and resignation that his heart went out to her.

"Find my daughter. Please. Please!"

His eyes met hers, and he saw there a grief so deep that he was shocked by the raw emotion. "We will, don't worry." As soon as the words "Don't worry" escaped his lips, he knew it had been a stupid thing to say.

Back at the station, alone in his office, Stewart thought about asking Rosina to look over the site but decided against it. He knew she was probably exhausted after last night's awful business, but he made up his mind to call her tomorrow. He needed to talk to someone who could help him think through this. First the curate, then the body on the beach, and now a missing child. Each of the cases presented aspects he just couldn't wrap his head around. He'd been a cop for a very long time, but this was the first time he had ever found himself so totally perplexed that he didn't know where to begin.

Feeling inadequate and depressed, he lit another cigarette.

TWENTY-SIX

Stewart rang the bell of flat number three. He could hear it ringing inside, along with the excited voice of a child. The door opened a crack, and an old woman peered out at Stewart. A small girl of about eight or nine years clung to the woman's legs and shyly peeped to see who was at the door.

"Oh, I'm sorry. I think I have the wrong flat," Stewart said.

The old woman just looked at him without saying anything.

"I was looking for Rosina," he explained.

Then he heard Rosina call out from somewhere at the back of the apartment.

"Who is it, Mama?"

"Rosina, it's me, Paul," he shouted past the old woman, who now opened the door wide.

"Paul, what are you doing here?" Rosina asked as she appeared behind the old woman.

"I wanted to speak to you. I'm sorry. I thought you lived alone."

"It's all right, Mama. He's a friend from work."

The old woman nodded and disappeared into the kitchen. The little girl took Rosina's hand and held it tightly.

"Paul, come in please."

He stepped inside. The apartment was small but nicely furnished.

Stewart felt a bit awkward. He'd had this visit all worked out in his head, but there were obviously a few things he didn't know about Rosina's personal life.

"Paul, this is my daughter, Sasha. Say hello to the nice man, Sasha."

The child eased herself shyly behind her mother.

Rosina looked quizzically at Stewart. "Is something wrong? A problem at work?"

"No, no. Nothing wrong." Stewart felt his face redden. "I just wanted to talk, that's all."

Rosina smiled. "Can you come back later? This afternoon, perhaps?"

"Yes, of course. I didn't mean to intrude."

Rosina put her hand on his arm. "You aren't. It's just that we are about to leave for church."

"Oh, I see." He had almost forgotten it was Sunday. And some people still went to church on Sunday morning.

"You can come with us if you want."

"Thanks, but no. I, um . . . have some things to do," he lied.

Rosina smiled again. "Come back about four o'clock, and we'll have some tea, just like the English do."

Walking back to his place, Stewart felt down but didn't really know why. He enjoyed his work—it was something he'd always wanted since he was child watching TV shows about cops and robbers. But lately it all seemed to be a chore. He was irked, too, at his inability to make any progress with these recent crimes, if indeed they were crimes. He had always prided himself on possessing an uncanny ability to see below the surface, to figure out what was really going on, even if all the clues pointed elsewhere. This time, however, he felt that he was missing some vital information. It annoyed him to think that maybe he was just getting old and maybe his faculties of detection were growing dull. He feared he was losing his appetite for the job.

He pulled out a cigarette. Concentrating on the smoke, he tried hard not to think anymore, but it was impossible. A series of vivid images filled his mind: The dead curate sprawled out on the stone path in a pool of blood. The mutilated corpse on the beach. A distraught mother screaming into the night. This was rapidly becoming his own waking nightmare.

He returned to Rosina's flat at four, and she let him in. He took a seat on the empty sofa and asked where her mother and child were.

"They are sleeping. They are both at that age where they need an afternoon nap. We have at least an hour to talk undisturbed." Rosina hadn't sat down yet. "Do you want coffee or tea?"

"Coffee, please. Strong and three sugars."

"Three sugars! You are crazy. Are you a diabetic?"

"No, I don't think so. Why?"

"Well, believe me, you soon will be."

He laughed, and she went off to the kitchen. She returned a few minutes later with two mugs. The one she gave to Stewart had a bright logo: a red heart framing the words *I love Poland*.

"Do you miss your country?" he asked, making small talk.

"Yes, of course, but I love it here, too. I am making a good future for my daughter."

"You still have family in Poland?"

"Not really. A few cousins and some distant relatives. My father is dead. He was a policeman like you. He was killed in a shootout with some drug smugglers in Krakow."

She stood and went to a shelf on the wall. She returned with a framed photograph of a man in uniform and handed it to Stewart.

"Is this your dad?"

"Yes, on a very special day. He was awarded a medal for rescuing a young boy from the river. The boy would have drowned. It's funny, but many children in Poland don't know how to swim."

"You miss him." Stewart seemed to have gotten stuck in the groove of asking questions.

"Yes and no. If he had lived, I would not be here. And many good things have happened to me since coming to this country. But I am sad that my daughter didn't really know her grandfather. He was a good man. A kind man."

They sipped their coffee and lapsed into a brief silence.

"So, Paul, what is on your mind?"

He shifted his body on the sofa so that he faced her. "I guess . . . I'm not sure. I used to be so certain of things when working a case. Catching criminals isn't terribly difficult. Most of the time they're idiots. They leave clues to their whereabouts or identity all over a crime scene." He smiled ruefully. "Why am I telling *you* this? You know, yeah?"

"Yes, of course."

"It's just that these latest incidents—I can't read them, can't work them out. It's as though there are dark spots I can't seem to figure out. Sometimes, just thinking about them, I feel like I'm going crazy." He heaved a sigh. "Like the dead clergyman. Where his body was found—it just doesn't add up. And now this poor girl whose child has been taken, I would swear blind she's telling the truth. But there's no evidence. None of it makes sense."

Rosina looked concern but said nothing.

"Rosina, you said something the other night. That poor guy on the beach . . . you mentioned the supernatural. You aren't really asking me to believe that the man was killed by something other than a human being, are you?" He looked at her pleadingly.

She looked away and said, "I only know that no human could have inflicted those wounds. And what the old man said—"

"Was all nonsense," he blurted.

She put a finger to her lips to remind Stewart to so as not to wake her mother and child.

She said, "In Poland, many strange things happen. Bad things happen to good people, and no one can explain how or why they happen. My father understood and believed that if there is a God from whom goodness flows, then there must be a devil who causes evil to flourish."

Stewart listened intently but remained skeptical.

She smiled, but the smile disappeared quickly. "My father used to say that sometimes the devil tempts us do bad things, but when he wants a job done quickly, he does it himself."

"Do you . . . believe in the devil? I can't believe I'm even asking the question."

"Yes, I do."

"Right, well, how does a cop do his job when the culprit is Satan?" he said a little too flippantly. "I can't very well get a warrant and arrest him now, can I?"

"Don't be silly. But you can learn to pray."

"I've never prayed for anything," he said, lowering his voice and his eyes. "I wouldn't know how."

"Are you a confirmed atheist, then?" Her blue eyes looked straight into his, trying to measure the man.

He shrugged. "An atheist? No, I suppose not. On the other hand, I've never given God much thought."

"Perhaps it is time you did." She went to her bedroom and came back holding a book. Sitting down again, she held it out to him. "It is my daughter's. A child's Bible. But I think it will be good for you until you have made up your mind. Then if you like, you can get an adult one, yes?"

He felt his face redden. He had come to Rosina for help, and here she was giving him a kid's Bible.

"Won't your daughter miss it?"

"She has more than one." Rosina still held the book out to him. "Take it. You can return it later."

Stewart took hold of the book, but she didn't let go immediately.

"Promise me you'll read it? Today?"

She smiled again, and he couldn't resist.

"Yes, I promise. Where do you suggest I start?"

She finally let go of the Bible and said, "Start with the Gospels, in the New Testament. Then we shall talk later next week, yes?" She picked up a piece of paper lying on the coffee table. A childish hand had scrawled the words *Jesus loves you* on it. Rosina opened the Bible to the beginning of the New Testament and placed the paper in between the pages as a bookmark.

"Start there, okay?"

"All right."

"And I shall pray for you every day."

"That'll be a first. Someone praying for me."

Sitting at his kitchen table with a coffee and a cigarette, Stewart found the bookmark, read the words on it, then carefully placed the paper next to his coffee on the table. At the top of the page that had been marked was the name Matthew in large letters. Stewart had checked his small pocket dictionary for the meaning of the word *gospel*. The definition referred to the teachings of Jesus but included the phrase "good news." *I could do with some good news*, he thought.

He began reading but soon got bogged down in the genealogy, all the "begats."

He decided to skip chapter one and moved on to chapter two. This part made sense, especially the description of the Jewish king Herod. Plenty of murderous villains around in those times, including a king up to no good. "Nothing much changes, does it?" he muttered.

When he came to chapter four, he stopped and flipped the pages to see how many chapters were in the gospel of Matthew. Twenty-eight in all. He was a bit daunted.

Some of the pages included simple drawings of Jesus and His followers. The sketches were very good, and Stewart could see how they would appeal to a young child. But he wondered how much of the book a kid would really understand. It was simply written with no difficult words, but the subject matter wasn't exactly typical of a children's book—King Herod slaughtering innocent children and stories of lepers and prostitutes.

A voice in Stewart's head told him to quit this now. After all, he was a grown man, and this stuff was just make-believe stories for weak people who couldn't face real life and all its knocks. He shrugged and started to close the book.

Rosina. Rosina had a quality very different from other women he had known. She was clearly a highly intelligent woman, and she believed.

He pulled out another cigarette, put it between his lips, and lit it with a match.

And he decided to read on to the end of Matthew.

TWENTY-SEVEN

After three days of discussion and bitter negotiation in the cathedral, the evangelicals had won the day. Much political maneuvering and deal-making went on before the electoral college made its decision as to who would lead the Anglican Church in northern Wales. The importance of the bishop's office could not be understated, for he would serve as pastor of the clergy and shepherd of the region's flock.

The conservative arm of the college had hoped to maintain the status quo. After all, didn't the scriptures confirm that God was the same yesterday, today, and forever? The late Bishop John had been an ultraconservative and opposed to any radical change, whether on a diocesan or parish level. During his term of twenty-four years, Welsh congregations had quietly diminished. A death in any congregation meant another empty pew in church. No effort was made to replace and renew. The waning vitality of the church in this region had been likened to an old man dozing off and simply waiting for the undertaker to call.

Bishop John's supporters had known it would be a difficult fight to elect another man like him, but they had numerous contenders to choose from and had been quietly confident that the brash and absurd tactics of the "new thinkers" would frighten the college members into making a sensible decision.

On the other hand, their opponents, the evangelicals, did not depend upon the machinations of church government and backroom deals. They believed that God's chosen would prevail. The evangelical clergy and, indeed, senior laymen had received scriptural confirmations. At prayer meetings, the Holy Spirit had made known His desire for change. Their candidate, Canon Nigel Jeffries, was a spirit-filled man with a reputation for taking action where it was needed. At crucial times, that meant getting on his knees and praying through the night. He had learned this discipline in the valleys of southern Wales, Evan Roberts country.

Accepted as an ordinand in the church as a young man, Nigel Jeffries had studied theology at Cambridge University. He did well there and early in his career was appointed chaplain at Wycliffe House School. His innovations and passion for the work got him noticed by the archbishop, who wasted no time in poaching Nigel for his staff.

Jeffries's special interest was the study of church history. Some imagined he would quickly retire to the dusty halls of church libraries, but this was far from the truth. His devotional studies and deep searches of the Old Testament were, for him, a way to grow closer to and become more intimate with a very personal God. Jeffries earned many honors and top-level job offers over the next decade or so, seemingly without effort on his part. Standing over six feet tall and quite bald, he was an imposing man but never intimidating. People meeting him for the first time found his manner warm and friendly. He was articulate and more than willing to get involved. Now, at the age of forty-nine, he was happily married with five young children and a host of responsibilities both personal and ecumenical. He felt ready to make his mark.

The new bishop's inauguration took place on the second weekend in November. The ceremony was a grand affair, but Bishop Jeffries was anxious to get down to the real business of reforming and revitalizing, of bringing clear thinking and biblical teaching back to a muddled church. His first order of business, he had decided, would be to visit as many of the churches in the diocese as possible. One of his first visits would be to St. David's in Penrhos Bay.

He had heard disturbing reports about the town, especially the spike in crime on Halloween and in the days after. Jeffries's spiritual antenna told him dark forces were at play. He also wanted to meet the vicar at St. David's in person, as during the elections Reverend Stannard had been one of his most vociferous opponents, and Jeffries wanted to know why.

As they sat in Stannard's study, the vicar was well aware he was being scrutinized by the new bishop. Upon entering the room, Jeffries had scanned the entire room, apparently taking the measure of the vicar. Stannard understood. He knew one could learn a great deal about a man by studying his habits and interests as manifested by the objects and books with which he surrounded himself. Stannard had not taken any trouble to hide his wants and desires.

"How old are you now, Stannard?" the bishop asked.

"Approaching sixty-three, Your Grace."

"Oh, please, call me Nigel. I don't feel comfortable with 'Your Grace.' I grew up in the south amongst the collieries. I can't imagine any of my dad's mates calling me 'Your Grace,' can you?"

Stannard winced at the use of the term "mates" but replied, "No, I suppose not."

"And what name do you go by? How do you like to be addressed?"

No one ever called Stannard by his first name. It was "vicar" or "reverend," and that was the way he preferred it. He did not encourage intimacy of any kind from his parishioners or even his friends.

"My name is Sydney. Sydney Stannard, Your Grace."

"Well, Syd then, is it?"

"I prefer Sydney, actually," he said rather peevishly. He was beginning to feel sick.

The demon Jusach stood at the vicar's shoulder, and he whispered into Stannard's ear, "Tell that oaf to get lost." Stannard shook his head suddenly as if to dislodge a flea from his ear.

"Now, Sydney, what's all this I hear about your late curate jumping off the church tower?" The bishop was not one to mince words.

Jusach said louder this time, "Go on, tell him. Tell him that Jones got what he deserved." Once again, Stannard shook his head irritably.

"Are you all right?" the bishop asked.

Stannard put his hand to his left ear to scratch it. "Yes. I'm perfectly fine, Your Grace."

The bishop placed the fingers of his hands together as if he was about to pray. He was looking straight at Stannard, waiting for an answer, and then for a moment his attention was drawn to the right of Stannard. He appeared to be looking directly at Jusach, who began to feel rather uncomfortable, although he was certain the bishop could not actually see him.

"Well, as you are probably aware, it was a most unfortunate incident," Stannard began.

"Quite." The bishop maintained his searching stare over the vicar's shoulder.

Aware that the bishop was not looking at him directly but focusing his eyes at something else, Stannard began to grow nervous. "Er, he was ill just before his death and, if I may say so, I believe that . . . well, he was not exactly in his right mind."

"Really? Are you suggesting he was deranged as a result of his illness?"

"No, not deranged, but momentarily unhinged and quite unable to control his faculties. This may have been due to his medications, which I understand were unusually strong analgesics."

Jusach suddenly felt an enormous pressure against his body. He knew what it was immediately, and realized he could do nothing to stop it. The prayer of a righteous man can do much to bind a servant of Satan. Clearly, this was this was bishop's doing. Jusach was slowly but inexorably pressed back against the far wall. As he tried to cry out for reinforcements, he discovered that the force exerted on his body had rendered him mute. Try as he might, he could not utter a sound. He was pinned to the wall as if he had been nailed there.

The bishop returned his gaze to Stannard and, smiling, said, "Prior to his death, was Mr. Jones hospitalized?"

"I don't believe so. He took some time off—several weeks, in fact—and I covered his duties."

The bishop smiled again. "That was good of you, Sydney. His care, then—how was he looked after? By a physician? A visiting nurse?"

"I believe so, yes."

"But you are not sure."

"Well, I had all of my duties and his to perform. It wasn't easy. I did telephone him to make sure he was not in need of anything," Stannard lied.

"I see. And the police and the coroner are satisfied there was no foul play involved?"

"Oh, absolutely. The verdict was death by misadventure," Stannard replied almost brightly, sensing the inquiry regarding Jones was nearing its end.

"I understand the local paper reported it as an accident, that the fall occurred whilst carrying out maintenance on the tower. Is that possible? Surely our curates are not normally encouraged to do repairs to the building fabric, are they?"

Stannard began to fidget once more. "To be honest, Nigel, the editor is a close friend, and I called in a favor. I thought it would do the church no good to have the newspaper dredging up all sorts of innuendo about the man."

"You knew he was a homosexual, then."

Stannard sighed. "Not until after he had joined us here. By that time, I could do nothing about his appointment."

"By that, you mean you wanted rid of him."

"Well, I certainly did not agree with his lifestyle. His sin was anathema to me. And yes, I would have moved Heaven and earth to have him removed if the option had been available to me."

"Where is the unfortunate man buried? I hope you gave him a decent send-off."

Stannard's heart was pounding in his chest. He chose to lie again. "Mr. Jones had no living relatives, so I administered a simple ceremony and had the local undertakers scatter his remains in the Memorial Rose Garden. I believe he would have liked that, as he was a keen naturalist. I planned to have a plaque made and erected there, but demands on my time have prevented it."

The bishop nodded but offered no further comment. "And the new curate? Richard Benton, Oxford man. Not a 'homo,' I suppose," he said with a wry smile.

Stannard flinched again. "No, as you say, not a . . . Mr. Benton is married and seems more suitable, but we have had the occasional difference of opinion. Why just the other day, he . . . well, I found his manner offensive. And I would welcome the chance to talk to you about it now, as I could use your help to discipline the young man and set him right." His manner changed as he was growing in confidence now. He had a genuine grievance to share, and he believed this would give the bishop an opportunity to side with him on an issue.

Saying nothing, Jeffries rose from his chair and perused the shelves of books. Stannard shifted in his chair uneasily. The majority of the books in his bookcases were on the subject of philately. Interspersed with these tomes were dozens of stamp catalogues ranging from the 1950s to the present day. However, there was one small open bookcase on the other side of the room, set as far from the desk as possible, that did contain some ecclesiastical works. There were a few Bibles— mainly the Authorized and King James versions—a copy of Strong's Concordance, Matthew Henry's commentary, and a small volume of Wesley's sermons. Dust had collected on these shelves, indicating this part of the room was not visited often. Stannard watched in horror as the bishop wiped the dust off one of the shelves with his index finger and examined it closely.

"Regarding your spat with Benton," the bishop said, "put it in writing and e-mail me with your thoughts on this matter. Do it today, please, and I'll read it tonight." He turned and extended a hand towards Stannard, who by this time was standing. "Well, I must be going, Sydney. Thank you for the tour. Most interesting and informative."

They shook hands, and the bishop motioned Stannard back to his desk. "Don't worry, I'll see myself out. Be sure to thank Mary for the delicious tea and Welsh cakes. God bless you."

As the bishop left the room, Jusach was suddenly released, and he fell headlong to the floor. Finding his voice again, he cursed the bishop with a litany of foul oaths.

Stannard merely stood dumbstruck. He felt he had been dismissed like a schoolboy. He was unable to utter anything, no benediction, not even a simple goodbye. He slumped back into his chair and said aloud, "God save me from all proselytizing evangelicals!"

"I'm telling you now, Richard, so that you know." Bishop Jeffries was visiting the home of the curate and his young bride. "I know this is going to sound crazy, and you'll probably think me a madman, but God has spoken to me. I have heard His command so clearly, and I am going to obey. No pussyfooting around. There are going to be some radical changes in this place."

Richard could not quite comprehend what had been happening to him as of late. First, he had been touched by the Holy Spirit while asleep on the pier. He was certain of it. His soul now felt as if it were on fire. When he read his Bible these days, the Word of God leapt out of the page with incredible power. Now the new bishop was standing in his kitchen, a mug of tea in one hand and a biscuit in the other, telling Richard and Sarah about his plans to reform St. David's, starting with an evangelical crusade.

"First, Stannard has to go. I will suspend him temporarily, but my mind is made up." The bishop's countenance was stern. "And anyone willing to confront his superior in the manner you did is a friend of mine. That took courage, Richard, and it tells me you prize justice over your own career."

Sarah cast a glance at Richard, a half smile on her face.

"No need to bother you with the details at this juncture. Stannard can stay in the rectory until after the crusade." Casting his eyes about the kitchen, the Bishop Jeffries said with a laugh, "I expect you're happy to remain here for awhile."

Sarah grabbed Richard's arm. "Oh, we love it here!"

"Good. I shall confine the vicar to quarters so that he will not be in the way during our work. I am putting you in charge of the crusade, Richard. We'll hold it in St. David's. I'm told it can seat over four hundred, though of late this hasn't been tested."

"But can we organize such an event in so short a time?" Richard asked.

"Yes! Yes, of course!" The bishop took a large bite of the biscuit but continued to talk excitedly, crumbs falling from his mouth. "I'll be here to help, and I'll bring some people from my office. It'll be good for them to get out into the real world." He paused for a moment as if trying to recollect something. "Ah, yes. I have fantastic news! We shall be joined by my good friends Simon James and his dear wife, Serena. They are marvelous messengers for Christ, and because of their music background, they should draw a crowd."

Sarah began to sing a song made famous by Simon in the early 1980s. "Bi-bi-bobbi, bi-bi-bobbi . . ."

"Well done, Sarah. Who would ever have thought that such a silly song would be used so greatly by God, eh? It's amazing. Or should I say, it's typical of God. I have heard children in small villages in the darkest parts of Africa sing it."

Richard was about to ask a question, but the bishop put up his hand, still holding half the biscuit. "Plenty of time for questions later. Simon and Serena are arriving soon, so we should get cracking. I'm staying over tonight. I'll deal with the awful Sydney Stannard in the morning, and then you and I will meet in the church at ten o'clock. Cancel all your appointments for the next two weeks. We have the Lord's work to do."

TWENTY-EIGHT

The powder-blue Mercedes-Benz sped along the highway on cruise control, the needle on the speedometer stuck on seventy. It was about two o'clock in the morning, and there were few other vehicles on the road. The woman driving looked at her companion, who sat snoozing in the passenger seat. Simon and Serena had been husband and wife for thirty-six years, and they had spent almost all their time together, on stage and off. They were still as much in love as when they had dated during rehearsals for *Jesus Christ Superstar* back in 1972.

When they first saw each other across the boards of the Adelphi Theatre in London's West End, Serena had recognized Simon immediately. After all, he was already a famous pop star with three hit records that had topped the British and American charts for weeks on end. He was handsome, tall, and slim and had a charisma that went beyond the usual celebrity sheen. She hadn't the nerve to speak to him directly, but she found herself staring at him all the time—and embarrassingly, he had noticed her attention.

She had been grabbing a quick coffee between rehearsals when she turned around to find his smiling face only inches from hers. "You're Serena Handley, aren't you?"

"And you are—"

But before she could finish the sentence, he leaned forward and whispered, "Yes, but please don't tell anyone!" He grabbed a coffee with one hand and with the other steered her gently toward a couple of vacant seats.

He said, "I saw you at the Empire in that wonderful musical by . . . by . . ."

"Epstein," she said.

"You sang and acted the part beautifully. I was quite impressed."

"Thank you. Since we are dishing out compliments, I love your music. But I have to confess I haven't bought any of your records." She blushed and looked down.

"Hey, don't worry about it. Everyone else has." They laughed, and then the bell rang signaling the start of afternoon rehearsal.

"Are you free on Saturday after the show?" he asked. "I know a great little Greek place on Frith Street in Soho. No one will recognize either of us there, I promise."

The rest was history. Their love affair made the newspapers and the cover of all the glossies. One night, just when they thought their lives were perfect and could not get any better, they received a phone call as they were relaxing in their Chelsea flat in London.

"Hello, Clint. How's business? We must get together soon to chat about my future."

Serena looked across the room at Simon. "Is that Clinton Roberts?" she mouthed silently.

Simon put his hand over the speaker and shouted, "Yes, it's Clinton Roberts, Darling." Then he grinned and said into the mouthpiece, "Carry on, old chap. What's up?"

Simon's smile died on his face as he listened to what was being said at the other end.

"Clint, seriously, I really appreciate your kind offer. But I don't know, it's not really my thing. I know it works for you but . . . Okay, okay, I'll talk it over with Serena . . . Yes, and I'll call you back. I promise."

Simon hung up the phone and then sat next to Serena on the sofa. "You can guess what that was about, can't you? Some big-time

American evangelist is in town for a show on Saturday night at Wembley Stadium. Clint is going to be singing, and he's invited us to come."

Serena said nothing.

"Anyway, we can't go. We're performing!" Simon said with a wicked grin on his face. "What a pity!"

"Simon, you know full well this is our weekend off. We could go . . . I mean, what's the harm?"

"Oh, come on! What's the harm? I love Clint, but I don't want to *be* him."

"Darling, there's something I've wanted to say, and I've been holding it back for weeks."

"Oh no, you're not pregnant, are you?"

"NO! You idiot." She hit him with a sofa pillow. "It's just that . . . well, we have this wonderful life—nice careers, plenty of money, really great friends—and yet sometimes I feel rather . . . empty." She looked at his face to judge his response before going on. "Simon, I love you, and I'm deliriously happy with you, but . . ."

Simon took her hand in his. "But what? What else is there?"

"I don't know, really, I just feel like something is missing."

"And you think religion might be the missing bit?" He said it kindly, not with his usual sarcasm.

"Maybe. I'm not sure, but I want to find out. This phone call just might mean something. Call Clint back for me, will you please, and tell him we are coming? I don't want to go without you, but I am going."

The stadium was packed. Clinton Roberts sung beautifully, as if inspired. Simon and Serena had been given celebrity seats, and Serena held Simon's hand tightly throughout the sermon as if reluctant to let go. The evangelist, Laurent Chavez, a preacher from Latin America, spoke eloquently and gently about the love of God, explaining that God loves each and every one of us, rich or poor, black or white. He explained that Jesus died on the cross to cleanse us from all sin, and that

God had prepared a way through the sacrifice of His Son so that we could be restored to fellowship with Him. Chavez went on to say that anyone could experience new life in Christ, that He alone could fill the emptiness inside. All a person had to do was to repeat a prayer. He walked the audience through the prayer of forgiveness slowly, before saying, "If you believe that Jesus died for you, if you accept His free gift of salvation, if you are willing to make Him Lord over your life, then come down here and show everyone that you really meant it."

At this, Serena let go of Simon's hand and slowly but surely made her way down the steps to the stage where many others were gathering. Simon watched her go and then moments later got up and followed her. They both gave their lives to Christ that day.

Simon was still dozing in the passenger seat.

Serena nudged him awake. "Honey, we're nearly there. It's just a few miles on, I think. Did you put the address in the GPS?"

"No, I didn't bother. I know the way there by now. You keep your eyes on the road."

Simon looked at the road ahead then suddenly screamed, "Serena! Look out!"

Serena stiffened immediately and slammed her foot on the brake. The car shuddered violently, the tires screeching and skidding as the vehicle came to a halt.

Simon flung open the passenger door and jumped out. He then ran back along the highway.

Serena was shaken. She set the handbrake, switched on the hazard lights, and climbed out of the car. Simon was standing about a hundred yards away, motionless, in the centre of the highway. Serena ran to him and threw her arms around his shoulders.

"Simon! What on earth happened? Why did you shout for me to stop?"

His countenance expressed utter confusion and shocked surprise.

She shook him. "Simon!"

Simon's haunted eyes turned to hers. "Didn't you see him? Standing in the road. I . . . I thought we were going to hit the guy."

"Who, Simon? Who? There was no one."

They both looked at the road behind them at the empty stretch of road. There was not a soul in sight.

"Come on, Simon. Let's go back to the car." Serena put her arm around his shoulders and tried to guide him back to the Mercedes. But he resisted, still dazed, reluctant to leave the scene.

They heard the sound of a car in the distance. Soon the headlights of an oncoming vehicle lit up the highway. Simon and Serena moved to the shoulder. As the car raced past, two teenagers shouted out their window, "Get out of the road, morons!" A beer can thrown from the car clattered on the concrete, tumbling and bouncing until it came to rest at their feet.

Then another vehicle, blue lights flashing, came into view and stopped just a few yards from the couple, who both raised a hand to shield their eyes from the lights. A young policeman climbed out of the driver's seat and approached them. The man showed them his ID and badge.

"Evening, sir. Madame. Is something wrong? Your car break down?"

Inspector Stewart, in plain clothes, stepped out of the car and slowly buttoned up his overcoat, pulling the collar up to ward off the night wind. He hated working the graveyard shift when the good people were tucked up in bed, leaving the night to the villains of the world. He walked over to where Simon and Serena stood talking with Sergeant Llewellyn. As if he didn't see the couple, Stewart said, "Sergeant, what seems to be the trouble?" He looked weary and sounded overtired.

"I was just asking these good people if they needed assistance, sir."

Serena stepped forward and tried to explain. "My husband thought he saw a man in the road. Only, I saw nothing. We stopped the car to be sure. We ran back along the highway but found nothing."

"I tell you, I saw a man standing right in our path. I was certain we were going to hit him straight on. And before you ask, I am not drunk. Nor am I having hallucinations," Simon insisted, quite agitated.

The detective and the sergeant both stared at Simon.

"With all due respect, sir, that may be for us to decide," Stewart said. "Which of you was driving?"

"I was," volunteered Serena.

"And what speed do you think you were doing?" Sergeant Llewellyn was now writing in his notebook.

"I know what I was doing, because I saw the speed limit sign back there. I slowed down to fifty miles an hour and set the cruise control."

"And neither of you has been drinking this evening?"

Simon turned to face Stewart. He was seemed to be regaining his composure and his senses. "We have driven up from Surrey. We are staying at the Alpha Hotel in Penrhos Bay, and we shall be there for a week. As you can appreciate, we are both extremely tired and really just want to get to our destination. And to answer your question, we have not imbibed any alcohol." His speech was polite but firm and delivered in a reasonably upper-class accent.

Stewart looked at them both for a moment. "I really should ask the lady to take a breath test."

Simon, exasperated, was about to say something more, but Serena squeezed his arm and smiled at the policeman.

"But as no one was hurt," Stewart said, "and no damage done. I guess we can dispense with that formality."

Serena reached out and touched the detective's arm. "Thank you. That's very good of you."

Simon still looked a bit put out.

Sergeant Llewellyn, his notebook and pencil poised, asked for their names.

Serena replied, "Mr. and Mrs. James. Simon and Serena James."

Stewart and the sergeant exchanged knowing glances. Both Serena and Simon knew that look and what was coming next.

"Not "Bi-Bi-Bobbi" Simon James," Llewellyn said excitedly.

With a glum expression, Simon nodded. "Afraid so. Banged to rights, you might say."

"Well, I never," Stewart said. "Fancy meeting a famous pop star in the middle of the night on my watch. And in Penrhos Bay, of all places."

Serena smiled again. "So are we free to go now?"

"Yes, of course. I am sorry to have kept you both. Don't just stand there gawking, Llewellyn. Escort Mr. and Mrs. James back to their car." Stewart gave Simon a little salute. "Good night, sir. And to you, madam."

Llewellyn walked them back to their car, and Stewart could hear him jabbering away the whole time.

Back in the patrol car, Llewellyn could not stop talking. "They're here for a crusade or something at St. David's. Here at the invitation of the new bishop. Friends of his, they said."

"Maybe we should interview them again on some pretext or other, and you can ask for a signed photo, eh?"

"Really, sir? That would be fantastic!"

Stewart just shook his head.

Stewart did want to see the Jameses again, though not strictly on police business. He left his card at the hotel, and Simon called him that evening.

"Is this about the incident on the highway, Inspector?"

"Yes and no. Sorry, that sounds a bit vague. I really want to hear again what you saw or what you thought you saw."

"I see. Well, if you come to the hotel about eight-thirty this evening, we shall have eaten by then. Should Serena join us?"

"Yes, of course. No problem. Three heads are better than one, they say."

"Good. We'll meet you in the bar."

Stewart arrived at the hotel at eight-twenty. He had walked across town to grab some exercise, of which he was getting precious little these days. He was a bit overweight but had little inclination to do anything about it. Beer, cigarettes, and food were his only comforts. He smoked on the way over, knowing he'd be unable to in the hotel bar now that smoking had been banned in public buildings.

He sat on a stool at the small bar counter and waited for Simon and Serena to arrive. The place was quiet, deathly quiet, with no other guests in sight. There wasn't even a bartender, so he sat without drink or cigarette, desperately needing both. He heard them before he saw them.

Simon was laughing as they came into the bar. He came straight over to shake Stewart's hand. "Good evening, Inspector. You are well, I presume?" Simon inquired politely.

Stewart stood and remained standing until Serena sat down at one of the nearby tables. "Yes, thank you. I'm fine."

"Drink, Inspector? What can I get you?" Simon had wandered around to the back of the bar. "Darling, your usual?" he asked Serena.

"Yes, please, but not a large one," she answered.

Simon poured a Diet Coke and added a wedge of lemon.

"Inspector? Are you off-duty? A scotch, maybe?"

"I am, as it happens. Yes, a scotch with a drop of ginger and no ice, thanks."

Stewart had figured out that both Simon and Serena were almost sixty, and yet they seemed so much younger, full of vitality. She was still quite attractive with long auburn hair, a slim build, and a face that shone with an indefinable quality. He, too, looked no different from photographs taken more than thirty years ago. Yes, he had grayed at the temples, but his hair was still thick and wavy. By contrast, although at least ten years younger, Stewart felt shabby and old.

"Your good health, Inspector." Simon held his glass of cola aloft.

Stewart looked puzzled. "I hope you don't mind me asking, but it's not many establishments that allow guests to help to themselves to the bar."

"Ever the policeman, looking for crime everywhere." Simon smiled. "Serena and I come here every year to do a show at the local theater. The original band comes with us, and we bash out all the oldies, even 'Bi-Bi-Bobbi.' It's all good fun, and the proprietors treat us like family. As you know, the hotel is closed for the season, but the owners said we could bunk down for as long as we want. But don't worry, I'll add the drinks to the bill. All above board, Inspector."

"I didn't mean anything by it." Stewart looked a trifle embarrassed and wished he'd kept his mouth shut.

Serena spoke up. "So what's this all about, Inspector?"

Stewart took a deep breath and launched into his tale of the odd circumstances of the curate's death. He told them of the grisly murder of the vagrant on the beach and the unusual nature of his wounds. Then he described the events of Halloween, culminating in the kidnapping of the child and the distraught mother's bizarre testimony regarding the carousel. Before continuing on, he looked at the couple across from him. Both Simon and Serena wore sober expressions, even seeming personally concerned. He was beginning to wonder if coming here and involving these kind people had been a good idea.

"I sometimes think I'm slowly going mad. None of these events make sense. Well, not to me anyway. And when you talked of seeing a person in the road who turned out not to be there, I wondered if this might be part of a pattern, if you get my meaning."

Serena spoke first. "May I ask, Inspector, are you a Christian? A believer in God?"

"That's the second time someone has asked me that recently."

"And?"

"No, I suppose not," he replied without a lot of conviction. "But a friend gave me a Bible—a child's Bible—and I've been reading it. The Gospels, mainly."

"Well then, even if you haven't gotten far in your reading, I am sure you have noticed an important theme—namely that there are two kingdoms in this world: the kingdom of God and the kingdom of Satan." She stopped to let her words sink in.

"I was afraid you were going to suggest something like that. But to actually entertain the idea that these events have been caused by supernatural means goes well beyond my experience and, I daresay, my jurisdiction."

Simon leaned forward. "We were once in that same place as you— full of doubt and unbelief. But as a wise man once said, 'Demons exist whether we believe in them or not.'"

"And you think that these events are the work of the devil?" There was more than a note of skepticism in his voice.

"At this point, that's hard for us to say, but it is possible. When the Lord is about to do a mighty thing, the enemy has been known to step up his attacks."

"Is the Lord, as you say, about to do a mighty thing?"

They both answered in unison, "Yes."

"We believe so," Simon continued. "We have come here at the bishop's invitation to preach the gospel and bring people to Christ. But it's the Holy Spirit who does the real work in the hearts of men and women, and we know He has come here for a specific purpose."

Stewart settled back into his chair, looking perplexed.

"Don't take our word for it, Inspector. You can read for yourself what happens when the Spirit of God moves in a specific location. I suggest you check the local library or look it up on the Internet. Search for 'Evan Roberts' and the 1904 revival in South Wales. Over one hundred thousand souls were saved there in just three months. The same could happen here in this town if God wills it. And if He is preparing such a revival to occur, then you can be certain there will be manifest opposition from the enemy."

They sat in silence awhile, sipping at their drinks.

Stewart was a bit dumbfounded. "So what do you suggest I do? I can't very well put cuffs on demons and toss them in jail."

Serena replied, "No, you can't. But as a born-again Christian, you would have the weapons to fight back."

Simon said, "You need to ask yourself, Inspector, 'If there is a God, do I want to know more about Him?'"

Stewart was beginning to feel overwhelmed.

Serena smiled and asked, "Do you mind if we pray about this situation right here, right now?"

Simon and Serena bowed their heads, and Stewart listened silently but intently. He was struck by the power of their simple words of faith. Serena's passion was apparent as she spoke fearlessly in the name of Christ, binding the devil and all his works in this place.

For Stewart, it was like hearing a new language, with strangely familiar words knocking at the door of his sparse vocabulary. He felt he was on the edge of some great truth but did not yet know how to grasp it.

At the end of the prayers he stood and said, "If you need security while you're in town, just let me know. I might be able to furnish you with a couple of discreet minders."

Simon smiled. "Thank you, Inspector. But we travel with our own security forces. The angels of God are never far from us, and we find they're quite handy in a pinch"

Stewart chuckled at this. Serena stepped up and hugged him. He hadn't expect this and responded a bit stiffly.

She said, "Now promise us you'll come to the event on Friday. Seven o'clock at St. David's. We'll save you a VIP seat—no, *two* VIP seats. Front row. Is it a deal?"

He felt he couldn't say no. "I guess it is. I think I know who to bring along, too."

Simon walked Stewart to the door and shook his hand warmly.

Stewart headed home not knowing what to think about what he had heard this evening. Years ago, he would have dismissed all this talk of angels and demons as nonsense. Yet something inside him was now asking him to take a leap of faith, despite how fantastic the idea seemed.

Twenty-Nine

Prince Rimmon sat upon his throne, brooding, a fistful of parchments clutched tightly in his claws. Lamps set in the cavern walls emitted a sickly yellow light, casting long, misshapen shadows among the sharp stalactites that hung menacingly over the assembled demon horde. Ganymede and Gathan and a few other high courtiers waited nearby for the outcome of their master's deliberations. They had been in this position for over an hour, in quiet attendance. They dared not speak amongst themselves, for fear of disturbing him.

The cavern in the mine was filled with all manner of devils, and the damned entities had begun to talk amongst themselves in a low muttering of unhappy voices. Rimmon seemed not to hear the murmuring, which was becoming perceptibly louder by the minute as the demons grew impatient. Gathan tried to catch Ganymede's eye to urge him to interrupt Rimmon, but Ganymede appeared preoccupied with his own particular ruminations.

At last, Rimmon stirred and, glancing up, indicated that he wanted Ganymede's ear. The horde of demons now fell silent, and every eye was on the dark lord. Ganymede stepped forward, bent low, and placed his ear dangerously close to Rimmon's fangs.

Shaking the parchments in his hand, Rimmon hissed, "What am I to make of these reports? Even my old ally Lord Salus makes sport of me for suspecting trouble in this pathetic place. He says I have been too long in the wilderness, that I am losing my wits. But I am convinced that something is afoot in this pestilential town. All my intuition tells me so. But here lies my predicament: Our great lord Satan will not entertain the notion and is on the verge of humiliating me for even raising the matter. If I dare speak again without hard evidence, I may spend the next thousand years herding frozen souls in Siberia."

Ganymede nodded in sympathy but said nothing.

Rimmon motioned to Gathan. "Gathan, tell me again what our lord's spies are saying."

The entire throng below the dais moved as one, surging forward en masse to try to catch what was being said.

Gathan bowed and then drew himself up to full height. "Reports coming in from all over the globe suggest that there are preparations underway for a major attack on our strongholds. Over the past few months, our agents have recorded the arrival of many high-ranking members of Heaven's host. They remain in secret places a few days before departing suddenly, and afterward much activity is observed with many warriors going to and fro between churches and other holy sites. One of our most trusted spies managed to secret himself in the cathedral chapter in London where he overheard the following conversation between high clergy. They said, 'So it comes to pass at Christmas then. We must rally the people and begin to pray in earnest.'"

Rimmon silenced Gathan with a wave of his hand. Gathan backed away, bowing low as he went. "What of the new bishop and his curate at St. David's?" Rimmon said peevishly.

Jusach stepped forward just one pace and said with false bravado, "The bishop is a fool, sire. He is more fitted to be a jester than a high priest. And as for the new curate, he is a stick insect with about as much power as a gnat in a hurricane."

"I can do without the diverting metaphors, sycophant!" Rimmon roared. "When I want amusement, I'll ask for it. Now get out of my sight."

Jusach scurried off.

Rimmon beckoned Ganymede with his finger, and the demon drew near once more.

"I am in sore need of good advice. What can I do when all these reports appear to herald a concerted offensive against our forces worldwide? I am persuaded that just prior to that unholy anniversary of the accursed enemy, we shall suffer an onslaught never seen before in this accursed universe. Lord Lucifer will not acknowledge it, but there is fear behind his countenance—he is terrified that this signals the Second Coming."

Ganymede threw his head back and laughed uproariously. "Surely not! Does he still believe in those myths just because some mad monk wrote them down from exile? It's been over two thousand years since the so-called revelation."

Rimmon held up a finger. "Guard your tongue, Ganymede. There are too many ears in this hall who would gladly report such loose talk back to Lucifer."

Now it was Ganymede who leaned forward to whisper in Rimmon's ear. "Sire, for sake of argument, let us take these reports seriously for a moment. Have there been any sightings of the . . . You Know Who, the third person of that ghastly trinity?"

"Good point, Ganymede. You are indeed my most trusted ally. I think the answer to your question is definitely no. If he had been in attendance at any of these meetings, we surely would have known." Rimmon's face brightened as a new plan began to formulate in his mind.

Ganymede added, "Might I suggest that where we do see evidence of He Who Shall Not Be Named, then that is where such an attack will come."

The prince sat back upon his throne with a look of supreme satisfaction. "Perhaps this putrid little nothing of a place will be our making. If the enemy strikes in Penrhos Bay, we shall be ready. And we will crush them utterly. Satan shall be amazed at our skill and ingenuity in routing the forces of good."

Prince Rimmon stood and addressed the horde of minions who waited eagerly for instructions. "My friends, you shall now applaud me, for I am magnificent indeed!"

There was a confused silence until Gathan stepped forward and shrieked at the top of his voice, "Hail Rimmon, our lord and master. Hail Rimmon!" Gathan made sure that the applause continued unabated until Rimmon spun around and vanished from their sight.

The clamor of praise immediately ceased and was followed by a collective sigh of relief.

THIRTY

The headline emblazoned across the front page of the local newspaper read, *Child still not found—Medium claims she can find Emily.* The article spilled over onto a two-page spread with photographs of Jezebel sitting at a séance table, of a carousel of the kind claimed to be seen by the child's mother, and finally, a photograph of Emily O'Reilly taken on her fourth birthday. The little girl in the photo was smiling and happy.

The reporter didn't pull any punches. His primary target for vilification was the police, in particular the efforts of Detective Inspector Stewart, whom the reporter said, "couldn't find a hundred-ton merry-go-round in a haystack, let alone locate the missing child." Stewart was quoted as saying, "We are continuing our investigation and are hopeful we can locate Emily unharmed." What the words said and what was meant by them was understood by the readers of the *Weekly Express*, namely that there had been no progress whatsoever and that the child was likely dead.

Another photograph showed Emily's mother, Melanie, holding a toy pony to her breast, seated with Madame Jezebel, whose hands hovered over a crystal ball. The caption under the photograph read, "Mother hopes Madame Jezebel can discover Emily's whereabouts." The article went on to say that the paper's editor had set up the meeting between Melanie and the spiritualist medium in the hopes that the "supernatural" might succeed where police methods had so lamentably failed. There followed a few heart-rending paragraphs describing the mother's sufferings and sorry state of mind. Readers were informed that she could neither eat nor sleep and had lost fourteen pounds since the disappearance of her daughter.

Melanie was quoted as saying, "Why did God allow this to happen? I thought he was supposed to be a God of love!" She complained of getting numerous cards and letters from people offering prayers. She didn't want anyone's prayers, she said; she just wanted someone—anyone—to bring her Emily home safe and sound. As for the police, Melanie had nothing good to say about them. She claimed she had been treated like a madwoman and forcibly restrained by uncaring officers. She felt Detective Stewart should be made to resign. She said he had made her feel like a criminal, that he hadn't believed one word of her testimony regarding the abduction. The newspaper's editor took up this call, saying that Stewart ought to face discipline and dismissal from the force. The article went on to challenge the police to publish its case findings in the newspaper to demonstrate that something credible was being done.

Melanie wept as Madame Jezebel comforted her, unaware that Emily was no more than ten feet away, hidden in a room directly above them. The demon Gathan was in attendance to ensure the proceedings went according to plan. Several reporters, including two from the local newspaper, were there with photographers. There was even a female reporter from one of the London dailies.

Madame Jezebel's round table was polished as glass, and the strange cabbalistic signs and symbols that decorated the surface shone like jewels in the flickering candlelight. An altar of curious design at the end of the room was flanked by two great black candles. The room had been carefully lined with damask-rose drapes of velvet-red hues and silken scarves of green and black. Here and there, silver and gold ornaments of astrological and occult significance had been expertly placed to maximize the flow of dark energies. To the casual observer, the décor was strictly for atmospheric effect, but in fact arrangement described the points of a pentacle incorporating satanic numerology.

Jezebel was dressed as a high priestess in a white robe trimmed with gold filigree and a loose hood draped over her black hair.

"Ma'am, do you think we could have some more light in here for my camera?" the photographer asked.

Jezebel's eyes flashed angrily. "Absolutely not! The environment has been perfectly attuned for my spirit guide to appear."

One reporter nudged his friend and whispered, "He got told, didn't he?"

His companion replied, "I'll be glad when this hocus-pocus is over. The whole thing gives me the creeps! You up for a pint afterward?"

"Silence!" Jezebel roared. Then she gathered herself and said with some menace, "I need absolute silence. And I warn you, do not approach the table during the séance. It may prove dangerous."

The reporters exchanged glances, winking at each other.

"We are here tonight to discover the whereabouts of this poor mother's child." Jezebel squeezed Melanie's arm to comfort her again.

Melanie was showing signs of strain. The deep circles below her eyes indicated weariness and lack of sleep.

"You may see and hear things that will shock and frighten you, or you may dismiss them in your disbelief. It is no matter to me, for I know the spirits to be true. After we have finished, you may check the room for hidden equipment or machinery. I assure you, you will be wasting your time. What you are about to experience is a reality that exists in a world parallel to our own. At such moments as this, the division between these worlds can be breached by the use of old magic."

There was a hush in the room now as everyone began to succumb under Jezebel's spell. She lit a candle at the centre of the table. Beside it lay three small oil pots which, now lit, gave off a sweet, intoxicating aroma. The smoke rose upwards, twisting and turning slowly like an immaterial snake. Melanie allowed herself to be mesmerized by the scene, its effects bringing a respite from the pain that had overwhelmed her.

"Son of Genghis, hear me. We desire your presence, lord. Gathan, come forth!"

Gathan smiled, for he loved being called "lord," even if by this stupid windbag.

Jezebel took Melanie's hands in her own and began to chant in a mysterious tongue, her head swaying from side to side. Her eyes were closed, yet she seemed to be gazing at something on the table. "Come, O Gathan, lord and master. We have need of your wisdom this night." Jezebel opened her eyes suddenly. The flame from the candle appeared to dance in her eyes, and the smoke swirled around and around the perimeter of the table, growing thicker by the second. Then the fumes coalesced into a mirage at the centre of the table. There, quite unmistakable, appeared the face of a Mongol warrior, his features sharply defined, the nose flat, the eyes almond-shaped, and the lips tight and thin, revealing jagged yellowing teeth.

The newspaper reporter stepped back into the shadows. One of the photographers raised his camera to shoot, but his hands trembled too much to get a clear shot.

Melanie tightened her grip on Jezebel's arm.

"Welcome, my lord. We are honored by your presence," the medium said, her head bowed low.

The vision in the smoke turned to gaze at the persons shaking in the shadows and uttered imperiously, "Who are these cretins who seek my favor?"

The nervous photographer now broke away from his confederates and ran for the door, dropping his camera along the way it.

"Yes! Run from my sight, fool! For I am Gathan the Destroyer!"

Jezebel raised her face to the phantasm in the smoky mist. "Lord, lord, we know of your mighty powers, but we do not ask you this night to fight on our behalf. Instead, we seek your wisdom on an important quest."

"What is it you seek?" Gathan asked, playing his part in the charade.

"The fair woman beside me has suffered a grievous loss. Her only child, a daughter, has been taken from her. She is distraught, as the soldiers here can do nothing to find the child or capture her abductors." Jezebel pleaded well.

Gathan grinned salaciously. "How can I assist this . . . damsel in distress?"

"Lord, you see all. Put this poor mother's mind at ease by searching the earth to find the child."

"But only if it is my pleasure to do."

"Yes, only if my lord wishes it so," said Jezebel obediently.

"Then chant the ancient words whilst I penetrate the darkness and seek the light."

Jezebel chanted low, sweet sounds, her voice like an oboe playing a haunting melody.

Melanie's head was now resting against the bosom of the spiritualist like a daughter with her mother.

The face in the smoke vanished and was replaced by a swirling mist from which emanated bursts of light and eerie sounds like birds shrieking in the forest. The reporters, now recovered from the initial shock, were busy scribbling notes, recording everything lest they forget later what they had witnessed.

The medium stopped chanting and announced, "My Lord is returning."

The face reappeared above the table. "I have found the child."

Melanie started, looking up at the apparition.

"Do not grieve, my dear. The child is safe. She sleeps. I, Gathan, son of the Great Genghis Khan, have warned her abductors that they will suffer a slow death at my hands if the child is not returned within seven days."

Melanie struggled to speak. "M–my lord . . . I . . . I'm so happy. Thank you. Thank you—" She thrust her hands toward the image as if to embrace it.

Jezebel swiftly pulled her hands back before saying, "Lord, you are mighty and gracious. Indeed, you are merciful. We are in your debt. Farewell, O Gathan."

The demon was happy with himself. His had been a compelling performance. As he rose from the room, he looked down at the pathetic group that had now rushed the table. *What is it the Creator sees in them?* he wondered. *How is it He is mindful of them, that He sends his angels to watch over them? It is entirely beyond my comprehension. If I had my way, I would annihilate the whole human race.*

THIRTY-ONE

The next day, front pages all over Wales carried reports of the séance and the extraordinary visions seen by the reporters and photographers. Melanie was said to be "ecstatic" that her daughter would soon be returned to her. Madame Jezebel, photographed outside her occult centre, said that the public was misinformed about white magic and the good it could bring to a community like Penrhos Bay. Included in some of the articles was a brief statement from Nigel Jeffries, the newly elected bishop, who said that the Bible clearly teaches that mediums and clairvoyants are serving Satan and that it was unfortunate that the mother of the missing child had been drawn into their web of deceit.

The superintendent of police in Penhros Bay issued a statement saying that the police "would always follow up on any information brought forward, but in this case no new data had surfaced that would be of use." The opinion pages were filled with letters from readers expressing their views—often passionate—concerning the case and the use of a medium.

Alone in her home, Melanie read and re-read the articles from several newspapers that were spread on the floor in front of her. Many of the articles included photographs of Emily depicting her from birth to the months leading up to her abduction. Outside, a noisy group of reporters and photographers waited impatiently for any news of the missing child.

Melanie wiped the tears from her eyes using a pretty little handkerchief adorned with flowers that she had given to Emily on her fourth birthday. The home that she normally kept so clean and tidy was now in disarray. She was neglecting herself and hadn't even bothered to buy food. Thankfully, a social worker had visited her earlier that day and promised to arrange a delivery from Food Share, a church-based organization that distributed food and other essentials to those who were, for whatever reason, unable to help themselves. Melanie definitely fell into this category.

Rosina and her friend Janet rang the doorbell and waited on the step. Each held a large box with enough food to last anyone at least a week. When Melanie O'Neill opened the door to them, a bank of cameras burst to life around them, and eager reporters shouted questions at the two women. As Rosina and Janet stepped through the door, the reporters surged forward as one, almost casing the women to drop their boxes. To escape the melee, they pushed into the hallway and slammed the door shut behind them.

"That's awful! How you put up with it all day?" Janet asked sympathetically.

"I don't really notice it anymore," Melanie replied sadly.

"Shall we put this food away for you?" Rosina asked, heading for the kitchen.

The kitchen was a mess. The two women looked at each other and then at Melanie and had the same thought. Janet put an arm around Melanie and directed her to the living room. "Look, you just sit down, and we'll put the stuff away. And then I'll make us all some nice hot tea and a sandwich. You look like you need it."

Melanie smiled weakly. "Thank you."

In the kitchen, Rosina was already busy cleaning and tidying. Janet set about emptying the contents of the boxes into the cupboards and fridge. In a short while, all three women were sitting together in the living room, sipping tea and nibbling on sandwiches and biscuits. Rather, the two visitors nibbled while Melanie ate voraciously.

Rosina said, "We both have young daughters. I can only imagine what you must be going through."

Melanie looked up and smiled, but try as she might, she couldn't stop another tear from falling onto her cheek.

Janet put her arms around Melanie to comfort her, and the young mother began to sob openly, a dam of emotion at the point of breaking.

"Let it out, Melanie. We'll stay with you as long as you want."

Melanie's body convulsed, the tears now flowing freely.

Rosina prayed silently for her.

After several minutes, Melanie dried her face and said, "I'm so sorry. I just feel so helpless, and I miss my baby so much. At times I feel that I can't cope."

"Please don't be sorry. None of this is your fault," Rosina said.

"I feel guilty anyway. Sometimes I think we shouldn't have gone out that night. I should have said no to Emily when she wanted to go on the ride. If I had been a good mother, none of this would have happened." She looked imploringly at Janet and Rosina.

Rosina knelt before Melanie. "The séance you went to . . . All the papers said you were happy afterward."

"I was, at first. But days have gone by, and I still don't have Emily back. I don't know what to believe anymore."

Rosina took Melanie's hands in her own. "Can I share something with you that may be hard for you to take in right now?" Rosina looked straight into Melanie's reddened eyes. "Nothing good can come from people like the woman you went to see. You were desperate, and I can understand that you would do *anything* to get your daughter back. But only evil can come of evil. That medium is in touch with demonic spirits, and no matter what you were told, it was all lies. I suspect the whole thing was concocted just to get this woman's name and picture in the paper."

Melanie had stopped crying and was listening intently.

"There is only one person you can turn to in these situations," Rosina said.

"Do you mean . . . God?"

"Yes."

"I *have* prayed. I used to believe once. That was before I the drugs. And Emily."

Janet wrapped her arms around Melanie a little tighter.

"Can we pray with you now?" Rosina asked.

Melanie nodded.

"Father, we ask that you give strength to Melanie and comfort her during this terrible time. We ask that you send Emily back to her mother, safe and unharmed."

Janet added, "Lord, you know how a parent feels when their child is taken. You know what she is going through. I pray, Father, that you would bring peace to Melanie's heart, a supernatural peace that comes only from you. We also bind the enemy, in the name of Jesus, that Melanie and Emily will never again be troubled by servants of the evil one."

Both Janet and Rosina hugged the young mother.

Rosina said, "If you like, we could come and visit you again."

"I'd like that. Thank you," Melanie said, sniffing, though her face was a little brighter now.

"Then we'll pop in tomorrow, okay?" said Janet.

The two women of God left the house, passing through the gauntlet of newsmen but saying nothing, though they were pestered right up to the door of their car. Janet pulled away from the curb and said, "I just kept thinking, *What if my daughter* . . ." She couldn't finish the sentence.

Rosina said, "We should contact the pastor right away and get others to pray. I truly believe that God is going to bring her daughter back."

THIRTY-TWO

The superintendent sat at his desk with several newspapers open to the offending pages. His hands lay flat, as if trying to hold the reports down as he studied them. Stewart sat, waiting for his boss to say something. He'd been called in just as soon as he had arrived at the station. The office was large and bare. There were no medals or trophies, no photographs of the superintendent with famous people or government officials. The superintendent was a private sort of man with no ambitions beyond his current situation as head of a small-town police force.

Nevertheless, e-mails from London and telephone calls from the commissioner of police had become a daily occurrence. Recent events that had culminated in the disappearance of Emily O'Reilly had caused a spotlight to be turned on his hitherto quiet existence. The superintendent was a good man, well liked by his subordinates. He was fair and showed no undue favor to anyone for any reason. He was one of the old school, a dying breed: a truly honest cop.

He didn't look up when he said, "I guess you've seen these articles? They're not very complimentary about us, and it seems that you, Paul, are their primary target."

Stewart simply nodded.

Superintendent Carlton looked up when he didn't hear a reply. He was shocked at Stewart's appearance. "Good heavens, Paul, you're a wreck! You're not letting these hacks get under your skin, are you?"

"Not really, sir. It's just that . . . I'm not sleeping too well."

"I'm not surprised. But you have to look after yourself, man," he said with some sympathy. "Look, this is going to sound harsh. I know the good work you've done since you came here, and I'm certain you're burning the midnight oil trying to bring this little girl home. But it's no longer just a local problem. The bad press we're getting has been passed up the line to my superiors." He stood up, stepped around the desk, and sat on the front edge. "You look sick, Paul. Seeing you like this has made up my mind."

Stewart looked up. He had a good idea what was coming next.

"I'm being pressured to take you off the case. It's already been decided. They're sending a team in. They're arriving tomorrow morning, and I've agreed that you don't need to do a handover. They will go over all the files and reports and contact you if, and only if, they need to."

Stewart sighed, not trying to hide his feelings.

The superintendent continued. "Listen, I know what sort of man you are, and I know you would prefer to see this through. But politics, the press, and the reputation of this station have all come into play. I hate it because it's got nothing to do with good police work. For most of my career, I've managed to avoid all this public relations nonsense." He began to stalk around the office.

"Boss, I'm sorry—"

The superintendent cut him short. Pointing a finger at Stewart, he said resolutely, "No. Don't you apologize. None of this is of your making. You haven't failed me, Paul—every department has unsolvable cases. The books are full of them. In any case, let's pray these boys find something we've missed."

Stewart sat hunched in the chair.

"I'm putting you on leave effective immediately. Full pay, no questions. Some hot-headed idiots in London wanted you summarily dismissed. I told them that won't happen on my watch. So if you go down, I'm going with you. Understood?"

"Thanks," Stewart said, his voice subdued.

"I want you to use the time wisely, Paul. Take that trip you're always talking about. A change of air will do you good."

"You know, there was a time I would have fought you on this. But now . . ." He drew a deep breath. "I need to find myself again, and this case has me beat. Nothing adds up. I don't know which way to go." Stewart stood up from the chair and held his hand out. "Thanks, Boss, I really appreciate your support."

The superintendent walked him to the door. "If there's anything I can do, just call me. And if these jokers find anything, I'll be sure to let you know. I'm not casting you out into the darkness, Paul."

Stewart walked silently through the outer offices, not turning to look at his colleagues. At the top of the steps outside, he paused and took a deep breath of cold autumn air. He instinctively went to his pocket for a cigarette but changed his mind. As he walked home, something the super had said nagged at him: *I'm not casting you out into the darkness.* Where had he heard that before? Then it dawned on him: It was something he had read in the Bible that Rosina had given him. He tried to remember the words, but only snatches of it came to him. He quickened his pace. Suddenly, he had an urge to get home and read more.

The next day, Stewart got up early and cooked himself a breakfast of ham, eggs, toast, and coffee, something he hadn't done for ages. Instead of leaving the dishes in the sink, he washed them up and put them away in the kitchen cabinets. He looked around the kitchen and thought maybe later he would tidy the whole place up. He had neglected the flat for too long.

After a shower he strolled over to the local barber shop. When his turn came, he sat down in the chair. "Hello, Janet. How's life treating you?"

She swung the gown over his shoulders and buttoned it up. She looked at Stewart in the mirror and gave him a warm, sincere smile. "Life's brilliant for me, thanks. How about you?"

"Funny you should ask. He whispered the next words. "I read the Bible this morning."

"Oh, yeah?" She paused, standing with scissors and a comb in her hands.

"Well, not all of it. But I can't seem to put it down."

"Wow." Janet smiled broadly.

"Honestly, I don't know what's happening to me." Stewart looked at her in the mirror and saw real, undiluted joy in her face.

During the next fifteen minutes or so, as Janet cut his hair, they talked about God and life. She invited him to her church, and he promised he'd see her there Sunday morning. Then Stewart departed, but not before leaving a big tip. He strode out into the morning feeling unspeakably happy.

As he crossed High Street, he decided to continue with his makeover. He visited the local Marks & Spencer, where he bought new shirts, trousers, socks, ties, a winter sweater, and a couple of new jackets. He was amazed when at checkout the woman asked him for nearly three hundred pounds. He hadn't spent that kind of money on himself since he'd been married. Unlike most men, he had enjoyed shopping with his wife and watching her try on new clothes. Happy times, now long past.

Stewart surprised himself by feeling quite light-hearted at the thought of his ex-wife. The past was past and he couldn't change it. He sighed, then smiled to himself. No regrets anymore. He made a promise to himself, and he intended to honor it.

Weighed down only with shopping bags, he hailed a passing taxi to take him home.

The next day he got caught up in housekeeping, cleaning and washing and tidying his bedroom, which was normally impassable. Then he went to the supermarket. He had long found the supermarket depressing. He'd throw almost anything into his cart as long as it fit a couple of basic criteria: First, could it be warmed up in a popty ping—a microwave oven—or consumed straight from the container? Second, would it keep for weeks and still not go bad? As a result, Stewart's diet consisted largely of canned baked beans, spaghetti, macaroni, soup, and custard in a tin.

But on this day, he found himself filling his cart his with meat, fish, freshly baked bread, cheese from the deli, and fruit and vegetables. He also purchased a French press and some Colombian coffee.

Wheeling around the aisles, he caught himself whistling a tune and more than once exchanged greetings with other shoppers. He felt like Ebenezer Scrooge on Christmas morning.

When Stewart arrived at church on Sunday, he had to ask if he was in the right place. The place seemed utterly unfamiliar, quite unlike any church he had ever visited, and he was at a loss for what to do. The building was the recreation centre of a caravan park located a few miles outside town and next to the beach. The room was outfitted with a long counter bar, and there were sofas and tables and chairs arranged as you might expect to find in a pub. At one end of the room was a raised stage with a half dozen musicians tuning their instruments and getting ready to play. There were a couple of guitars, drums, an electric keyboard, and a tall bass. Several microphones had also been set up.

Stewart was dumbfounded. The only church services he had ever been to were funerals or weddings, and those had been held in darkened naves with cold, hard pews and a forbidding pulpit at the business end. This was something else entirely. This was a bar, plain and simple. There were no pews, no crucifixes, and no minister in robes.

His confidence suddenly drained away, and he wondered what he was doing here. He glanced around at the other people who had arrived early to see if anyone would notice his retreat. As he turned to go, Rosina and her young daughter strolled in. She spotted him immediately and came straight over.

"Paul, what are you doing here?" she said with real warmth in her voice. She hugged him and said, "This is wonderful!" Then she turned to her daughter and said, "Sasha, say hello to Mr. Stewart."

The little girl was shy, but she smiled at him and then asked her mother if she could go and play with her friends.

"Paul, I am so surprised. Come and sit down." She guided him to a sofa. "To be honest, I was a little worried about you. I heard about the suspension." She placed her hand on his. "I am so sorry."

He shrugged. "I'm actually enjoying the time off."

She looked at him with disbelief.

"No, really, Rosina. I'm glad to have some free time to think about my life and my future."

"And?"

"It's too early to say whether I stay in the force or take retirement and do something completely different. But what I do know is that I need to make some changes. I can't go on as I did before. I find I'm beginning to gain a new perspective on life. I'm not sure what's driving it, but I want to explore it, whatever it might be."

Rosina was about to say something but held back and smiled instead. "You look different, too," she said.

"Yeah, I got a haircut and bought some new clothes." He stood up to show off his new look. "Speaking of haircuts, there's the lady responsible for my new coiffure."

Janet had spied Paul and Rosina and was waving from the door. She was standing there with her own daughter, Lauren, who was chattering away with Sasha. Janet and Rosina greeted each other with a long hug.

"You two know each other?" Stewart asked.

"She cuts my hair, too," Rosina said with a laugh.

"And our daughters play together. "So, Inspector, what do you think of our church? I guess I should have warned you," she said sheepishly.

"Honestly? I was just about to make a run for it when Rosina rescued me. And it's not like me to flee from a pub."

They all laughed at this.

"But I must say, it seems a pretty odd place to hold services."

Rosina spoke up first. "Well, Paul, I think you'll soon see that God isn't in the architecture, and Jesus Christ is not just a historical figure in stained-glass windows. He is alive, and He desires a deep personal relationship with every one of us. So it doesn't really matter when or where we worship Him. The real truth about church is that it's not a building; it's a family. People are the building blocks, and the mortar that holds us all together is the loving relationships we share with one another. Christ's church is here." Rosina pointed to her own heart, and then, to Paul's surprise, she tapped on his chest. "And if you let Him in, it will be here, too."

Stewart felt a tingling sensation in his breast where Rosina had touched him.

"Excuse me," she said. "There's someone I need to say hello to."

Janet asked, "Would you like some coffee or tea? Sit down and I'll get it for you."

The church was beginning to fill up quickly.

Stewart picked up a placemat from the coffee table in front of him. Written across the top was *God's Free Church*. The band started playing something that sounded like a rock song. The lyrics were displayed on an overhead screen against a backdrop of scenes of mountains, forests, and waterfalls. Everyone was standing now—men, women, and children—all clapping and singing loudly. A few people seemed to be dancing. Stewart had never in his life seen anything like this.

He decided he was going to jump in at the deep end. *Sink or swim*, he thought. He sang the unfamiliar words and soon found he was actually enjoying the experience. After a while, many of the children ran out of the main building for their own planned activities, though several stayed and settled quietly alongside their parents to listen to the sermon. Stewart could see that some people had Bibles spread out on their laps to follow the Scripture references given by the speaker. For those who didn't have Bibles, the text of the verses was displayed on the overhead.

The speaker, a tall man in his fifties, was casually dressed in an open-necked shirt. He had introduced himself as one of the pastors of the church. His style of delivery was dynamic and interesting, and Stewart found himself on the edge of his seat, carefully following every word. This was all new to him, but something inside him hungered for more. The sermon was followed by a prayer and then more music and singing. Afterward, most people hung around, talking and chatting.

Rosina and Janet had gone off somewhere to collect their kids, and Stewart was left sitting alone, though not for long. First a couple came over and introduced themselves, asking whether this was his first visit to the church. Then the speaker came over and shook his hand. When Rosina and Janet returned, they all sat down at a table and talked mainly about what he thought of the service. For once, he found he didn't mind being the centre of the conversation. Upon leaving, he kissed Janet on the cheek and warmly thanked her for inviting him. "What a strange place," he said to her. "But I have definite feeling I'll be back."

THIRTY-THREE

The offshore waters were mildly stirred by a gentle breath of wind. The delicate breeze plucked at the surface here and there, creating small undulations that were born in an instant and then vanished before the moment had time to speak.

Since his encounter with the Holy One, Samuel had seemed to grow in stature. No longer possessing the presence of a mere minstrel, he displayed the physique of a warrior of God. His whole demeanor shone brighter, a bravely earned gift from the Creator Himself.

"It's so beautiful here," he observed to the captain.

Bezalel and Samuel walked together upon the waters, a mile from the landfall of Penrhos Bay.

"Yes it is. I thought you needed a respite after your recent troubles, and I know you love the seascape."

"Troubles?" Samuel stopped.

"Not your troubles, exactly, but those of the couple in your charge."

"I am not troubled, though, Captain. Isn't our duty to care for and protect the saved?" There was a note of uncertainty and inquiry in Samuel's voice.

"Of course. Please do not stumble over my poor choice of words."

They continued to stroll parallel to the shore in the general direction of the Great Ulm. This truly was a stunning vista, though the rocks and cliffs of the Ulm must have seemed a hard, forbidding place for those who lived here in ancient days. The delightful seaside town of Penrhos Bay was relatively young. Only two centuries earlier there had existed here only a wide sweep of mud flats between the eastern and western shores. This had been a wild place inundated daily by the ocean, where only the birds of the air and sea creatures that scampered over the mud between tides and could survive. To the south the dark hills of Snowdonia were capped with new falls of snow.

Bezalel said, "I brought you here to talk of things to come. This town will soon be under siege by the enemy, and a great battle will ensue. The Lord God has chosen this humble place to be the start of a mighty awakening among His people. We have been given only a glimpse of what He intends to do, but it will be great, and its effect will be felt across the earth."

"I knew something of the kind must be coming after the Spirit of the Lord spoke to me and gave me the sword." Samuel's voice was reverent. The sword hung about his waist in a silver scabbard. As he spoke, his right hand instinctively clasped the hilt.

"You have a very important part to play in His plan, Samuel." The captain halted. "You will be required to fight alone. In this way, the enemy will not suspect that the one you guard is the key to a revival that will unleash the power of the Spirit."

"The man Richard, the new curate. He is the one?"

"Yes. Richard will suffer much travail in the days to come. The Lord has placed much trust in you in this vital affair. Be assured the Spirit of God will be at your side, yet he will remain undetected by Rimmon's servants. Nonetheless, you must engage the enemy using only your strength and wits. The Spirit will guide you, but He will not intervene. This is the will of God."

Samuel became pensive, a question growing in his mind. "But, sir, surely there are warriors among the hosts far more skilled and capable than I?"

"You're right. There are."

Samuel lapsed into a deep silence.

"I shall be nearby with ten thousand handpicked warriors, though we shall be hidden. However, I will arise with our host at the right time and vanquish the enemy."

Samuel's eyes grew bright.

"Together, we shall deal such a mighty blow to Satan's forces that they will be scattered throughout creation."

"Praise God!" shouted Samuel. Quite spontaneously, he began to sing of the glory of God in the sweet tongue of angels.

Waves now splashed over their feet. The wind was rising and bringing with it storm clouds.

The companions rose, climbing together to the heights, the captain's arm draped about his friend's shoulder in unconditional brotherly love.

THIRTY-FOUR

For those with eyes to see into the spirit realm, the sight would have been an odd one—a large and fiercely imposing angel, armed with a shining scimitar, standing guard in front of the small seaside hotel. Indeed, the clergymen arriving and those already gathered inside were unaware of the angelic presence. A heavy rain was blowing in off the sea and lashing the entry to the hotel. For most sensible Welshmen, this was not a night for venturing out on any pretext. Yet it seemed that none had refused the curious invitation.

The grandfather clock in the hall struck seven. Simon looked at his watch and announced, "I think we shall wait for another ten minutes for any who may be delayed by the weather."

"Is it always like this in North Wales this time of year?" Serena asked genially, hoping to stimulate some conversation as there had been precious little so far. Though all members of the body of Christ, the local clergy seemed ill at ease with one another. But for a moment everyone was quite happy to chat about the weather.

Simon and Serena mingled to while the minutes away. A few latecomers arrived, two elderly men and a large middle-aged woman. The men were a Methodist minister and the pastor of the evangelical church at the edge of town. The woman was one of the curates from Holy Trinity.

To put the assembled group at ease, Simon explained that they had not been invited to hear him and his wife sing, especially not "Bi-Bi-Bobbi."

Someone muttered loud enough for all to hear, "Thank God for that."

Simon laughed. Taking stock of his guests, he understood quickly that the task ahead of him was not going to be easy. He could tell by the way the clergy had seated themselves—leaving a vacant seat between them and the next person until the last possible moment—that they were not inclined towards meeting together. Before continuing, he said a silent prayer asking for God's leadership and wisdom.

"As I said to each of you on the phone, I've invited you here to tell you all about this weekend's concert and crusade. Let me make it clear that I am not here to 'sing my own praises.' I'm simply asking that you and your church support us in this kingdom endeavor."

A few chairs moved as the occupants shifted uneasily in their seats.

"You are already aware that Bishop Nigel Jeffries, whom some of you have already met, has asked Serena and myself to lead this event. Please be assured that this is not our first time in the trenches. Serena and I have been doing outreaches like this for over thirty years now, but I hasten to add that we are here to serve *you*."

A man in a collar raised his hand. "Simon, I am Archibald Cowell of the Reformed church in town. Might I ask, why is the event being held at St. David's and not in one of the other churches?" The minister waved his hand from side to side, indicating his brethren. I daresay, any one of us has better facilities than St. David's."

"Archie, to answer your question, it is being held at St. David's because the idea for the event came from the bishop who, in choosing not to with us here tonight, is sending a clear signal that this is not an Anglican event but rather, he hoped, a combined effort of the body of Christ. He is simply providing the venue. On a more practical point, to change venues at this stage would cause some difficulties. I can assure you that St. David's has more-than-adequate facilities for an event of this kind."

Cowell seemed satisfied with the answer, so Simon continued. "Bishop Jeffries has told me of the recent spate of awful occurrences here in town. He said that God has spoken to him and that what the Lord requires of us, the Christian community in Penrhos Bay, is to link arms and defend this place against the principalities and powers of this age."

A man suddenly stood up in an agitated state and exclaimed in a strong Welsh accent, "If God has spoken, then why has he spoken only to the bishop and not to the rest of us? Does God want to put us under the control of the Church of England? I say to you, young man, that my ancestors fought against English tyranny, and many gave their lives fighting for that just and holy cause. What do you say to that?" He sat down again, arms folded, and stared aggressively at Simon.

Simon glanced at his wife, sending her a subtle but urgent signal for prayer.

Without rising from her chair, the lady curate from Holy Trinity spoke up. "Jane Seymour, Trinity. Concerning Halloween, I am certain that most of the troubles on Halloween were just hijinks on the part of young people imbibing too much alcohol."

"Weren't there also some serious crimes? A grisly murder and a kidnapped child?" Simon replied politely.

"Yes, that too. But pick up any newspaper in the land, and you'll read of similar tragedies." Before Simon could comment further, she went on to say, "I have been curate at Trinity for seven years and Bishop Jeffries is head of our diocese. But his predecessor, who held the position for over two decades, never once announced that God had commanded him to do anything at all, let alone with *other* churches. I am of the firm opinion that it is ordained by God that there be different denominations. In that way the church reaches everyone in the community, whatever their particular point of view on religion. For my part, I think this whole crusade business is a trifle naïve. This is the misguided notion of an inexperienced bishop trying to force his ideas on a community which, may I say, has weathered every storm of the past without help from the outside."

Another individual rose to speak. It was the minister from the Presbyterian church. He was a balding man with gray hair, dressed in a dark-gray overcoat and scarf, which he had not removed despite the warm temperature inside the room. "I think I can speak for many of us here, being the senior clergyman in Penrhos Bay." There were a few grumblings at this remark. "I think we all would have been more disposed to support this so-called *outreach* if we had been given time to put it before our committees and trustees and then, of course, seek the Lord's guidance. I suggest a period of at least six months' preparation would be suitable. Is that something you can oblige us with?"

"I am only here until next Sunday," Simon replied rather curtly, having become a little fed up. He sighed and was about to carry on when a young man stood and asked if he could speak. Although already weary at the unexpected direction of the meeting, Simon sat down and gave the man the floor.

"I am a new Christian," the young man said, "and I am just so surprised to hear you all talk this way. We all worship the same God, don't we? This man and his wife have come to Penrhos Bay to help us, and all we seem to want to do is throw up obstacles in their way. I'm afraid I don't understand." The young man looked genuinely confused.

"May I inquire as to which of our churches you belong to?" one of the ministers asked in an offhanded way.

"God's Free Church," the young man said.

"I thought as much. You are aware, I suppose, that your pastor is not an ordained minister and has no formal religious qualifications?"

"I didn't know that, no. But what does that matter if people are coming to Christ? People, like me, who had never thought of stepping into an orthodox church?"

The minister scoffed. "You are presumptuous, young man, to even ask such a question." He looked away and addressed the assembly.

"Why, theirs is not even a proper church—they meet in a café! Cappuccino Christians, is what I call them. A cup of no substance and with froth on top. 'Come in, dear atheist Have a cup of coffee, we'll have a chat about Jesus and—presto! Pack your suitcase because you're going to Heaven!'"

Simon had obviously had enough and was just about to dismiss the meeting when, quite suddenly, the bottles of hard liquor lined up behind the bar at the back of the room began to shake and clink together. The lights flickered on and off and on again, and the glass chandelier hanging from the ceiling trembled. The tables began shaking, and a gust of wind blew through the room, enveloping the gathering.

The Methodist minister shivered, turned up the collar of his overcoat, and cried out, "Could someone please shut that door!" All turned to see who had entered and left the door to the hall open, but there was no one. The door was closed tightly.

There was a palpable prescience in the air, as if something remarkable was about to happen. To everyone's astonishment, a small but intensely bright flame, like that of a large candle, appeared in the space above Serena's head, and she began to speak in a language not of this earth. Yet the tone was clear, the words strong and full of warning. Many of the clergy, recognizing the presence of the Holy Spirit, fell on their faces while others merely quaked in fear. The female curate wore a strange expression on her face, a look of disbelief, and stood staring at Serena. The young man from God's Free Church wore a broad smile and could barely contain himself, he was so excited. Then Serena ceased speaking, and Simon drew closer to her, taking her hands in his. The flame above her head had disappeared.

Then the Welshman who had complained that he had not heard from God rose from his chair. The flame had appeared above his head, and the anointing of the Spirit was upon him. He spoke in a gentle and tender voice. "You are all My beloved children. Yet I have this against you: that you fight among yourselves like vultures over carrion. Are you not all My sons and my daughters? Are you not equal in the family of love? If I were to choose favorites from among you, who would stand? Are you not members of the same body? Behold, I will do a mighty thing in this place—with or without you. There are those here who need healing and comfort. Bind up their wounded hearts and bring them the gospel of peace. Tell them of my Son so that they may know My joy eternal. How will you accomplish my will if you are divided? Let those who have ears to hear listen and understand! Pray now and consider your ways. Stand together and you will know My victory. Or choose desolation and know a wilderness of your own making. The Lord your God has spoken."

The flame was extinguished, and the man fell heavily onto his seat, visibly shaken.

Silence reigned, as though none dared speak. Then there was a quiet sob, followed by a low cry of anguish from another, until the entire assembly of clergy began to weep. The female curate cried out pitifully, her voice tremulous with emotion, "O Lord, forgive me! I see clearly now that my thoughts are not your thoughts. I have sinned against you, and I have not kept your ways. I confess, Lord, that I have harbored enmity against my brothers in Christ." She stopped and looked at each person in the room, her eyes flowing with grief. "Brothers, I ask—no, I *beg* your forgiveness."

The tall Presbyterian minister stood and strode across the room, pushing chairs roughly aside, to where the Welshman sat. Grasping him by the arms, he lifted him to his feet. "Ian, you and I were good friends many years ago, and now look at us. We haven't spoken a civil word to each other for nigh on twenty years. God allow us to repent this night for our folly."

Ian threw his arms around the much taller man and hugged him, tears streaming from his eyes. "Andrew, it is I who should seek forgiveness." He searched deeply in his friend's eyes. "Will you forgive my stupid ways?"

"Yes, yes! My friend, yes!" Andrew cried deliriously.

Simon and Serena had become mere bystanders. Simon's meeting, for all its good intentions and human endeavor, had been hijacked by the Spirit of God. Serena squeezed her husband's hand and kissed him on the cheek.

Then curate from Trinity stepped over to the young man from God's Free Church. "I am sincerely sorry for what I said about your church. Perhaps I could visit one Sunday?"

"And have a cup of frothy coffee with me?" the young man said, grinning.

"Actually, I *despise* coffee," the curate replied. "Perhaps a nice cup of tea?"

They both roared with laughter at this.

No one wanted to leave this place, and so they sat and talked and prayed together into the wee hours of the morning. Before leaving, each made generous offers of help to Simon and Serena, promising to do their utmost to assist in the crusade. They all agreed to pray day and night leading up to the event to bind the works of Satan and to make straight the way of the Lord in Penrhos Bay that many lost souls might come to know Christ as their Redeemer.

The meeting was closed with everyone gathered in a circle, on their knees, praying and worshiping God, thanking Him for His mercy and timely intervention. Like sheep who had gone astray, they had now come home when they heard the call of the Shepherd's voice.

The angel on guard outside the hotel remained vigilant. The pack of demons who had gathered at a safe distance knew that something extraordinary was happening. They had sensed the presence of God and withdrawn to a safe place in the darkness. Now seeing the faces of the departing clergy, who were talking animatedly and walking arm in arm, enlivened and invigorated by their experience, the demons wondered just what had actually occurred behind those doors. Troubled deeply, they flew in haste to Rimmon's lair in the caverns below the Great Ulm to acquaint their master with these portentous and disturbing tidings.

Richard and Sarah, who had been unable to attend the meeting at the hotel because of a prior engagement with the bishop, were astonished as Simon described the clergy's encounter with the Holy Spirit and how deeply it had affected them all.

"You should have seen it, Richard! It was like night and day. I don't mind saying I was ready to walk away. I have never witnessed such animosity between leaders of the Christian church. Then the Spirit rushed in and everything changed."

"Oh, I wish we had been there!" Sarah said.

"Don't fret about that," Serena replied. "Those who needed to be there were present, and boy, did the Lord get their attention!"

THIRTY-FIVE

Captain Bezalel held a war council in the medieval castle at Conwy, which had temporarily become his headquarters. Guards were posted all about the high battlements and towers to watch for signs of demonic activity.

The main hall was filled with fifty warriors of the first order. These valiant, battle-scarred officers had commanded battalions of the Lord's host in numerous encounters with Satan's horde, and they knew well the fiend Rimmon. Every single warrior gathered within the confines of this ancient castle was spoiling for the fight, ready to engage the enemy. Their moment would arrive soon enough, but each one knew that for victory to be certain would require their patience and unflagging obedience. Rimmon was a ferocious adversary, and they knew from past campaigns that he should not be underestimated.

The captain said, "Even now Rimmon will be preparing his assault on the town. The dark deeds perpetrated by his foul devils on Halloween night will no doubt seem like a picnic in the park compared to his plans for this crucial weekend."

The officers murmured and whispered among themselves.

Bezalel raise his hand for silence.

"Even now, our brother angels are engaging Satan's forces in minor skirmishes around the world to divert attention away from this region. To the ears and eyes of the enemy's spies, it will seem that no great defensive force of angels has been gathered here. Even though he has knowledge that Spirit is moving, he will believe that God has blundered by underestimating Rimmon's hold on this town. We know that he has conscribed additional legions that he will use to instigate chaos and undermine the faith of Christians hereabouts. By upsetting the balance of power in his favor, he believes he will gain supporters among those in earth's ruling places. There are many mortals in this region who would benefit much if Rimmon were to seize control.

"The Lord has informed me that on Friday evening several of the surrounding towns and cities will suffer violent assaults from demon brigade working in concert. Our response will be an appropriately measured defense, doing just enough to stem the tide. Rimmon must not be made aware of my participation, nor must he suspect more than the regular angelic presence. Rimmon will expect us to retaliate to his initial attacks, but we shall give ground in some of the skirmishes. He is a vain lord, and he will be unable to resist the opportunity to summon all his demons in one great, all-out assault upon the heart of the crusade, St. David's Church. It is there that we shall spring our attack on Saturday evening. We shall hit them hard and send them all to the pit of judgment. Our forces shall come at them from three sides, from both flanks and from above to cut off their escape. At the same time, another force will splinter off to decimate Rimmon's lair under the Great Ulm. We will utterly annihilate his headquarters, once and for all."

A great cheer went up from the assembled officers.

"I want all section leaders of legions of five thousand to stay. The rest of you, go and make your warriors ready for the battle. Be alert, remain vigilant. All glory to God!"

The senior officers gathered around Bezalel to review the final strategy and tactics to ensure that victory would be swift and certain.

In a private room off the main cavern, Rimmon's emissary had been on his knees before his master for more than an hour. Ganymede, Gathan, and Rimmon's other lieutenants stood by, waiting.

Rimmon tore up the parchment a sixth time and threw it at the emissary's head. "If I ask for much, my request is declined," he snarled. "And if I ask for too little, it seems a trifle in Satan's eyes and he declines my request."

The prince glared at Gathan who shrugged his shoulders and contorted his features in an odd expression of sympathy as if to say, *We understand your predicament, lord, but . . .*

Rimmon scowled and turned his gaze to another of his sycophants. "Ganymede, you are often craftier than I. Why can't you tell me what to write?"

Ganymede wondered if this was a compliment or an accusation but could not decide, and so he chose the simpler option of being obsequious. "I, my Lord? Nay, I could never be as cunning as you. And as for advising you, I merely pick at the edges. It is your own wisdom that cuts to the quick." He bowed low.

"Yes, yes, all right. You may be inferior to me in all matters, but I command you to conjure up some bit of cleverness for this moment. Then you can go back to bowing and scraping."

Seizing the opportunity, the others backed slowly away, leaving Ganymede to face Rimmon alone. Even the emissary relieved his pain by prostrating himself, thus relieving the agony in his knees and neck.

Ganymede, seeing that he could not deflect attention to the others, tried to think of something that would please his Lord. But the more he reasoned, the more his mind went blank. Becoming flustered, he tried to articulate a sentence that he hoped would make sense.

Rimmon leaned forward, pen poised, ready to record Ganymede's words.

"I . . . I think . . . under these special circumstances . . . given the delicate balance of power and the inadequacies of our adversary . . .

notwithstanding the recent visit of the unmentionable third Person of the . . . um, thoroughly distasteful trio of—"

Rimmon stood and bellowed, "What are you gibbering on about, you imbecile?! Gathan, pull his arms off!"

"Lord, have mercy on your faithful servant. It's just that I normally hesitate to speak before my thoughts have coalesced fully."

Rimmon studied Ganymede's eyes. "Then I give you five minutes to think silently. But choose your next words carefully, for if I am displeased, they will most certainly be your last words."

Ganymede had always been able to assuage Rimmon's anger by some artifice or another, but it was plain that Rimmon would not be mollified in this instance. Clearly, the prince feared for his own safety because of this wretched town. Ganymede's thoughts wandered to when he had been posted to Paris during the eighteenth century, a time of drunkenness and debauchery, fine wines, and lace handkerchiefs. He sighed at the memory.

"You seem deep in thought, my friend," Rimmon said. "By my reckoning, you have sixty seconds to formulate my answer."

Ganymede caught sight of several grinning demons who were becoming excited at the prospect of seeing his arms flung across the room.

His own mouth was as dry as a desert at high noon. Then suddenly he laughed out loud as a brilliant, simple thought formed.

Composing himself, Ganymede stepped closer and whispered, "May I, lord? This is for your ears only."

Rimmon dismissed all but one from the room. The emissary was commanded to remain and make ready to carry his message to Satan.

"My lord, the answer to a complicated problem is often the simplest," Ganymede explained.

"Yes, get on with it. My patience is running out."

"Well, if you do not know what to write, then do not write anything!"

Rimmon's face darkened.

Ganymede held up a finger. "Anything, that is, that may place you in an adverse position with our master."

Now intrigued, Rimmon glanced at his lieutenant who continued.

"I am sure you will appreciate the elegance of what I propose. Instead of asking for some fixed number of reinforcements and possibly angering our master, simply lay out the problem as you see it and then ask *Him* to allocate the number of demons required to win the day as he sees fit."

Rimmon had gotten lost somewhere along the way and was now looking puzzled. "So what you are saying is, that I should . . ."

"That you should let his highness provide the answer. That way, you cannot be held accountable for any failure due to insufficient forces, although defeat is inconceivable." Ganymede knew this was untrue—Satan would have Rimmon's head in the event of failure, no matter the cause.

"Yes, I see it now. Very clever of you, Ganymede." Looking smug and satisfied, Rimmon said, "Now tell me exactly how I should phrase the request, and then this poor fellow can be on his way."

THIRTY-SIX

Richard and Sarah Benton had their hands full. They had been thrown into the deep end by the bishop in a clear case of sink-or-swim. Richard, in particular, wondered if he was capable of carrying out the task of organizing a crusade in such a short period of time. He had shared his misgivings with Sarah one night as they lay in the darkness, minds racing while waiting for blessed sleep to come.

"I should have been there," he said.

"Richard, just because you weren't at the meeting when the Spirit spoke, you have no reason to feel inadequate. The Lord knew exactly who was to be there, and that is that. You can't second-guess God."

"You're not being very sympathetic, Sarah."

"But I am. I would love to have been there too, but we weren't. Doesn't that tell you something?"

"No, it doesn't," he said petulantly.

"Richard, you're behaving like a child. Have you forgotten already how you felt that night on the pier? You told me yourself you'd been touched by God."

He turned over in the bed away from her.

She put her hand on his shoulder. "Listen to me. The bishop has great faith in you. He's going to give you St. David's after that Scrooge, Stannard, has been formally dismissed. He wouldn't have put you in charge of this whole thing if he didn't have confidence in your abilities. Simon and Serena and the bishop himself will be at your side. Instead of seeing this as a trial, look at it as an opportunity to serve a community in desperate need of God. Trust in Christ, and you'll bless Him. He has blessed us wonderfully, and I think sometimes we ask too much without giving enough back."

As Richard lay still in the dark, he could feel Sarah's breath on his neck. He turned over to face her. "You're right, as usual," he said tenderly. "What would I do without you?"

"Probably sink into oblivion."

"And which oblivion would that be?" he joked as he dug his fingers into her ribs to tickle her.

"Richard, don't, please . . . don't!" she cried, laughing through tears.

The next day, they were at the church very early. Before morning prayers, and with help from other church members, they had assembled the temporary stage for Simon and Serena's performance. Other volunteers were busy cleaning so that the whole church would be spick and span.

Later that morning, Simon and Serena arrived to oversee the setting up of the sound system. It took hours to adjust the levels to the satisfaction of Simon, who wanted everything to be perfect. During the sound check, Sarah had time to sit and have coffee with Serena. It was a delight to hear about their lives and their conversions when they had both been on the verge of stardom. Afterward, Simon suggested that Richard join the three of them for a time of prayer.

They sat in a corner of the church hall, and Serena led them. She soon began praying in tongues, and Sarah could feel Richard stiffen and go quiet, retreating into his Anglican shell. Yet Sarah could feel the power of Serena's entreaties, even though she couldn't comprehend their meaning. Simon closed the session by praying in English and asking God to bless every detail of their preparation for the event.

Serena then said, "Come on, Simon, we still have a lot to do." Giving Sarah and Richard friendly hugs, they hurried from the hall.

Richard sat down again. "I think I could do with a cup of coffee." He looked up at Sarah.

"I'll get it for you. Just sit and relax for a minute."

Returning with the coffee, she sat down beside her husband. "It's the speaking in tongues, isn't it?" she said. "It bothers you."

"I'm sorry, but it doesn't sound real to me. Sounds like babbling, in fact. Did you know the word for speaking in tongues, *glossolalia*, means just that—meaningless prattle in a nonexistent language?"

"But Saint Peter and the apostles spoke in tongues on the day of Pentecost."

"Yes, but the book of Acts also says that those listening heard their own languages being spoken and understood clearly, which means the apostles weren't speaking gibberish."

"All right, but do you think someone so devoted to God like Serena would speak gibberish while praying? Come on, you've seen the kind of person she is, honest and loving. I don't see her engaging in some shabby theatrics to make herself look good."

Sarah looked at Richard and waited for an answer, which was slow in coming.

"Use your logic, Richard. What makes sense here? Do you trust Simon and Serena?"

"Yes, of course. But you're doing it again!" he complained.

Sarah raised her eyebrows as if to say, *Doing what?*

"You know, pushing me up against the ropes, then sneaking in a cross to the chin."

She wasn't about to let her husband off the ropes, either. "Doesn't Saint Paul say that it is good and right to desire the gifts of the Spirit? Including the gift of tongues?"

"Y-yes."

"Besides, I know someone else who prays in tongues. Someone quite close to you, in fact," she said mysteriously.

"Who?

"Me, silly."

"You? I don't believe it. I've never heard you pray that way."

"First of all, I don't tell you everything. A woman has to have some secrets. Second, I use it when I'm praying on my own for really important things, like when you rushed out that night and left me."

"Really?"

"Oh, Richard, it feels so intimate, as if God Himself is in the room with me."

"And do you know what you're saying?"

"No, not in words. But it goes deeper than mere words. It's as if my heart is speaking to God directly, without my mind getting in the way. It's difficult to explain, really."

Richard saw that her eyes shone brightly as she spoke about this.

"Do you trust me?" she asked, grasping his hands.

"Of course I do."

"Then promise me this: Ask God every day over the next few days to give you the gift of speaking in tongues. Will you promise?"

He hesitated before answering, making sure he meant the promise undertaken.

"I promise," he said.

"Thank you, my love. I think you'll be amazed," she said affectionately. "Come on, now. There's loads of work yet to be done to get this show on the road."

THIRTY-SEVEN

The uniformed commissionaire manning the door of the Grand Hotel looked up at the steel gray sky as the first drops of freezing rain came in on the wind and fell upon his face. He adjusted his peaked cap and drew up his collar to ward off the cold. Stepping back into the lee of the main doorway, he pulled on a pair of black leather gloves. John Maxwell had been forced to take early retirement from the London Metropolitan Police due to a serious gunshot wound sustained in the line of duty. Unfortunately for Maxwell, the incident had left him with minimal mobility in his right leg, and he felt fortunate to get the job at the Grand. The hotel seemed to think it was good business having an former police officer on the door.

The Grand Hotel, situated on the promenade, was far too ostentatious for this small seaside town, but it had been built about the same time the new championship golf course was opened. Penrhos Bay boasted the finest links course in the north of Wales. At this time of year, however, when most golfers had fled with their clubs to Spain or Florida, the Grand Hotel was quiet. There would be a small rush at Christmas time when the Grand put on a splendid holiday vacation for those who could afford the exorbitant rates, complete with name entertainers performing at the New Year's Eve Ball.

Maxwell pulled back the sleeve of his overcoat to check his watch. It was nearly time for a much-needed break of hot coffee and toast and butter in the hotel kitchen. His assistant Gerald would cover for him, and Maxwell could put his feet up for half an hour or so. The sleet would soon turn to snow, as the color of the clouds over the cliffs of the Great Ulm heralded a coming storm. The commissionaire was just thinking to himself that he should bring up a broom and some salt bags to keep the steps clear of ice and snow when three limousines glided slowly to a stop outside the hotel entrance.

Grabbing a large umbrella, he scrambled down the steps. He wasn't sure which car door to cover with the umbrella. All three cars were immaculate pre-war Rolls-Royce models. The first and third were black, while the central vehicle was a deep blood-red color. Maxwell couldn't see into the cars, as all of them had dark tinted windows, so he simply waited for a door to open. He wondered who this might be, as the manager had not notified him of any guests arriving this morning. The driver's door of the middle car opened, and a uniformed chauffer in gray jodhpurs, jacket, and peaked cap ran around to the rear door and smartly opened it. Maxwell quickly hopped over, umbrella held high. Emerging from the vehicle was a pair of petite, red high heels and two shapely legs in sheer black stockings that swung elegantly onto the pavement.

"Welcome to the Grand Hotel," Maxwell said.

The woman who stepped out of the car was stunningly beautiful, dressed in a white fur coat with red trim at the hood, sleeves, and hem. Long blonde curls fell over the open neck of the coat. She strode forward, not showing any cognizance of the commissionaire. As she went up the stairs, Maxwell could barely keep up, but she waited at the top for him to come and open the door for her.

Once inside the lobby, she went immediately to the desk and addressed the female receptionist. "Please get the hotel manager."

The receptionist looked her up and down and for a moment thought of saying, "Can't I help?" But one quick glance into the woman's cold green eyes convinced her otherwise, and she said rather meekly, "Right away, Miss."

Maxwell stood inside the lobby door, watching the woman while keeping one eye on the vehicles just in case another guest decided to enter. The woman's perfume lingered in the doorway. The scent was strangely alluring, heady yet sweet, with some indefinable quality that made him feel uneasy.

The hotel manager, Aubrey Westbrook, was a product of the old school, an anachronism in this day and age perhaps, but he had the right manners for the type of guest who frequented the Grand. Middle-aged and tall, dressed in a dark pin-stripe suit with a carnation in his lapel, he was the very image of a high-class servant.

At first he was a bit peeved at being disturbed. But when he saw the woman in the fur coat, his whole demeanor changed. "Madame, welcome to the Grand Hotel," he said with a broad smile on his close-shaven face. "I am the General Manager, Aubrey Westbrook." His accent spoke of Eton and Oxford, though it was certain that Westbrook had been to neither. "If you will follow me, we can discuss your needs in my office."

As the woman entered his office, he turned to the receptionist and said, "Julia, be so kind as to bring us some tea."

The woman dropped her hood and unbuttoned her coat to reveal an exquisite and no doubt expensive dress. She wore a single, elegant string of pearls and matching earrings. Westbrook noted the six diamond rings on her fingers. She crossed her legs as the manager sat down behind his wide oak desk. He tried very hard not to stare at her legs.

"So, Madame, how may I be of service?" he asked, trying to keep his smile as natural as possible.

"It's Miss. My employer, Count Rimmon, plans to stay here several days, along with his entourage."

Aubrey Westwood was good at recognizing accents, but he was nonplussed by her manner of speech. It contained a variety of subtle qualities he thought might originate in France or Russia, perhaps even the United States. The more he listened, the more confused he became. Her mannerisms were also unusual and spoke of breeding and elegance, yet he was at a loss to classify her in his mental filing system.

"The Count requires a suite for himself and at least six other rooms all on the same floor, preferably the top floor. Is that possible?"

Her green eyes shone like sparkling emeralds.

"Well, let me see." He turned to his computer screen on the desk. "I think we can accommodate your party."

"Are there any other guests staying on that floor, or booked to stay?"

"No one there at the moment, Miss . . . ?"

"You don't need my name, Mr. Westbrook," she said coldly.

"No, of course." He glanced back at the screen and tapped the keyboard. "There are some guests arriving in a few days' time who I am sure will not be of any trouble to you. They're a group of elderly—"

"Please, put them somewhere else."

"Er . . . yes, I am sure that can be arranged. Now about the bill. I could give you a splendid discount, I'm sure."

"Discounts do not matter. I will pay in cash. How much?"

"Well, there are in fact ten rooms on that floor, so let me just calculate the costs. Will you be dining with us?"

"You will have all food sent up as and when required. Just include a generous amount on the bill, especially for champagne."

The hotel manager coughed and tried to come up with a suitable amount. By his calculations, the fee would be enormous. Nevertheless, he added twenty percent. "By my reckoning, the bill will come to nearly twenty thousand pounds."

The lady showed no emotion at all. "That is good. Let's say twenty-five thousand to cover any contingencies. I will speak to the Count right away."

Removing a mobile phone from her handbag, she spoke into it without dialing. Westwood was unable to identify the language, which was very strange and somehow seemed ancient.

She then stood and said, "The Count is satisfied with these arrangements. One of his assistants will bring an attaché case with the money right away. You may keep the case if that is convenient for you. Do you have an underground car park where the vehicles can remain during our stay?"

Westwood nodded. Westbrook was feeling somewhat unnerved, as if he were being dictated to and his hotel being commandeered.

"Yes? Good. And my employer can access the hotel via the car park without publicity? He is a very private man, you see."

"Why yes . . . yes."

"Are the rooms ready for occupation?"

"Yes, we are always ready for our guests," he said proudly.

"Good, then let us go."

Rimmon stood in the centre of the room, in human form, sipping a glass of chilled champagne and staring at Ganymede.

"I'm not sure if I like you as a human female."

"I am not sure I like it myself," replied Ganymede, inspecting himself in a full-length mirror. "Though I think I could get used to it, except for these things." He cupped his hands under his full breasts. "As appendages, I can't imagine why mortal men drool over them."

Gathan looked at Ganymede with an expression of disgust. "Then why didn't you choose a masculine form like we did?"

"I thought it might be fun, Gathan—a concept that you simply cannot comprehend."

"Now, my friends, let's not bicker," Rimmon said. "We are here on 'vacation,' after all."

Gathan made himself busy, while Ganymede sat down on a sofa and started to paint his long fingernails.

"Have you posted sentinels at all the entrances?" Rimmon asked.

"Just as you requested, my lord," Gathan replied.

"Do we have any uninvited 'guests' watching us?"

"A few, not hidden—three or four of Bezalel's lesser fighters."

"Good. Ganymede, have you done what I asked?" Rimmon asked sarcastically as the demon in disguise continued painting his nails.

Ganymede looked up. "I have done exactly as you instructed. I have created a cloud of unknowing all about the hotel. The watchers will be able to see and hear, but what they see and hear will be quite different from what is actually happening. Although . . . there is no hiding the truth from the One who sees all and knows all."

"True, but He will not intervene. He has no stomach for further conflict with Lucifer."

Rimmon strolled over to the French windows, opened the doors, and stepped out onto the balcony. Large snowflakes had begun to blanket the area. Rimmon held out the palm of his hand, and a snowflake landed upon it like a dying butterfly. He studied the flake closely. "Ah, the wonder of creation! His compound fractals are the stuff of genius, but lo, what happens if I step into the warmth?" He turned around and stepped into the room, and the snowflake melted. "One day we shall see all of His creation melt away, just like this flake."

Ganymede clapped at this.

Rimmon smiled, admiring his own wit. Then he grimaced, remembering an unpleasant task. "Where is that pest Jusach?"

Gathan stuck his head out the door and shouted down the hall, "Jusach, get in here!"

The demon came scurrying in just as Rimmon sat down.

"Ah, Jusach, my friend. What is this I hear about a mere mortal getting the better of you?" Rimmon asked playfully.

"Master, I was taken by surprise. I was certain the bishop could not see me, when all of a sudden I felt his eyes upon me and he started to pray. I was pushed against the wall by some godly force."

"And you could not free yourself?"

"I could not, my lord." Bowing low, he expected a tirade of abuse in response.

"You may go," Rimmon said tersely.

Jusach backed out of the room as fast as he could, heaving a sigh of relief as he went.

"It seems I must deal with this new bishop myself. He could prove a great hindrance to my plans." Rimmon looked across at Gathan. "Let's ask our friend the Reverend Stannard to come and pay us a visit. Organize it straight away. I will entertain the eminent vicar this afternoon, and we shall learn more about this troublesome upstart."

Stannard took the elevator to the top floor, fingering a business card that read *Count Rimmon, Philatelist. Collector and Purveyor of Rare Stamps.* No address, no telephone number, no e-mail. He had thought about bringing along the penny Victorian stamps, but decided against it, choosing instead to play his cards close to his chest. The lift doors slid open, and Stannard was confronted by two large men, both over six feet tall and weighing in excess of two hundred and twenty pounds each. Both were dressed in dark-blue suits, shirts, ties, and black shined shoes.

One of the men said in a thick Russian accent, "Follow me."

Stannard heard the doors of the lift close behind him and began to feel nervous.

The guard knocked gently on the door of Rimmon's suite. Zurvan, one of Rimmon's attendants, cracked opened the door.

"Lord Rimmon's guest is here," the guard announced.

Stannard thought to himself, *Lord?*

Zurvan opened the door wide. "Please come in, Reverend Stannard. My master is expecting you."

The scene that greeted Stannard was like something out of an American gangster film. There was Count Rimmon, seated in an ornate, high-backed regency-style chair, dressed in a cream-colored bespoke double-breasted suit, striped shirt, and silk cravat, pinned with a gold brooch studded with diamonds. White spats covered his brown patent leather shoes, and a pink carnation was neatly set into his jacket buttonhole. A knockout blonde, her long legs crossed, sat idly on the sofa, painting her nails. A towering black man stood quietly behind Rimmon, wearing dark designer sunglasses.

Stannard hesitated.

Count Rimmon did not rise from his chair. "Gathan, bring a chair for our guest," he said, smiling at Stannard.

The oversized bodyguard brought the chair, placing it just a few feet away from where Rimmon was seated. Stannard sat down.

"I understand you wanted to discuss some stamps, sir?" Stannard said quizzically.

"Yes, yes—all in good time. Reverend Stannard, your reputation precedes you. I understand you have a keen eye for a bargain, especially for penny blacks."

Stannard shifted in his seat. "I have dealt with the purchase of such stamps, but I have always paid a fair price."

"That is very interesting," said Rimmon, staring intently into Stannard's rheumy eyes. "But I am being an inhospitable host. Would you care for some coffee? Or tea perhaps? I know how English clergymen adore tea!"

"Thank you, no." Stannard fidgeted in his chair. "Could we get down to business?"

"Why, of course, if that is what you prefer."

"Yes, that is precisely what I would prefer," Stannard said a bit more sharply than he'd intended.

"Ah, but first I would like you to meet an old friend. Zurvan, ask my other guest to join us."

Zurvan left the room by a side door, leaving it ajar. Stannard fixed his eyes upon the door.

"I think you two gentlemen have met before?" Rimmon said.

The person who came through the door cause Stannard to jump to his feet.

The man was dressed in a clergyman's collar and was carrying a smart black attaché case. Stepping into the room, he stood silently staring at Stannard. It was the Reverend Alexander Martin, the man from whom Stannard had obtained the penny blacks.

Stannard looked from Martin to Rimmon in an agitated fashion. The woman momentarily ceased painting her fingernails to watch the drama unfold.

"Please, Reverend Stannard, sit down. Mister Martin, set the case over here on the coffee table."

Stannard was in shock as he sat down slowly and gazed at Martin. Crazy questions were spinning around his brain. How could this man be here? And what was his business with these foreigners?

Martin did as he was told and then took a pace back to stand beside Gathan.

"Does it not say in your Bible, Stannard, that one day your sins will find you out? I am afraid that for you *this* is that day."

"I don't understand what is happening. Why have you brought me here?" Stannard asked in a perturbed tone.

"All will be revealed, my friend. Have patience. Let us examine the facts, shall we? I believe you purchased a stamp album from this man for a paltry sum, which admittedly would have been very generous had the album not contained some extremely valuable items. Is that not true?"

Stannard's face had drained of all natural color. Unable to speak, he just nodded.

"The items in question are, conservatively speaking, worth about twenty thousand pounds, I think."

Stannard nodded again.

"Good, I am glad you do not bother to dispute these facts. I see that you can be an honest man when you wish to be."

Rimmon leaned forward and opened the attaché case. He spun it around on the glass surface of the table so that Stannard could see its contents.

Stannard stared at the case in horror and pushed himself back into the chair. Gathan stepped around to the back of the vicar's chair and placed his hands on Stannard's shoulders.

"Look, I'll make restitution," Stannard said, now perspiring heavily. "I'll turn over the album and the stamps, and Martin can keep the money." His hands began to tremble.

Rimmon turned to look at Martin. "Well, Reverend Martin, I think the vicar's offer is a fair one. What do you say? Shall we accept his offer?"

Martin smiled, looked straight at Stannard, and said, "No."

Stannard's demeanor visibly changed from one of fear to utter dread. He looked down at the attaché case. It was filled with bundles of new fifty-pound notes which, together, must have amounted to several thousand pounds.

But it wasn't the money that attracted his attention. It was the gun.

"Ah, my friend, do you recognize the handgun?" Rimmon asked.

Stannard stammered, "It's— it's . . . an army pistol."

"You're right, it is. A British officer's service pistol from the Sixties, if I'm not mistaken." He paused.

Stannard did not look up.

"In fact it is your own pistol."

Stannard tried to stand, but Gathan's strong hands held him down.

"But it can't be. It's not possible. I threw it into the Thames when I was ordained as a priest."

"So you did. But the past has a way being dredged up, if you'll excuse my pun."

Stannard looked anxiously at Rimmon and then at Martin. "Do you mean to shoot me? Over the stamps? I said I'll repay you. I'll do anything, but please don't kill me!" He began to whimper.

Rimmon smiled. "Whatever gave you such an incredible idea? Do you think we are gangsters? That we'd gun you down in the Grand Hotel and dispose of your body in the dumbwaiter?" Rimmon laughed out loud, which set his compatriots all laughing.

Stannard began to wonder if he was in a madhouse, or if this was nothing more than a horrible nightmare.

"Come, come, dear fellow. Don't jump to conclusions. I simply want to make you an offer—one I feel you will not want to refuse. Martin, get the vicar a glass of water. On second thought, make it a whisky."

Rimmon waited while Stannard drained the drink in one gulp.

"Now listen carefully. The cash in the attaché—and by the way, they are not forged notes, you have my word—amounts to exactly fifty thousand pounds. I am prepared to hand it over to you. You can even keep the penny blacks should you agree to my proposal. All in all, that amounts to more than seventy thousand pounds. Add that to your own nest egg, and I am sure you could live out the rest of your life quite comfortably."

Stannard looked utterly miserable. "What is it you want me to do?"

Rimmon smiled. "I want you to kill the bishop."

"Good heavens, are you mad! Why on earth would I do such a thing?"

"Because if you don't I shall order Gathan to tear your limbs off one by one. And then he will decapitate you with his claws."

"What do you mean 'his claws'?"

Gathan's hands pressed down upon him, and Stannard cried out in pain. He turned his head to see Gathan's long, black claws digging into his shoulders. In abject fear, he then looked upon Gathan's face.

Stannard screamed in sheer panic. Gathan clamped one of his demon's claws over the vicar's mouth as Stannard began shaking uncontrollably. He looked around the room and saw not the well-dressed quartet from a gangster movie but saw instead four gruesome, unearthly beasts. He urinated involuntarily, the liquid waste dripping through the fabric of his slacks and onto the carpet.

"I see we have influenced you quite enough, Reverend Stannard. Are you now prepared to listen to my proposal?"

Stannard felt his blood turn to ice water, and he passed out.

"Get some water, Gathan, and revive him," Rimmon ordered testily.

Gathan removed the champagne from the ice bucket and emptied the bucket's contents upon the vicar's head.

Stannard came to immediately, gasping and spluttering.

Gathan grabbed Stannard's head and forced him to look upon Lord Rimmon, who had resumed his human form.

"Now, my friend, I am only going to say this once, so mark my words: You will take the case with the money and the pistol. On Saturday, we will arrange it for you to be able to walk up to the bishop and shoot him dead. If the young curate is with him, kill him also. When you have done this deed for me, I shall have you spirited away to anyplace of your own choosing. My companions will be watching at all times, so do not even think of betraying me. If you do, I shall make sure you keep an appointment with Gathan to suffer a horrible death beyond even your wildest imagination. Is this clear?"

Stannard managed to nod his head.

"Good, we have an agreement. You may go. Zurvan, escort our friend home."

Zurvan shape-shifted back into his prior human form. Stannard had to be assisted from the room. Zurvan picked up the attaché case and, taking Stannard's arm, led him away.

Just as they reached the door, Rimmon spoke. "I say, Stannard. I suggest you use some of that cash to buy another pair of trousers."

The others in the room broke into raucous laughter, and the woman, unable to control herself, fell off the sofa.

THIRTY-EIGHT

Stewart arrived back home from the local supermarket to find an e-mail from the boss waiting for him:

> *I know you're on leave, Paul, but something has come up, and I don't want these new boys getting their hands on it. Seems an ex-cop is doing security at the Grand and would like to have a chat with us about a strange bunch of guests. Do me a favor and pop over there to have a word with the guy. John Maxwell is his name, late of the Met. It's probably nothing, so keep it low-key and informal. Thanks. Keep me posted if it amounts to anything.*
>
> *P.S.—Missing you around the place.*

Stewart checked his watch. It was nearly noon. He decided to rustle up some lunch before walking over to the Grand Hotel.

Yesterday's snow had turned to slush. The skies were still gray over Penrhos Bay—more snow was on the way along with subzero temperatures.

Stewart found the commissionaire sweeping melted ice from the hotel steps. "You Maxwell?" he asked in an open and friendly way.

Maxwell looked down at him. "That's right. You from the local nick?"

"Detective Inspector Paul Stewart. Good to meet you." He held out his hand.

Maxwell hobbled down the steps and shook Stewart's hand firmly.

"You were with the Met?" Stewart asked.

"Yeah, that's right. Twenty-six years, until I was invalided out."

"How did you get that?" Stewart asked, pointing to Maxwell's bad leg.

"Got blasted by a young thug. Shattered my knee. Still hurts after seven years."

"And the bad guy?"

"We got him, all right. He'll be inside another ten years."

"So justice was done then."

"Maybe. Not sure my knee would agree," Maxwell said dryly.

"I was in the Met force, too, but after you, I should imagine."

"Yeah? How'd you end up here? This is a bit of a comedown after the big city."

"Don't I know it. Personal problems, but that's water under the bridge now."

Maxwell nodded.

"The super says you might have a problem at the hotel. That right?"

"Let me put the broom away, and then we'll talk."

Maxwell hobbled up the steps, went inside with the broom, and reappeared moments later without it. Taking Stewart's arm, he eased the detective away from the hotel entrance toward the rear of the building. "I've got something to show you first. Come and have a look at this."

At the back of the hotel, they stopped at the top of a wide concrete ramp that led down to the underground car park. There were only about half dozen cars parked there, but Stewart immediately saw what Maxwell had brought him down for. All lined up neatly in a row were three immaculate antique Rolls-Royce limousines. Two were black and the third a crimson red. Stewart walked over to vehicles and lovingly placed his hand upon the bonnet of one of the cars, stroking it as though it were a rare and precious animal.

"These all belong to our guest Count Rimmon and his entourage," Maxwell said.

"A count? There's no such title anymore, is there?"

"Manager thinks he might be Russian."

Waving his hand at the three cars, Stewart said "Silver Ghosts?"

"No, last Ghost was made in 1925 or thereabouts. These are from about a decade later. They're all Phantoms." Maxwell had done his homework.

Stewart walked around the car nearest to him, admiring the lines and the paintwork. "You can almost smell the luxury. What are they worth, do you think, in this condition?"

"At a guess, at least two hundred thousand apiece."

Stewart gave a low, admiring whistle.

"Odd thing I noticed about the license plates," Maxwell said, "they're indecipherable."

Bending down to examine the plates, Stewart said, "I see what you mean."

"To be honest, I didn't it a thought at first. I just assumed they were registered in some foreign country. But having looked at them again a few times, that script is nothing I recognize."

Stewart ran his finger over the script. "It's more like ancient cuneiform. Babylonian, at a guess."

"You an expert on that kind of stuff?"

"No, not at all. Just a hobby. I like to watch the History Channel. Gets my mind off work."

"Tell you what. I'll take a photo and e-mail it to my daughter Toni. She's a senior lecturer in linguistics at Warwick. Clever girl. She'll know what it is. Or if she don't, she'll know someone who does."

"Sounds good, John. Let me know what you find out. But you didn't bring me over here to admire the Count's taste in automobiles."

"No, I didn't. Let's nip into my cubby hole and have a mug of tea, and I'll tell you what worries me about this rum bunch."

Maxwell led the way through a door to a sparsely furnished room with a table, two chairs, and a monitor showing multiple images from the hotel's closed-circuit television cameras. "How do you like your tea?"

"Strong and sweet, thanks."

Waiting for the kettle to boil, Maxwell pointed to the screen and tapped the keyboard. "Take a look at this. I can zoom in on just about any part of the hotel. That is, I could until the Count and his friends moved in. Now I can't access the top floor at all."

Stewart looked at the monitor. It showed various hallways and public areas in and around the building.

"When I bring up the top floor, this is what happens." He tapped a key. The screen images disappeared and were replaced with snowy interference. "I had the maintenance man check it over, and he can't find a fault."

"Anything else?" Stewart asked.

"Since they arrived, no food has gone up—only ice buckets and champagne, and plenty of it. Housekeeping staff are turned away, and even the manager was told to shove off when he went up there. One of the Count's people said his boss was indisposed and not entertaining visitors. He told Westwood to come back later, but the goon said it in a way that suggested to Westwood he was not welcome in his own hotel."

"A very private party, then."

"Very. And that's not all. They paid in advance—in cash—twenty-five thousand pounds. That's a lot of spondulicks in any language. The manager was afraid they were forged notes. So I took them straight over to the bank and had the manager there examine them."

"And?"

"All kosher. New fifty-pound notes and genuine British currency."

"That's a lot of cash to be carrying around."

"The bank manager wondered out loud about Russian money laundering, which is why I contacted you fellows."

Maxwell poured hot water into the giant tea mugs and handed Stewart the milk and sugar. "Oh yeah, and another thing. Yesterday, the Count had a visitor during the afternoon. Stayed about an hour and left with one of the thugs. He looked a bit worse for wear after the meeting."

"Anyone you know?"

"Only by sight. Never made his acquaintance, but from what I've seen of him, I don't think I want the pleasure. It was the vicar from Saint David's. Stannard's his name, I think."

"Stannard!" Stewart scoffed. "I met him a couple of times several months back. He's a cold fish, all right. Obnoxious, as well."

"But what does Stannard have to do with these guys?"

Stewart thought this over while the two of them sipped their tea in silence. Then he said, "Tell you what, John. Why don't I go up to see this Count. Flash my badge. They dare not refuse me entry. I'll tell them I'm checking on reports of a large amount of cash, etcetera."

"You want me to come with you?"

"No, I'd prefer to do it alone. I'll stop by and see you afterward."

The elevator doors opened at the top floor, and two burly guards barred Stewart's way, not allowing him step out of the elevator.

"Tell your boss the cops have arrived."

"Show me some ID," said one of the men coldly.

Stewart offered his badge. The man took it and disappeared down the hall. The other thug stuck a foot in the elevator door to stop it from closing.

A few moments later, the first man reappeared and beckoned to Stewart to follow him. When Stewart stepped into the suite, he quickly surveyed the room. Two men were playing chess at a table near the French window. A sultry blonde was sitting on the sofa,

reading a book. Light piano music played in the background. Count
Rimmon was seated at a desk writing a letter on hotel stationery.
He rose from his chair as Stewart entered and greeted him warmly,
shaking his hand and returning his badge.

"Ah, Detective Inspector Stewart, how good of you to call. Have a
seat and tell me how I can help you."

Stewart sat down. The others didn't seem to take any interest in
him. "Merely a routine visit. Our way of welcoming guests to our fair
town, you might say. The hotel manager deposited a large sum of cash
at the bank yesterday, which he received from your staff in payment
for your stay. Is that correct?"

"Why, yes. Have we done something wrong, Inspector? Mr.
Westwood seemed quite satisfied with the arrangement."

"No, I don't believe you've broken any laws. It is just that when
such a large amount of cash is deposited into a British bank, it tends to
set off alarms. Money laundering by foreign nationals is big business in
this country, I'm afraid."

"I see. In that case, I'm happy to explain of the provenance of the
money. The cash was withdrawn from Coutts, my bank in London,
after being transferred electronically from a bank in Switzerland. I can,
of course, provide copies of the transactions."

Stewart was fumbling in his overcoat pocket for his small
notebook and pen. He withdrew a pocket-sized New Testament and
laid it on the glass table. Every eye in the room was suddenly on him.

"What are you so assiduously searching for, Inspector?" Rimmon
asked politely.

"My notebook, sir. I just want to take a few notes."

"And what is that on the table?"

"It's a copy of the New Testament. I've recently become interested
in the Bible," Stewart said distractedly, still rummaging through his
pockets for the notebook, which he finally located in his inside vest pocket.

"The Bible? Really? How quaint. A book of myths and stories
more suited to children and the weak-minded than an intelligent man

like yourself. Much overvalued, I believe, and an anachronism in this modern world. Wouldn't you agree?"

"Excuse me, I guess I should have brought along a dictionary. Anachro-what?"

"Anachronism, Inspector. That is, belonging to another time."

"No, I don't agree. I've found it very interesting," Stewart replied with some conviction. He returned the Bible back to his overcoat pocket. "You are not a believer in God, then?"

"Oh, but I am! A passionate believer, but you must be careful not take as truth everything you see in print. There are always two sides to a story, and in this case, I and my associates subscribe to another version of events," Rimmon said cryptically.

"Well, I confess I'm pretty new at this, so I'm not sure what you mean. Perhaps I could continue with my questions?"

"Yes, of course."

"I don't think we need to see copies of your bank papers, sir, but thank you for offering. Can you explain why the hotel staff is not allowed to enter this floor to carry out their normal duties?"

"Perhaps you suspect felony where there is none. I am a very wealthy man, and I'm sure you will understand that a man in my position has enemies. That is why these dear friends travel with me, to protect my person and my interests. The reason for withholding entry to this floor from nonessential personnel is merely one of security. My own staff cleans the rooms, and I want for nothing."

"Apparently, you haven't ordered any food from the kitchens."

"Is that a crime? Again, a very simple explanation. I have a rare gastric disorder, and my food is specially prepared for me."

"And your men? I assume they have normal appetites?" Stewart asked with just a touch of sarcasm.

"They prefer to eat outside the hotel." Rimmon stood. "Now if you please, Inspector, this interview is becoming tiresome." One of the men playing chess rose from his chair and stood close to Stewart.

Stewart stood and put away his notebook. "One last question. I understand the Reverend Stannard visited you yesterday but looked poorly when leaving. Any particular reason why he should in worse condition than when he arrived?"

"Inspector, am I my brother's keeper? Should you not simply ask the Reverend Stannard yourself? Nevertheless, I will oblige you. Stannard came here to discuss business. He has some rare postage stamps to sell, and as a collector, I am interested in buying them. As for his health, he complained that he was suffering from the onset of influenza and, not wanting to catch anything myself, I terminated the meeting and asked that we reschedule another time."

Stewart shook Rimmon's hand. The Count's grip was ice cold. The detective looked into his eyes and saw animosity there, despite the polite manners.

On his way out of the hotel, Stewart described his meeting to Maxwell. Stewart had to admit that everything seemed above board and that there was nothing special to report.

"And the cameras?"

"I don't know, John. Perhaps they have some kind of jamming device."

"My best hope, then, is that they leave soon, and good riddance to them all. They're a queer bunch," said Maxwell.

"I agree. As for Rimmon himself, I would go so far as to say that there's something *evil* about the man. But what it is exactly is beyond me."

"Stop in for another cuppa sometime. I could do with the company. And I'll be sure to get you that information on the license plates."

Maxwell called Stewart a few hours later. "I don't know if this is going to help or hinder your inquiries, Paul, but my daughter recognized the script on the plates of the red Rolls-Royce. It's an old Sumerian language, apparently, and roughly translated means 'Hades' or 'Hell.' So I'm guessing our esteemed visitor has a nasty sense of humor. Maybe he's a big shot in a criminal underworld—though which underworld, I wouldn't like to speculate."

Paul didn't say a word in reply. He felt as if someone had just walked over his grave.

THIRTY-NINE

Samuel was sticking close by Richard Benton, ensuring that the enemy did not come near him. A great deal depended on the curate over the next few days. Richard and Sarah had labored day and night to organize the crusade, which was now only two days away. They had arranged all the logistics for the weekend and had attended several meetings with the various church leaders who had pledged to help. They had led prayer sessions across the town every night, often getting to bed in the wee hours of the morning, quite exhausted, only to rise early to start all over again.

The young couple had plenty of helpers, but even these people needed to be managed. Everyone needed to be told what to do and when to do it and what was to be done if something went wrong, such as some key individual not turning up. The bishop was most insistent on carrying out the arrangements to the letter. He was in the habit of saying, "If you get the little details right, then the Holy Spirit will take care of the rest." On top of everything else, Bishop Jeffries was expecting the enemy to do their worst to disrupt the proceedings, extending their mischief to even the mundane details like the electricity and lighting. "Have plenty of candles, matches, and flashlights on hand," he insisted repeatedly, "and make sure the batteries aren't dead. We don't want to end up in darkness now, do we? That would suit the enemy very nicely."

In truth, the planning and preparation were going well, making Richard the man of the hour. His reputation was growing by the day. He had become well respected in the town and beyond, where news of his prayer meetings had been received with excitement. Since his encounter with the Holy Spirit, Richard had begun to comprehend the tenets of Evan Roberts: First, confess all known sin; second, rid yourself of anything of dubious value in your life; third, be in constant readiness to obey the Spirit of God; and fourth, confess Christ openly and publicly to the world.

Some people were talking of another major revival in Wales. Richard himself was acutely aware of what was being talked about in the churches across the region, and knowing he had been irrevocably changed by the Spirit, he believed himself ready for whatever God had in store for him. His longtime dreams of saving souls were becoming a reality, though he would never have guessed as to the location of his missionary field.

Sarah busied herself marshaling the ladies of the churches, who were coordinating refreshments and counseling. Several teams were working to provide parking, security, and first aid, while those charged with welcoming guests were preparing themselves as well. The bishop had sent out personal invitations to many dignitaries and local politicians, and he was expecting them all to attend, such was his enthusiasm for the event.

Samuel was in awe of the effort, of the industry and hard work that went into each person's appointed tasks. He had never seen anything like it before. He was beginning to enjoy his posting on the earth and wondered whether, if called, he would want to return to the celestial choir. Shadowing Richard these past days had made him aware that humans in the service of God, though made of clay, were vitally important to the Lord's plans to usher in His kingdom. Samuel knew now that the unseen guardians of men had an extraordinary responsibility, and he felt a sudden, encompassing wave of pity flow over him for those fallen brothers who would never know the joy and wonder of the new Heaven and the new Earth.

The shortest route from Penrhos Bay to Conwy was to follow the railway. The line departed from the centre of town, traveling south for a mile or so, with the golf course on the left and the sea on the right. The track then curved gracefully, heading west before straightening out. As it neared Conwy, the line looked as if it were heading directly into the castle itself, but the railway began to decline gradually, disappearing into a wide tunnel cut right through the granite rock under the castle's foundations.

The castle had been the brainchild of master mason James of St. George, who worked for Edward I. Completed in 1285, Conwy Castle had never been captured by enemy forces. The castle was impregnable, a stone fortress with eight towers that overlooked the estuary, the river, and the land about. Connecting the towers were monumental stone walkways that soldiers could easily move along to meet an attack at any quarter. Edward had the castle fortifications built after fighting in the Holy Lands, where he had seen Crusader castles and noted how ingeniously they had been constructed to resist attacks and sieges. He applied this knowledge well.

The castle's layout meant that an entire army could be hidden there, a fact that Captain Bezalel used to his great advantage. Because the recent demonic activity had been centreed on Penrhos Bay and in the towns along the southern coast, he knew that Rimmon and his spies would not be watching Conwy. Indeed, only a few demons had been diverted to the area to make a quick reconnoiter but had seen nothing to report. As far as they were concerned, nothing came out of Conwy, good or bad. The river had silted up years ago, the local fishing industry had died, and the town's only revenue came from tourists visiting the medieval castle. They came, took their photographs, and moved on to the next stop on their itineraries.

The hour of the battle was fast approaching, and the captain was putting the final touches on his plans. He and his officers had already decided that their route into the heart of the enemy's territory would be along the railway. The hosts would drop into the dark tunnel under the castle and move at lightning speed, following the iron rails until they reached their destination. Rimmon's forces would be wreaking havoc in the town, thinking they were about to demolish the meager squad of angels guarding St. David's, when suddenly they would be overwhelmed by a tidal wave of angelic warriors.

Bezalel rolled up the maps and plans and announced to his faithful band of officers that all they had to do now was stand in readiness and wait for the call.

FORTY

Richard busied himself around the church, double- and triple-checking every last detail to make sure all was in readiness. He rushed over to Serena, who was standing talking with Sarah.

"Excuse me for interrupting. I just wanted to be certain you and Simon are happy with the sound system."

Serena said that everything was fine and he shouldn't worry.

"Good advice, Richard," Sarah said.

Serena made her apologies and went off to find Simon.

Sarah brushed a bit of lint off his coat lapels and gave him a reassuring smile. "Look, Richard, if you don't stop worrying, you will be the *cause* of something going wrong. Find a quiet place and spend a few moments in prayer. And ask God for a spirit of calm." She gave him a playful shove. "Go on."

"All right, then. I'll be upstairs. But come and get me if something happens."

"Richard!"

"All right, all right! I'm going."

Bishop Jeffries was talking to Simon on the stage when Serena came up and hugged them both. "I think something wonderful is going to happen tonight. I can feel it in my heart," she exclaimed.

The bishop had a look of excitement in his eyes. "My dear, I would expect nothing less with the two of you here."

Simon asked, "Are you sure Richard will be okay? He seems a bit anxious."

"Oh, he's a young man, and I think this is his first real stab at responsibility. But I knew the first time I laid eyes on him he was right for the job, and I think the Lord is going to raise him up in a remarkable way. Just mark my words."

"Well, there's no time like the present," Serena said. "Let's pray for Richard and ask that everything goes according to God's plans."

They formed a circle, arms around each other's shoulders, bowed their heads, and prayed.

A few minutes later, one of the people assigned to the door came running up the nave. "I think you should all come and see this," he said, and then ran back toward the doors. "Come on!" he shouted.

The bishop glanced at his companions as if to say, *What's this all about?*

Loud voices could be heard coming from outside the church. Someone threw open the doors, and Serena put a hand over her mouth in an expression of pure glee and laughed. Simon and the bishop exchanged glances and stood on the threshold, quite dumbfounded. Outside were hundreds of people waiting to enter. The queue went down the path and disappeared around the corner of the church.

"Hey, bishop! Aren't you going to let us in?" someone shouted good-naturedly.

Sarah arrived, and seeing the crowds, gasped. "I think I should get Richard."

The bishop made a grand gesture with his hands and, bowing before the mass of people, cried out, "Welcome, my friends! Right this way!"

Richard arrived and saw the mass of visitors pushing up the nave and into the pews. "But it's not time yet!" he said, looking at his watch.

Sarah smiled at him. "Well I guess you'll just have to ask them to leave and come back in fifteen minutes."

Richard grabbed her by the elbow and pulled her aside. "It happened," he blurted. "Just now, when I was upstairs."

"Really?" She threw her arms about her husband.

"I was just praying normally when I felt the Spirit take hold of me. The next minute I was praising God in this wonderful, strange language. It was like a taste of things to come beyond death."

Richard and Sarah both shed a tear in this, their last private moment before the crusade.

Outside the church, hundreds of angry demons were attempting to gain entry in hopes of disrupting the event. They loosed wave upon wave of fiery darts and arrows at the angelic guard, but the Lord's host, wearing full battle armor, wielded great shields to protect themselves from the onslaught. The devils cried out loathsome obscenities and blasphemies, hoping to goad the angels into leaving their post. Once in a while, one of the demons rushed headlong to engage an angel face to face but was quickly dispatched to the pit of fire by the sharp two-edged sword of the defender. Even more foolhardy were the devils who tried to breach the main door, where there stood two great cherubim in armor. These were the same angels who guarded the gates to the Garden of Eden after Adam and Eve were expelled. The huge swords they held aloft were perpetually alight with fire. Those hapless demons who tried to engage the cherubim were instantly destroyed in a flash of light.

Many of the demons were tasked with influencing the men and women waiting to enter the church. The fiends whispered all kinds of arguments, sowing doubt among the guests as to why they had come in the first place. Demons cajoled and threatened, but nothing seemed to work. Neither subtlety nor coarse means had any effect, as if an invisible force were keeping the humans immune from such odious entreaties.

Trying another tack, a squad of demons possessed a crowd of noisy drunken youths who happened by. The youths then jumped over the church wall and began to scream and shout at the lines of people. But the bishop had foreseen that this kind of thing might happen and had requested the presence of peacekeepers from the local constabulary. Detective Inspector Stewart and several of Penrhos Bay's finest were congregated behind the church, keeping a low profile until needed.

The police emerged from around the corner of the church like a band of marauding soldiers. Within minutes, those thugs who had not fled in fright had been overpowered, handcuffed, and bundled into police wagons. The people in line cheered and clapped as the last youth was secured and peace restored.

The demons were becoming distraught, seeing that none of Rimmon's machinations had proved effective.

Rimmon was watching from across the street, atop a high building, with Ganymede at his side. "This is too painful to watch, Ganymede. It's a debacle. Your plans are failing miserably!"

Ganymede thought, *My plans, indeed! Why is it I am always to blame?*

"At least Gathan can be trusted to deliver," Rimmon said irritably. "He will arrive soon with the body of the child, and that should put an end to this spectacle."

FORTY-ONE

Jezebel sat on the bed next to the child. She was nervous and tired. She checked her watch for the tenth time. Gathan had said he would be there to pick up the child an hour ago. He was going to take the girl and place her safely at the back of the town supermarket. Then Jezebel was to go to the police station and say that she had seen her whereabouts in a trance, directing the police to the location only a few streets away. Jezebel's heroics would be front-page news, and everything would end well.

She looked at her watch again and then down at Emily sleeping. The child was pale and looking thin. Jezebel wondered how the child's mother must be coping. She had never had children of her own, but she could imagine the pain Melanie must be going through. She was cheered by the fact that in a short while it would all be over and the mother and child would be reunited.

The air in the apartment turned cold, and suddenly Gathan stood before her in his true demonic form. Jezebel recoiled in horror at his gruesome appearance.

"Stand aside, woman. I am here for the child!" Gathan shouted.

Jezebel trembled, but something deep inside told her to stand her ground. "What are you going to do with her, lord?" she asked, her voice breaking.

"What do you think? I am Gathan the *Destroyer*. Fool of a hag! I have amused myself with you long enough."

His hot breath blasted her face. She withdrew onto the bed, trying to distance herself from this hideous creature.

"You think you have power?" he snorted. "You are nothing but my slave, my puppet. Even so, if you were younger and prettier, I might spare you from death. But I have no further use for you."

"Stay back!" she screamed. "Go back to hell where you belong!"

Gathan laughed uproariously. "I am going to crush your skull in my claws and feed your body to the rats. Then I shall take pleasure in extinguishing the life from this little doll and discarding her remains outside the crusade."

Jezebel threw her body over the child to protect her. Gathan mocked her cruelly and, laughing derisively, showered her with obscene profanities. He took a step toward her and was just about to pull Jezebel off the child when a great crash behind him made him spin around.

Standing before him was Samuel, his armor shining brighter than the sun.

Gathan cried, "What is this? A youth in toy armor? Come for another beating, have you? Is this all your God can muster, a puny choirboy?"

Samuel stood resolute. "I am here for the child, Gathan. Step aside or meet your doom."

"Ha! You jest with me!" Gathan towered over Samuel by at least three feet, his body as solid as iron, his muscles black as ebony, and his fanged teeth now dripping with saliva as the battle heat overtook him. He leapt forward, but Samuel darted to the side, sending Gathan sprawling over the furniture, shattering glass ornaments and spraying trinkets across the room. Jezebel bundled the child into her arms and ran for the bathroom, locking the door once inside.

Gathan turned his hateful eyes upon Samuel. "I am going tear you apart, angel! You will cry out for your God, but He will not come to your aid." Again, he sprang forward, this time knocking Samuel aside with such force that the angel hit the wall with a sickening thud. He had only a moment to restore himself as Gathan lunged forward once more. Samuel managed to swing his body to the right and in so doing avoided the monster's clutches.

The demon turned slowly and faced Samuel. "So we play games, eh? You run and hide, and I chase. Is that it?" Gathan's gaze was fixed upon slaughter of the angel. The demon crouched low, his body stiffening with awful power. He was like a savage beast, a lion about to spring upon his prey.

Preparing himself to withstand a mighty blow, Samuel heard a voice whisper, *"Let him come."* Gathan sprang upward and crashed into Samuel with such terrible force that the momentum carried both of them through the wall and into the street. Shards of brick, timber, and glass fell onto the hard paving below. The combatants spiraled through the air, but it was Gathan who took the brunt of the impact as they thudded onto the concrete. He gasped for breath, momentarily winded, and Samuel pulled himself free.

Hearing the commotion, three demons who had been creating havoc of their own sort nearby, rushed to see what was going on. Spying Gathan flat on his back and confronted by a single, puny angel, the demons' first impulse was to laugh and mock the fallen demon, but knowing what Gathan was capable of, they thought better of it. Instead, they sped to Gathan's aid, grabbed Samuel from behind, and were about to dispatch him when Gathan shouted, "Hold, curs!"

Gathan rose up to one knee, speaking with rage, "Stay your hand, or you will regret your actions. This one is mine."

Rising up to his full stature, Gathan withdrew his sword from its sheath and brandished it above his head. "I will carve you into little pieces so that the crows of the morning will have something to eat." The demons released the angel and fled.

Samuel reached over his shoulder and withdrew the sword that the Spirit of the Lord had given him.

"Aha!" Gathan grinned. "The child has a knife, but I think it is for slicing apples and sticking grapes!"

He came at Samuel with surprising speed. All Samuel could do was leap aside. When the demon's mighty sword clashed with his, Samuel felt the vibration run through his body, shaking him to the core. The next attack came as swiftly as the first, but this time Samuel was ready and braced himself to parry Gathan's blows. The unearthly sounds of battle reverberated along the narrow street, and Gathan's war cries intensified the violence of the deadly duel.

Gathan's physical power was immense, and Samuel knew he could not win on that score. Only his speed and agility kept him alive as the demon thrust his sword at the angel's vulnerable points. Time and again Samuel managed to dodge the fierce strike of his enemy, but he felt himself beginning to tire.

Samuel parried a blow weakly, and Gathan drew breath and smiled as if knowing his quarry was done for. Samuel prayed silently, *Lord, I need your help. Come to my aid.*

As the gargantuan demon raised his sword to strike the fatal blow, Samuel's own sword began to shine with such brilliance that it dispelled the darkness of the night. Gathan swung his sword in a deadly arc, intending to part Samuel's head from his shoulders, but the sudden light blinded him and his sword whistled cleanly over Samuel's head. In the same instant Samuel sidestepped the bulk of the demon and thrust his own sword deep into Gathan's left breast.

Gathan's huge sword fell from his grasp and clattered noisily onto the concrete. His right hand went to the wound in his side. His gaze drifted to Samuel. A terrible look of disbelief passed over the demon's ashen face as annihilation took him to the pit. Gathan's form disappeared from the face of the earth, never to return.

Placing his sword back into its scabbard, Samuel knelt to thank God for his victory. Rising high above the building, he sang out a victory cheer that resonated across the town and beyond. Demons nearby heard the angel's cry of triumph and trembled at the sound.

Turning, Samuel made his way back to Jezebel's apartment where he assumed human form. He pried open the door to the bathroom and there found Jezebel crouched upon the floor in the corner, still trembling but still shielding the child with her own body. Samuel knelt beside her. Stroking her hair, he said in gentle tones, "Come, Grace, let us go. There is nothing to fear now."

FORTY-TWO

Bezalel was waiting patiently with his captains and lieutenants on the highest tower of the castle when he heard Samuel's call come as clear as a bell ringing through the night air. The captain addressed his valiant troops in a loud voice that echoed around the castle walls. "Angels, do your duty and flinch not in the face of the enemy. They have chosen a dark path with Lucifer, but Satan shall not prevail! I desire nothing more than to see this town rid of his pestilence. Show no mercy. Stand tall, for when God is with us, none can defeat us!'"

There was a great cheer from the angelic host.

Turning to his officers, he said, "Give the order. Let us go to war!"

The vanguard of the angelic army surged forward into the railway tunnel, heading swiftly toward Penrhos Bay. Hundreds and then thousands of battle-hardened warriors of Christ now hurtled along the track, keeping low to the ground so as not to warn the enemy of the deadly force approaching their position. By the time the front line of soldiers had turned the bend by the river's edge, Bezalel had caught up with them and was leading the charge.

No sound was heard upon the air as Bezalel and the vanguard arrived at the railway station arch, passed through, and scattered in all directions to catch the enemy unaware. Behind them came the bulk of the angelic force, and bringing up the rear were splendid cherubim astride white stallions that flew high into the night sky, ready to fall upon their prey like hawks swooping down for a kill. Everything profane on this night would know the full weight and power of the heavenly host.

All about the town demons suddenly realized they were under attack by a formidable force. Fear seized their hearts as it seemed the warriors of Heaven had appeared out of nowhere. After the initial shock, captains of the demon horde tried desperately to rally their troops, ordering their underlings to regroup and resist. But as soon a group of demons managed to form a defense, hundreds of angels swept down upon them and slew them without mercy, consigning each to the pit of Hell.

"Master!" Ganymede screeched. "We must flee!"

Rimmon looked to the skies and saw two terrifying beasts bearing down upon them. "Satan save us!" he cried in abject fear.

Rimmon and Ganymede wasted not a moment before vanishing into the deepest dark.

The two horsemen reared up, and pulling on the reins, turned their steeds to seek other prey, too late to catch the arch-demons.

Bezalel and his forces were engaged in skirmishes all over the town. On the rooftops, in the alleyways, and on the byroads, the angels quickly vanquished their foes. Thousands of demons had already been dispatched to the pit of judgment, but the angels of heaven gave no quarter, seeing to it that none should survive the battle.

Bezalel cried out to the passing cherubim astride their gleaming stallions, "Benjamin, Aster! Any sight of Rimmon or Ganymede?"

"Yes, they have flown."

"Pity! I was hoping to meet my old adversaries face to face."

The seraphim rode on, having spied a group of escaping devils. They harried them across the sea and on into the dark night.

Bezalel rose high above the town to see how the battle fared. Three of his guards kept pace with him. All across the town demons were fleeing, chased by warrior angels in close pursuit.

Meanwhile, under the Great Ulm, several brutish demons fought hard to prevent a squad of angels gaining entry to Rimmon's cavern.

"You shall not pass!" shouted the massive demon guard at the head of the formation.

An angel, showing no fear, lunged forward to silence the demon, but as he advanced a large arrow came whistling out of the dark. The arrow struck the angel full in the chest, piercing his armor. The angel cried out in pain, and his legs crumpled under him. As several angels jumped over his form to finish the job their brother had begun, two other angels came to the aid of their fallen comrade. As the attackers came abreast of the lead demon, they leapt as one and simultaneously fell upon the brute, their swords plunging deep into the demon's form. He immediately vanished in a cloud of sulfurous smoke.

Seeing this, the second rank of demons turned and ran, screaming like banshees, but their retreat was in vain. There would be no escape for them. In a short space of time the deed was done. As the last demon disappeared en route to Hell, the company of angels gave a great cheer.

Bezalel, searching the main thoroughfare, saw Samuel in human form walking towards St. David's Church with a woman at his side. He bore a small female child in his arms. From the church Bezalel could hear praises being sung to Almighty God.

FORTY-THREE

Though a spectacular battle had been waged by spiritual forces in the skies over Penrhos, the inhabitants of the town were for the most part ignorant of the tumultuous struggle. A full six hundred of the town's citizens could be found at St. David's, where every available space for sitting or standing was filled. People sat in the nave and in the aisles, content to squat or sit cross-legged on the floor after all the seats had been taken.

Sitting in the front row were Paul Stewart, Rosina Padelski, and Melanie O'Reilly. Rosina had persuaded Melanie to come, although the mother was understandably still very emotional and sorely depressed at the loss of her precious daughter. She needed comfort in these hours of anguish.

Stewart listened intently to Simon and Serena as they gave their testimony, describing the height of their stardom when they were recognized on the streets and had so much money in the bank they didn't know how to spend it all. The glitz and the glamor and the celebrity status, Simon explained, had left them both surprisingly unfulfilled and searching for real meaning. Stewart recognized elements in their story that corresponded to his own thoughts over the past few weeks, and he began to understand what he needed to do next.

When Serena announced a thirty-minute refreshment break, Stewart headed for the door to get some air.

Samuel and Jezebel were just coming through the covered lychgate at the end of the path leading from the church. To Samuel's surprise, the path to the church entrance was lined on either side by dozens of his comrades. There were angels on the roof of the church and on the tall tower, perched on nearby buildings, hanging out of trees, and standing all along the perimeter wall. The illumination radiating from the host chased away the darkness and made the night seem as day.

Samuel hesitated at the gate. He turned to Jezebel with tears in his eyes. "Ma'am, I wish you could see what I see!"

"Perhaps she can—just this one time." Bezalel now stood beside them both. He placed his hands upon Jezebel's shoulders and made a silent request.

Immediately, her eyes were opened, and she saw the host of angels. Her face shone with wonder, and she gasped. "Samuel, this is . . . magical!"

"No, Jezebel. Not magical. Just heavenly."

Samuel proceeded to carry the child, who was beginning to stir from her long slumber, to the entrance of the church.

Paul Stewart emerged from the church in time to see Samuel with the child and Jezebel walk up the path. He thought nothing of it at first until Samuel stopped and spoke to him.

"Inspector Stewart, this is the missing child, Emily O'Reilly. Would you please take her to her mother?"

Samuel gently passed the child into Stewart's hands. The detective was dumbstruck.

Samuel turned and gazed into Jezebel's eyes.

She beamed back at him. "Thank you, Samuel, for saving Emily. I have seen more good this night than in the whole of my sorry life."

Samuel embraced her tenderly. "You were very brave in the face of much evil. Please tell the mother that her daughter was not harmed and will have no memory of this episode in her life."

Bezalel then spoke kindly to Jezebel. "You had better go inside. You will have to try to explain to the police how the child came to be reunited with her mother. They will probably think you mad. But stay here tonight with these good people, and you will be blessed." As he turned to go, he hesitated and said to Jezebel, "I think it's time you start using your given name, Grace."

Grace took one last look at the gathering of angels, trying to imprint the scene and every detail onto her memory. Slowly, the image began to fade until her world took precedence once more.

Inside, Melanie O'Reilly heard someone at the back of the church crying her daughter's name, but she couldn't see anything past the mass of people. She climbed onto the pew to get a better view and spied Stewart carrying Emily, who was now fully awake and shouting happily for her mother. Rosina grabbed hold of Melanie, propelling her down the nave toward Emily. Stewart stopped and without saying a word passed the little girl into her mother's waiting arms. Melanie was wailing tears of joy, and Emily hugged her mother with all her might. Rosina dropped to her knees and started to cry, which set off many of the people gathered around them, until it seemed everyone was bawling his or her eyes out.

The news of Emily's return spread through the church like a wildfire in a dry forest. Bishop Jeffries found Melanie and Emily at the centre of the throng. He knelt down beside them and said to Melanie, "You must be the happiest mother alive." Standing, he turned to the crowd of onlookers. "Okay, let's all return to our seats and give them some breathing space. We'll get started again shortly."

As the crowd began to disperse, Stewart managed to pull Grace aside. "You and I need to have a little talk. You have a lot of explaining to do concerning the mysterious return of the little girl. But I guess it can wait until the end of the service."

"Yes. I do have a story to tell, but I don't know if you're going to believe any of it," Grace replied.

"Indeed," Stewart said. "You might be surprised."

FORTY-FOUR

Dignitaries from all over the region had been invited to attend the crusade on Saturday night, regardless of their faith or denomination. The bishop had personally contacted members of the British and Welsh parliaments, the heads of multinational corporations, and personalities from the worlds of sports and entertainment. It remained to be seen who would actually accept the invitation.

Angels patrolled the town in large numbers, but there was no visible sign of demonic activity in the vicinity. The angelic victory had been a complete rout, and Bezalel was glad to be rid of Rimmon's presence. The cherubim had returned to Heaven with their flaming swords, their work here done.

Samuel stood alone atop the church tower, thinking on the events of the past weeks and days. Only a short time ago, he had been dismissed from the heavenly choir, and now he was being treated by God's own warriors as a hero. The Lord had given him the sword of truth when He could easily have chosen a stronger, more experienced angel for the honor rather than a novice like himself. Yet he knew that God often chose the weak to confound and overcome the strong and powerful. The Old Testament was full of such stories, including the shepherd boy David slaying the blasphemous giant Goliath with a single stone and a sling.

After the initial furor surrounding Melanie and Emily had died down, the bishop had preached a sermon of repentance and forgiveness, and more than five hundred men and women came forward to accept Christ as their Lord and Savior. There were so many souls seeking Christ that the bishop was quite overwhelmed. Richard and Simon had stayed by his side throughout the night to help lead these new saints in prayer.

The next afternoon, reports poured in of the Holy Spirit's bringing other souls to Christ. Crowds of people had come knocking on the locked doors of churches all over town, desperately seeking spiritual guidance. By midnight, ministers across Penrhos Bay found their pews full of people wanting to know more about Jesus. In one extraordinary instance, about forty people, including many young people, had congregated outside the police station. When the sergeant on duty came out to investigate the ruckus, the people on the steps demanded that he bring out a Christian policeman to minister to them. He returned with Constable Colin Knightley, and led by the Spirit, the constable preached about Christ right there under the blue lamp, in uniform and all. Not one of those who were gathered in front of the station refused the call, and to the officer's utter amazement they all knelt and worshiped God.

Bishop Jeffries listened to these stories and could only express wonder at the power of God. "What shall we expect tonight?" he asked, looking at the small group gathered with him.

"More miracles, I should think," Richard said.

"Let's pray, shall we?" the bishop urged.

The dignitaries began arriving in black limousines and trendy hybrid cars and were escorted into the church by stewards. The bishop greeted each arrival personally, thanking them profusely for coming and supporting the crusade, even though many clearly saw this as a social affair and not a religious function. The inevitable photographers snapped shots of celebrities standing beside Simon and Serena with their arms about their shoulders, trying to make it look as if they'd been friends for years.

Richard opened the evening with a brief prayer before Simon and Serena took the platform and performed a few of their hits from the Eighties. By the time the first break came around, the audience was thoroughly enthralled and entertained by the charismatic duo.

At the break, the bishop motioned to Richard to follow him outside. "Richard, my boy, take a look at those stars! How brightly they shine, as if the skies have been cleared of Satan's polluting influence." The bishop put an arm around Richard. "I wanted to tell you how much I appreciate all your hard work in making this event a success." Richard was about to say something, but the bishop held up his hand. "Credit where credit's due, Richard. You've earned it. You and your lovely wife Sarah are just what this parish needs, and I have decided to appoint you vicar. I hope you will accept the posting."

"I don't what to say, sir. I never expected a reward, and I never had a vicarage in mind at all."

"I know that, and that's why I have so much confidence you will do me proud. Will Sarah agree to the appointment?"

Richard smiled. "Oh, I think she'll be ecstatic."

"Then let us shake on it. Reverend Richard Benton, welcome to your church."

At that moment, a lonely figure walking along the street turned into the church grounds. It was Jonas Silth, the petty thief who months ago had attempted to rob the poor box at St. David's. Richard and the bishop watched him approach and noticed that there was something quite odd about his manner.

Silth walked straight up to them and spit in their faces. He shouted, "Ha, I see you! I know who you both are! Gloating over your victories! Destroyers of the fallen! Where is the mercy of the Lord when He judges and condemns the sons of Lucifer?"

The bishop stepped in front of Richard to confront the man as he continued sputtering profanities. Richard was unsure what to do.

Silth pushed his face right into the bishop's and, calling him obscene names, grabbed the bishop and tried to wrestle him to the ground.

But the bishop was a strong man and resisted. "Be quiet! I command you!"

Silth laughed derisively. "Who are you to command us?"

"Richard, this man is possessed," the bishop shouted. "Take hold of him now!"

Grabbing an arm each, they tried hard to secure the man, but Silth struggled and freed himself. Whatever possessed this unfortunate man was powerful indeed.

Silth's voice changed in an instant, becoming deeper, coarser, and more menacing. "Our lord will not be defeated! He will return to this cesspit and claim his rights. He will enslave these puny people once more, mark my words!"

The bishop said, "In the name of Jesus Christ, I command you to tell me who you are."

Silth recoiled and his body contorted in painful agony. The voice inside was tremulous now. "We shall not pay heed to you, churchman. We will not obey your words."

The bishop repeated, "In the name of Jesus Christ, I command you to tell me who you are."

The words came out of Silth's mouth broken and sharply separated. "We. Are. Legion!"

From behind the bishop and Richard, another figure approached in the darkness, using the dark shadows to remain hidden from sight. It was Stannard, and he carried the loaded pistol Rimmon had given him.

"Now is your opportunity," barked Silth. "Do not fail us!"

Stannard edged closer, his hand shaking. He raised the gun and placed his finger on the trigger.

From above, Samuel was ready to spring upon Stannard to upset his aim, but Bezalel placed his hand on his companion's arm and restrained him. "This time, it is not our fight. Let us trust in God."

The bishop was addressing the demons. "In the name of the Father, the Son, and the Holy Spirit, I command you, come out!"

Silth threw himself to the ground, writhing in agony as if having a seizure. His hands clutched desperately at his head as if trying to contain something writhing inside him.

The bishop leaned over Silth and once more abjured the demons to depart. "Be gone from this man, I say!"

"Do not send us into the void!" Many voices now screamed from inside Silth. "Give us another soul to inhabit. Mercy! Be merciful, O Great One!"

"Be gone, I tell you!"

The poor man's body shook and quaked, and then his mouth opened impossibly wide. From inside him came an evil stench, and a dark vapor issued forth which seemed to contain hideous forms in its very essence.

The disembodied demons spied Stannard and flew past the bishop and entered the disgraced vicar. Stannard squeezed the trigger, but the gun fired upward as he was thrown back by the force that entered his body. His head crashed down upon the hard concrete, killing him instantly, the gun still in his hand. Blood began to ooze slowly from his scalp.

The demons had chosen ill, for now their only recourse was to take hold of Stannard's screaming soul and transport him straight to the netherworld.

At the sound of the gunshot, several people came running from inside the church.

Silth lay still upon the ground. As his eyes slowly opened, he saw Richard kneeling over him. The bishop had rushed over to where Stannard lay in the hope that he could help the man, but it was too late. The bishop removed his coat and placed it over the vicar's head. He said, "Someone telephone the emergency services for an ambulance, will you please? Tell them someone has been killed. I'll stay with the body until the emergency people arrive. Everyone else, please go back inside the church."

The bishop went to where Richard was helping Silth to his feet. The man seemed confused and dazed, but appeared to remember nothing of the incident.

"What's your name, friend?" the bishop asked.

"It's . . . er . . . Jonas. Jonas Silth. Am I under arrest, sir? I swear I didn't take the money. I put it all back!"

"Arrest? What on earth for?." The bishop turned to Richard. "He's in shock, I should think. Richard, your first duty as vicar of St. David's is to take this unfortunate fellow and give him a hot mug of tea and plenty of cake."

Richard took Silth's arm and led him away.

The bishop looked towards the heavens and said a silent prayer of thanks to God for saving his life, though his heart was grieved at the death of Sidney Stannard.

EPILOGUE

Detective Inspector Stewart had already been to church and arranged to meet Rosina and Sasha for lunch at the Castle Hotel. Since he had given life to Jesus Christ, he'd felt differently about a lot of things. He had even entertained the idea of sparking up a romantic relationship. With Janet? With Rosina? He was almost old enough to be their father. Besides, he wanted to wait and see what else he might do with his life. It sounded crazy, but he felt that God had something for him to do.

He had an hour to spare, so he walked over to St. David's. Along the way he considered the demise of Sydney Stannard, the late vicar. Stewart admitted to himself that he couldn't feel any sympathy for the man. From what Bishop Jeffries and Richard Benton had told him about Jonas Silth and his "possession" by demons, he wondered if there was something more to the incident. Now looking down at the bloodstained concrete, he convinced himself that Stannard must have slipped just as he was about to assassinate the bishop. Had God intervened at just the right moment, or was it simply an accident and entirely coincidental? Stewart strolled to the opposite side of the church and stopped at the spot where Maynard Jones had met his end. He scratched his head, still stumped. Then he became aware that someone was standing behind him. He turned quickly to find a smart young man smiling at him.

"Can I help you?" Stewart asked.

"More to the point, I think it's how I can help you, Inspector," Samuel said kindly.

"Wait a minute. I know you, don't I? You're the man who handed Emily to me at the crusade." Then Stewart's face clouded over. "But Grace claimed an angel helped her that night."

Samuel simply nodded. "That was me. And I have been given permission to enlighten you. God does not want you to live in darkness, Paul. Please take my hand."

Stewart felt a trifle foolish as he reached out to take hold of the young man's hand, but as soon as his flesh touched the angel the world around him disappeared and day suddenly became night.

He found himself suspended in mid-air high above the church tower. What he saw below astonished him. A violent struggle was taking place between two fantastic beings that he could only guess were a demon and an angel. Stewart could see that the angel was no match for his larger opponent, but still he fought valiantly to wrest from the demon a human captive. The man in the demon's grasp was the late curate, Maynard Jones. Then angel was brutally cast aside, and at that moment the demon dropped his captive. Stewart heard the angel cry out in despair, and he saw Jones plummet to the ground. He looked away before the body impacted the earth.

Then the vision shifted. It was night still, and Stewart saw Richard Benton and the bishop frantically trying to overpower Jonas Silth outside the church. As he watched, Stannard stealthily emerged from the shadows and pointed a gun at the bishop's exposed back. What he saw next troubled his own spirit. He watched in horror as the hideous creatures that had possessed Silth flew screeching out of his prone body and rushed straight into Stannard, causing him to jolt backwards in terror. The gun fired harmlessly into the air.

Stewart turned to speak to Samuel, but the angel had gone. Stewart was alone again, standing once more on the church pathway in the midday sunshine. Now he knew without doubt that the spiritual realm was a terrifying reality. But what of himself? Where did he stand? Suddenly, Stewart felt as if something wonderful was pressing in all around him, and he knew then that he had to make a choice to know more of God personally or live the rest of his days in unbelief. He didn't need his notebook to figure it out this time. He knew what he had to do.

Bezalel and Samuel sat on the roof of the church, looking out at the Sunday shoppers. Samuel asked, "What will happen to Grace for her part in the kidnapping of the child?"

"God's grace covers a multitude of sins," Bezalel replied. "She may or may not be brought to account for her part in the affair but she has seen the error of her ways and given her life to Christ."

Samuel's serious expression reflected his thoughts. "She told me that she would prefer to burn the New Age centre to the ground but will have to be content to just shut-up the place take everything to the town dump."

"That is good."

"And the Inspector, sir, what of him?"

"He has a long journey ahead of him still. But the insight you've given him will pave the way to greater understanding. And he will receive help from the Holy Spirit every day from now on." Bezalel turned to Samuel and said, "As for you, you are to continue guarding Richard and Sarah. Much responsibility will be placed on their shoulders in the years to come. They will know triumph but also much tragedy, I am afraid." Bezalel's face darkened with sorrow. "And you can be certain Rimmon will not let this town remain in our control without another fight. But we shall be ready for him."

"To be sure we will, my captain."

Neither spoke for a while as they watched the townspeople go about their business.

Then Bezalel patted Samuel on the back. "By the way, I have decided to give you a promotion. Henceforth, you shall be known as Lieutenant Samuel, angel warrior first class."

Samuel whirled around and spun into the sky, singing at the top of his incomparable voice.

Later that night it snowed, and a thick blanket of white covered everything. The light from the moon caused the snow crystals to sparkle with an icy brilliance, as if God had given a sign that the dark things of the town had been made good again and were now unblemished, pure as newly fallen snow.

The End

AUTHOR'S NOTES

A number of the scenes portrayed in this story are based upon fact. The incident involving Richard and Sarah watching the sky and asking God for a shooting star really happened to the author and his wife. The brightest, most beautiful shooting star darted across the heavens, and we heard it *whoosh* as it traversed the night sky. Mere coincidence?

The scene in which a crowd of people outside the police station, calling for a Christian policeman to come out and lead them to salvation, occurred during the Scottish Revival of 1949–1953. For more information about this happening and the South Wales Revival of 1904, simply interrogate any good internet search engine.

Also, I can personally attest to the astounding incident in which a group of pastors, who had known each other for many years, but did not fellowship with each other because of their ingrained religious differences, encountered the Holy Spirit on the eve of a crusade. It happened in Connecticut in the United States in 1988, and I was in attendance at that extraordinary event. The elder pastor of the town told me privately afterward, "It's just like God to bring a man from another country, an Englishman, to shine a light on our darkness.

That was your mission. That's why you were brought here—to bring us back to God. It might not have happened without you."

F. John Hurr
Colchester, Essex
United Kingdom

25 November 2014

The second book in the series entitled '**Light of the Holy**' will be published by XLIBRIS in the summer of 2015. To whet your appetite here is chapter one.

Light of the Holy – Chapter One

Rimmon waited with much fear and trembling and more than a little resentment. He was sore afraid, having been summoned by his lord and master. To be commanded to appear before the mighty one was indeed a great honor—or a great disgrace. In light of his recent failure, Rimmon knew why he was here. His feelings of dread were well founded, for many were called to Satan's private chambers, but few emerged alive and well. Rimmon knew the lord of Hell showed little or no interest in his subordinates, and no one demon had special access to Satan or was ever shown favor for long. The Dark Lord had no use for the bickering and infighting of his sycophantic horde for he was at all times preoccupied with thoughts of vengeance. Ever since his ignominious expulsion from Heaven's courts, Satan had busied himself plotting the fall of his enemy and all those who worshiped Him. Elohim had found rebellion in the heart of Lucifer and cast him down into the outermost regions, to abide there in darkness until summoned. Satan now was bent on one thing, and one thing only: to usurp the throne of God.

Where there was love, he would sow hate. Where there was faith, he would sow doubt and unbelief. Where there was hope, he would sow despair. Where there was light, he would sow darkness. And where there was life among God's followers, Satan would gladly bring death. Havoc and disaster, torment and pain, lust and greed—these were the tools of his trade. His one abiding aim was to corrupt and destroy all that God called good. To this end he plotted, labored day and night, age upon age, to set himself free from the yoke of God and assume lordship over all.

Prince Rimmon was fully aware he was nothing more than a pawn in Satan's plans. He had long served as one of Satan's commanders on the earth, but his future now appeared grim, for Rimmon's forces had suffered a humiliating defeat in a nothing of a Welsh backwater. The debacle had almost led to his own capture by an old friend and longtime adversary. Rimmon wracked his brain, struggling to understand why his foe had been so eager to protect that insignificant little cesspit of a town. Penrhos Bay was a miserable dunghill with a scattering of only a few men and women loyal to God. Why? Why?

As Rimmon waited in the antechamber, he fumed, deploring the fact that his lieutenant Ganymede had not also been summoned. He should be here to stand alongside Rimmon and face the wrath of the Prince of Darkness. After all, losing the battle had been Ganymede's fault entirely. Rimmon had trusted his friend and ally to carry out the battle plans to the letter. If Ganymede had done as he had been instructed, victory would have been assured. It was Ganymede's incompetence—and, of course, that oaf Gathan's lack of cunning—that had led to their defeat. He sincerely hoped that Gathan was this very moment immersed in the unquenchable fire suffering agonizing punishment in the place reserved for the enemies of God. Rimmon felt no pity for him whatsoever.

Now that Rimmon was to stand before his lord, should he attempt to place the blame on Ganymede and Gathan and thus assuage his own complicity in the defeat? He pondered this strategy. Perhaps even now he could save his own skin by incriminating his lieutenants. This thought intrigued him momentarily but was quickly dispelled. Satan would see through that subterfuge straightaway. Rimmon sighed deeply. He knew he alone would bear the blame, for he was standing in Satan's court and they were not.

Then another thought came to mind. Perhaps he could salvage the situation by simply accepting full responsibility for the failure at Penrhos Bay. What if he stood tall and take his punishment honorably? After all, he had served Satan well for many centuries. There was a possibility his master would be merciful. Yet as Rimmon thought this through, he couldn't stop his hands from shaking. His lord was called Satan, a name given him after the great schism. The very name meant "the accuser."

Rimmon felt dreadfully sick in the pit of his stomach. He had the urge to vomit but fought it back. He felt faint and steadied himself by leaning against the wall. These may well be his final minutes before annihilation.

Two great, ugly demons stood guard outside the throne room. They stared at Rimmon with pitiless eyes, clearly tasting his apprehension and smelling his fear. They were enjoying every moment. Each demon held a large curved scimitar raised high to bar entrance to the chamber. The massive doors to Satan's inner apartment were crafted from precious metals mined from the depths of the Earth. Satan plundered freely, stealing indiscriminately from the world's resources, always diminishing precious metals and jewels. He stripped the forests bare and laid the green places waste. He was strangling nature, slowly, inexorably extinguishing the very life of the planet.

Ostentatious gems studded the framework of the doorway in intricate designs cruelly crafted from diamonds, emeralds, rubies, and pearls. The sins of the flesh and symbols of evil were set intaglio into the hard fabric. These were sculpted and cut from ivory and bone, taken from animals long vanished from the earth. The door handles were gold and silver, fashioned as ripened fruit like that found in the Garden of Eden, site of Satan's greatest victory. Torches burned bright on each side of the doors, illuminating the space about the guards while, just a few yards away, Rimmon stood disconsolate in the shadows.

Then from beyond the doors came a discordant melody, haunting music made by flute, pipe, and voice. Rimmon listened intently, straining his ears to hear the strange melody that emanated from within Satan's inner sanctum. As the music played on, the doors slowly opened. The guards stepped aside and, lowering their swords, bade him enter. Stepping forward as the condemned to the scaffold, Rimmon halted for a moment upon the threshold and bowed low his head, his fear growing.

"Rimmon, you may approach," the Dark Lord's voice beckoned.

The doors behind Rimmon closed shut. There was no escape, for he was now alone with the terrible god of this age.

Strange music filled the vast room. Rimmon looked around but saw neither musicians nor singers. There was a fragrance in the air, an exquisite perfume, full of subtlety, dominating the atmosphere, intoxicating. The music floated like smoke blown on the air, dancing on a breeze. The music was capricious, feral, and completely spirituous, with a quality both beguiling and intimidating. Rimmon was oddly exhilarated by the scent and the sounds, yet his keen senses alerted him to something poisonous within. The effect was one of inebriation, and he began to hallucinate psychedelic visions, shapes and scenes he had never before seen or even dreamt of.

At the very center of the great room was a golden throne, and upon it sat his satanic majesty. The diabolical dais upon which the throne perched was made of rough-hewn rock of purple porphyry, and it appeared as an island rising out of a dark sea. The seat of power was fashioned from pure gold, unadorned by precious jewels, and its surface shone like mirrored glass. Satan sat upon the throne, regal, imperious. His whole demeanor spoke of arrogance, and his countenance was full of pride. Above the throne was a high domed ceiling made of pure crystal, imitating the heavens of the universe. But in this private domain, it was always dead of night.

The design of this domed space suggested the verisimilitude of space and the universe. Brilliant stars shone and vibrated in the firmament above Satan's head, while numerous suns and galaxies waxed and waned. Filling a quarter of this cosmic vault was Earth, God's own favored creation. The planet turned on its axis slowly, its blue-green beauty marred by scars of brown and black, pockmarked places where Satan's hand had blighted the landscape. Indeed, it was his desire to see this world totally blackened, barren and devoid of every living thing.

The floor of the chamber was made of transparent glass, and below its surface was a translucent sea of cobalt blue and emerald green. Beneath the floor a strange amorphous liquid moved as if it were a living thing. Rimmon's eyes were drawn to its depths, and he watched spellbound as mysterious coagulations of bloodlike forms glowed with crimson light, moving through the mass and then dissolving into the fathomless blue, deeper, deeper to where the waters thickened into velvet, inky blackness. Strange and peculiar shapes unlike anything found in the oceans of the earth moved about in the depths—slithering, sickly pale things, boneless entities formed out of Satan's thoughts.

"Come, friend, enter my realm. You are welcome here."

Rimmon's rapt attention was broken. He gazed at his master and saw that the music he heard and the perfume he breathed issued from Satan's body. From pipes and flutes lodged in his flesh the sounds came forth. From open pores the fragrance came. Words from the accursed Scriptures came to mind: Thou wast perfect in thy ways from the day that thou wast created, till iniquity was found in thee.

Before him the solid surface at his feet melted away until only the sea remained. Rimmon drew back, fearing lest he succumb to its frightening depths.

"Have faith, my dear one," Satan said. "Trust in me. Walk upon the waters."

The demon prince hesitated as Satan watched.

"Come, come to me."

Rimmon stepped out onto the waters, and the surface held him. He took another step. And then another, quickening his pace until, striding forth, he made his way towards the throne.

Satan smiled at him. "Place your faith in me and no one else, and you shall live."

"My lord and my king, I . . . I worship you!" Rimmon exclaimed.

Then the smile on Satan's face waned.

The tranquil sea became troubled.

Small waves lapped against the rocky island where Satan sat serene.

Rimmon's ankles dipped below the shifting waters, and he began to panic. Two fiery red eyes were rising up from the depths to meet him. The demon prince wanted to cry out, but he could not. He continued slipping slowly downward. His knees were now covered, and his eyes widened as the creature from the deep began circling him. Rimmon could now clearly see the colossal serpent gliding effortlessly through the turbulent sea. In one swift motion, the creature struck, coiling its sinuous body about the demon's legs and then his abdomen and chest, constricting his breath. The monstrous head of the snake rocked to and fro before Rimmon's face, gazing into his eyes.

He wanted to scream, but no sound issued from his mouth. The serpent was mesmerizing him while slowly, slowly crushing him in its deadly embrace and drawing him down toward the murky depths. The demon struggled for breath as he felt the waters spill over him. He could do nothing to resist. Terror filled his heart. Despite being fully submerged, Rimmon felt the foul breath of the beast upon his face and the stench of its entrails in his nostrils. He could feel his life ebbing away. He now understood this was his fate, to sink into the depths and join the other countless victims who had come to Satan's lair. He would himself become one of the hideous forms he had glimpsed what seemed like hours ago, swimming about this pestilent lake for all eternity.

With one last desperate struggle, Rimmon fought to save himself, knowing even as he did it was useless to even try. Failing miserably, he finally acquiesced and submitted himself unto slow annihilation.

Suddenly, the awful moment had passed, and he found himself lying exhausted, utterly spent and prostrate before Satan's throne. The Dark Lord looked down upon him, a sardonic smile on his face, and Rimmon knew full well he was prepared to do anything—anything—for the Father of Lies.

F. John Hurr
November 2014
Colchester, UK

Lightning Source UK Ltd.
Milton Keynes UK
UKOW04f0152241214

243623UK00002B/169/P